ALIUS ACADEMY

ELEMENTAL MAGE SERIES BOOK 1

LARA WRAY

Copyright © 2023 by Lara Wray

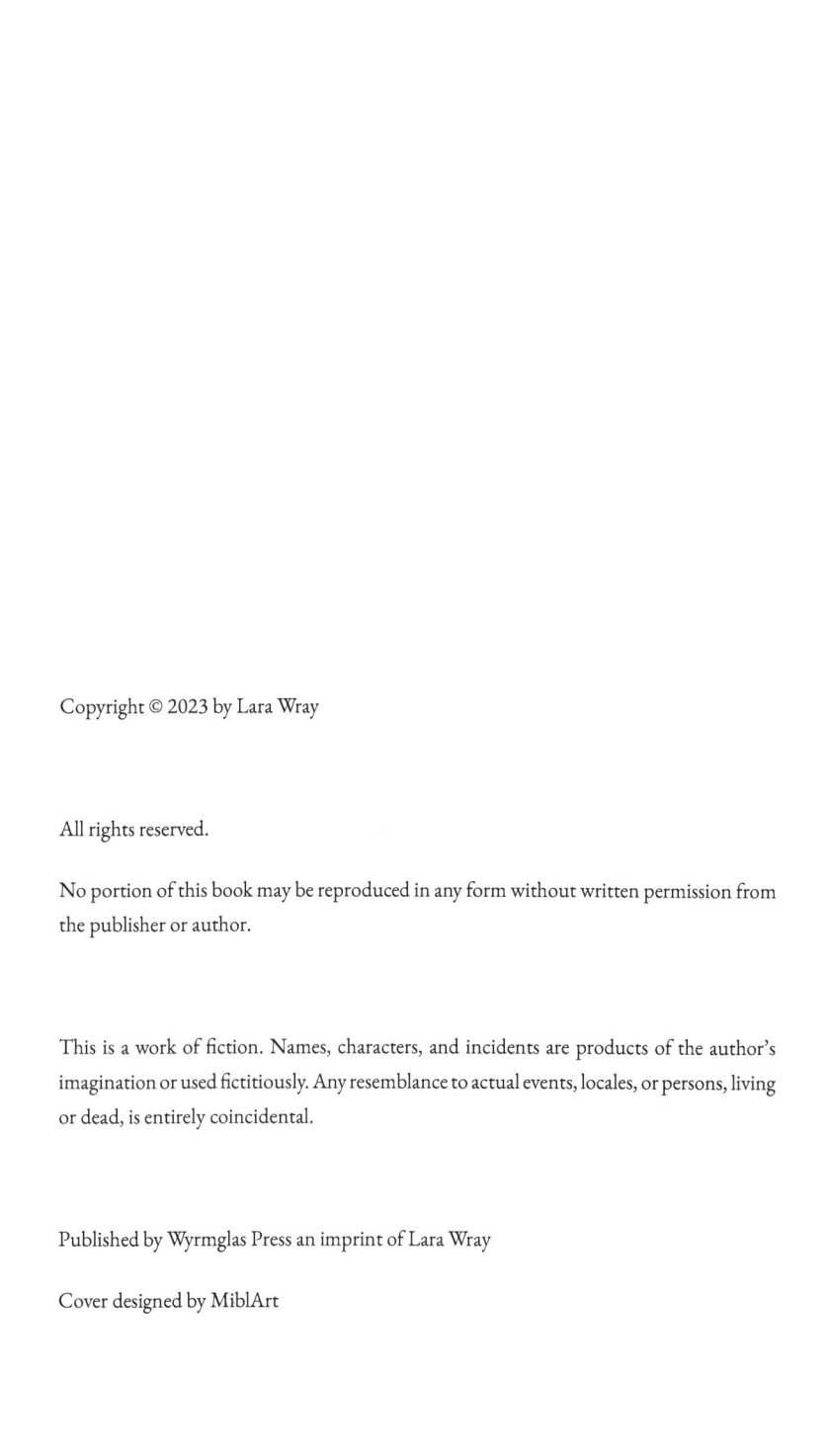

All rights reserved.

No portion of this book may be reproduced in any form without written permission from the publisher or author.

This is a work of fiction. Names, characters, and incidents are products of the author's imagination or used fictitiously. Any resemblance to actual events, locales, or persons, living or dead, is entirely coincidental.

Published by Wyrmglas Press an imprint of Lara Wray

Cover designed by MiblArt

Contents

1. PROLOGUE — 1
2. CHAPTER ONE — 6
3. CHAPTER TWO — 18
4. CHAPTER THREE — 38
5. CHAPTER FOUR — 51
6. CHAPTER FIVE — 67
7. CHAPTER SIX — 83
8. CHAPTER SEVEN — 95
9. CHAPTER EIGHT — 104
10. CHAPTER NINE — 119
11. CHAPTER TEN — 127
12. CHAPTER ELEVEN — 134
13. CHAPTER TWELVE — 148
14. CHAPTER THIRTEEN — 158
15. CHAPTER FOURTEEN — 167

16.	CHAPTER FIFTEEN	174
17.	CHAPTER SIXTEEN	189
18.	CHAPTER SEVENTEEN	201
19.	CHAPTER EIGHTEEN	215
20.	CHAPTER NINETEEN	230
21.	CHAPTER TWENTY	251
22.	CHAPTER TWENTY-ONE	263
Also By		277

PROLOGUE

"Wake up, Landi, wake up now!" Grandmother Adrianiss spoke sharply as she shook Eilandia's shoulders.

Landi's eyes snapped wide open. She squinted as her eyes adjusted, focusing on her grandmother's face, wreathed in shadow, and the shaft of low light filtering through the skylight and slicing through the dim of the attic room.

Her grandmother bent down and peered closely into her eyes. "How do you feel?" she asked softly.

Eilandia blinked and sat up. The brew the soul-melder, Barbira, had given her to drink had made her sleepy.

"I was dreaming of Mamai," she croaked, remembering. Her eyes lined with tears; she scrubbed them away with her fists. Even at eight years old, she knew her grandmother didn't like it when she wept.

Grandmother's dark eyes were sad as she looked away. "We must go. But first see your reflection, so you know yourself."

"Did it work?"

"Better than we hoped for. No one shall see Eilandia, Princess of Eassus, in the girl that stands before them. They shall only see

Laurel-Leah Fields, daughter of Elizabeth and Daniel Fields of Summerton."

Landi drew back her covers and stood up from the single oak-framed bed beneath the eaves, making her way hesitantly to gaze in the full-length mirror. She saw a stranger.

Her silvery-flaxen hair was now mousy brown, her olive skin now white. Gold-amber eyes had become forest green. Her heart-shaped face was now long. She was sturdier, stronger. The symbols Barbira had marked on her body had disappeared. Her hands shook, and her breath hitched when she reached out to touch her reflection.

Grandmother knelt beside her with a grimace and a sharp intake of breath, then embraced and gently rocked her, inhaling deeply. Landi buried her face in the nape of her grandmother's neck. Her skin smelt of eldaraflowers and her black-silver hair of rosemarian mint.

"Do you remember what we spoke about?" Grandmother pulled back to observe Landi. "Your brother will unbind your magic, and your memories will be restored when you're older and stronger. Then you will reunite and return to Eassus, as your brother has foreseen." Her lips were a tight line, her dark eyes solemn but determined. She released Landi, who straightened her dress. "Recite to me what I have asked you to remember."

Grandmother planted a foot forward from her kneeling position, her face twisted in pain. She braced her side beneath her ribs, where her wound lay, and bared her teeth as she rose. Landi watched, eyebrows knitting.

"Recite it," Grandmother repeated. Her light brown skin had taken on a tinge of yellow as she sat heavily in the chair beside the mirror.

"I will be bound in a soul-suit, with the essence of my great-grandmother of Earth, to change my appearance," Landi recited. "My powers will be bound, and I will be placed with Earth parents whose memories will be altered to believe I am their child. My memories will also be altered to believe they are my parents. Aldisill will awaken my powers when I am older and stronger. Together, we will return to Eassus and fight." Her lip wobbled as she finished. She eyed her grandmother's side, where she had been clutching.

"We will meet your new family tonight; they will love you as their own. All else will be forgotten, for a time." Grandmother's voice was strained and cracked.

"Will I ever see you again?" Grandmother had not mentioned it. Landi knew she was in pain, but Grandmother shushed her whenever she asked about it.

"Old ladies are not your concern." Grandmother narrowed her eyes at Landi as if to silence her.

Landi's eyes brimmed with tears; her vision blurred. She dared not blink for fear that if she released one, her grandmother would chide her once more. She sniffed and wiped her eyes with the back of her hand, her lips pulling down at the corners.

She was so scared she could barely breathe. It felt the same as when she had been little, before her magic emerged and before she'd learned how to swim. Her older brother, Aldisill, and her friend

Thenn had been sneaking a boat out onto the castle lake alone, with no adults.

Her brother had been about to return to magical school, and Landi hadn't wanted to be left out of the fun; she hadn't wanted to be left on her own. And even though she was frightened by her nursemaid's tales of the monster who lived in that lake, when Aldisill told her she couldn't go, she fussed until he yielded. He made her swear on a Third Fringe bear tooth she wouldn't tell anyone about it, and that she wouldn't go into the water. Delighted, Landi had agreed.

Aldisill and Thenn had rowed the boat to the centre of the lake, told her they wouldn't be too long, and dived in, leaving her alone on the boat. Landi waited and waited, but when they didn't return to the surface, she worried. Calling out to them, she stared into the black waters, waiting.

Maybe the monster got them, she'd thought, frightened, when they still didn't resurface. Too small to row the boat back to the shore on her own, she scowled at the water and the imagined monster and jumped in to find them.

She didn't have her floaters on. She'd kicked and flailed, gasping for air only to go down again, gulping water, lungs screaming, staring at the sky from beneath the depths, willing herself to live.

It turned out later that the boys had gone into the lake to go monster-hunting. Little Landi had forgotten Aldisill and Thenn now had elemental water control and could stay under water for days if they wished. She was rescued by a creature – the lake monster her nursemaid had told her tales of. But she never forgot that feeling of drowning, and she practised and practised her swimming so it would never happen again.

And now she was back in the lake alone, powerless, not knowing how to swim.

Grandmother leaned in towards Landi and tilted her chin up to meet her gaze, her eyes softening. Gripping Landi by her shoulders, she spoke in a resolute tone, as if this was the only thing that mattered.

"You are young. You will live. You will be safe."

CHAPTER ONE
Ten years later

There must be more to life than this.

As pathetic as it was, that had become my daily work mantra.

Now I'd finished my A-levels, I'd gained full-time employment in my once part-time job. It was great earning a full-time wage, but the inharmonious odour of floor cleaner mixed with sausage, bacon, and eggs frankly made me want to vomit. Mercifully, I'd reached the end of five nightshifts and an onslaught of overtime at Murray's – the only twenty-four-hour greasy spoon in the grim Heights of Bawshall, Seddingham, England.

For the past two days, two of our day-shift staff, Alice and Ben, had called in sick last-minute, causing my nightshift hours to bleed into the day and increasing my twelve-hour stint to no less than eighteen hours – or whenever the boss, Murray, found cover. Our newest waitress, Princess, and I had managed the best we could, but she was part-time, and I'd already worked seventy-two hours over five days. And today, I had something better to do than overtime.

Princess sidled up to me from behind the food-service counter. She removed her cap and fiddled with her always perfect braids.

"I've washed down the counter, and the food is ready to be served, but—" She raised a long finger and lowered her voice, glancing over her shoulder at Murray through the window into the kitchen. "Neither Alice nor Ben have called in sick, but neither of them have shown up yet. And I don't know about you, but *I'm* not doing any more hours this week," she said, a determined glint in her eye.

"What, neither of them? They should have arrived ten minutes ago!" I craned my neck to peer past Princess into the kitchen.

Murray was on his phone, his already ruddy complexion gaining a purplish hue by the second. His fifty-year-old face was creased like a balled-up piece of paper. He looked pissed off, but since the divorce began, that was nothing new.

"I like the money," I admitted, squinting, "but…"

I knew how this would play out: how it always played out. It would end with me caving to his requests and staying, as I always had since I'd started working here two years ago.

"But… I want a day off now. He needs to get other workers in – agency staff, anyone – just not me." This time, I would stand my ground.

"Last I heard, he was effing and jeffing down his phone on a voicemail message for Ben. What we need to do is cut through the kitchen like ninjas – get our bags, then slide out the back door. Are you with me?" Princess asked, eyes wide and hands in judo-chop position.

I giggled at her dramatics. "I'm with you, but I need to empty the mop bucket first – so he'll have more than enough time to ask me to cover the shift."

Rolling my eyes, I wheeled the mop bucket toward the kitchen door. The most annoying part was that Ben's sickness was almost certainly less a sickness and more of a two-day hangover. All he'd talked about last week had been the plan for an alcohol-fuelled night at a club opening with his new date, Natasha.

That made me reflect on how long it'd been since my last date. Since exams had finished, all I'd done was work, but today I was meeting my best friend, Vita, for coffee in the afternoon, and we'd be dropping into Jake Thornton's house party tonight.

Jake was Vita's ex-boyfriend, and their relationship had ended *badly*, so I wasn't sure going to his party was the best idea. But she wanted to show him how fabulous she was without him and had insisted we go. As the best friend, it was my duty to accompany her for moral support – and to make sure she didn't get sucked into that vortex again. That was... if Murray didn't guilt-trip me into working.

Vita was leaving for university in Italy in two days. I'd already missed a party over the weekend, and I was determined to hang out with her before she left. I wouldn't do more overtime – not when I had a day off.

But... I needed this job, and I hadn't yet looked for anything else. I steeled myself and straightened my spine, sure I'd fold like an accordion.

"Right, let's get this over with," I said to Princess, marching with mop and bucket to push open the kitchen door. "Alright, Murray?" I made a beeline for the sink to my left.

Princess moved with the speed of an eagle, squawking non-stop as she flew through the kitchen. "See you on Saturday, Murray, great work, the best shift—" Her voice cut off as the door swung back into the kitchen.

"Princess!" Murray bellowed after her.

"She must not have heard," I said, pouring the contents of the bucket down the sink, along with my last chance to get away. Setting the bucket down and still hopeful of escape, I made a break for the door.

Murray blocked my escape route with the bulk and speed of a bullet train – but just then, the bell at the front door rang and someone entered the café. It was Alice, fifteen minutes late for her shift.

Propping open the kitchen door with a broad hand, Murray asked, "Alice, did you see Ben outside?"

She backed out of the café, fair head surveying the street. "No sign of him," she confirmed.

I tiptoed toward the back kitchen door and edged it open.

"Lori, Lori!" Murray shouted. His voice could have pierced the clamour of a crowded Sunday fish-market.

Dammit!

"Ben hasn't shown up. I've tried calling, but he's ghosting me. Now..." He pursed his lips, flipping his phone from one hand to another. "I know you've worked an extra day and stayed behind for two days. And I will call for agency staff. But... can you stay until they arrive?" He bit his bottom lip.

I had my speech prepared for all the reasons I couldn't do it. But all at once, above Murray's fog-horn tones and the noise of the extractor fans in the kitchen, a ringing started in my ears.

"I..." I began, but the sound seemed to put pressure on my brain.

"Look, I know you've just done sixty, er... seventy-plus hours—"

That was all I heard. His mouth was flapping, but the ringing sound swelled to a deafening pitch. I pressed my hands to my ears to block it out, but it was coming from inside my head.

My face heated, head splintering with the unbearable pain of it. Breath coming fast, I slid down to the floor. Murray bent over me, his mouth moving soundlessly, his eyes panicked.

Rolling to my side, I vomited. Alice sprang back, covering her nose and mouth with both hands.

The noise ceased, but there was someone screaming.

It was me. Tears wet my cheeks when I silenced myself.

Ben charged through the kitchen door. "What the bloody hell's going on in here?! It sounds like someone's being murdered!" His eyes darted around the place, taking in the scene.

"Ben, you're late and you didn't answer your phone!" Murray snapped. He gazed down at me, his left eye bigger than his right. "Lori's overworked and... might be having a breakdown," he added when I didn't speak.

His arms were folded, and there was a deep look of concern on his crumpled face. It was an expression I'd never seen from him in the two years I'd worked here. He knelt beside me. "Shall I call an ambulance, Lori, love? Can you stand up?"

This was the most mortifying experience of my life.

Murray called me a cab home and ordered Ben to clean up my vomit.

It took fifteen minutes to get home to my two-up, two-down on the ironically named Lovely Lane, feeling wretched. I never wanted to return to work. Ever.

I hooked my coat onto the stand in the hallway, head finally feeling clear and the nausea had eased. I wouldn't mention the fiasco at work to my parents. Not now, anyway – I barely wanted to think about it myself.

"Hello, darling, are you back home?" My mum called her usual greeting, asking the obvious, from the kitchen at the back of the house.

I caught my reflection in the coat-stand mirror. "Hi Mum, I'm back!" My skin was pale, but I *had* just worked way too many hours in five days.

When I entered the lounge, mum's stag ornament greeted me from atop the radiator cover, behind my usual spot on my two-seater sofa. I hated that thing. It creeped me out, but no matter how often I relocated the ornament, it always ended up behind me.

My parents were way older than the other kids' parents in my year at school. My mum had had me at forty, when my dad had been forty-seven. They told me I was their miracle baby and named me Laurel-Leah, for the laurel wreath worn by the ancient Romans, representing triumph. After eight years of trying, I supposed I was their triumph over infertility.

Dad was sitting in his usual spot behind the lounge door on his recliner armchair – covered with throws to hide the threadbare material – with the TV blasting out the news. At sixty-five, his hearing and health were ever-declining, and he'd been ill with too many conditions for years. He turned his gaunt face toward me.

"I didn't realise you were home. Good morning, daughter. How was work?"

Intelligent jade-green eyes, a touch darker than my own, peered from beneath wayward grey-white eyebrows and over his silver-rimmed spectacles. He was wearing his striped bathrobe with matching slippers, and a blanket covered his legs.

"Hi, Dad. It was fine," I lied as I adjusted the stag's position, turning away its perilous horns, then plopped into my usual spot on the adjacent sofa. I shivered; the house was cold. We used blankets to save on heating bills, but this morning there was an icy bite to the air.

"Another two people found dead—strangled. The police suspect a connection to the other strangulation cases," my dad said, bending his grey head over the remote control. No matter how many times he used it, he always had to look for the correct buttons.

The news footage showed police cars at the front of a taped-off mansion.

"Where is that?" I squinted.

"In Cressing Village, down the road."

That was a wealthy area of Seddingham. After my dad had had his first heart attack six years ago and could no longer work, we'd moved from the small southern town of Summerton to Seddingham, as my grandad lived in the area and the cost of living was lower.

Since moving to this northern city, I had hardened myself to the constant reports of murders and the gang-related gunshots I heard some nights. The police helicopters often flew low over the house, searchlights flashing through my drawn bedroom curtains. I realised that it was a part of city life. Now I only worried about serial attacks when victims matched my description.

The victims in this news coverage were a man aged forty-eight and his son, twenty-one, attacked in their own homes. I blinked away that uncomfortable feeling home invasions churned up and looked at my dad, glad both he and my mum were safe. And happy my parents had, despite their meagre earnings, sent me to self-defence and martial arts lessons, after that kid threw a brick at my head. Bawshall was a rough area, but even in Summerton, kids had hung around bus stops, looking for a fight. Self-defence lessons might not help against guns, but they came in handy as a deterrent or when fighting off local ruffians. I was also more than grateful my parents had sent me to school outside the area, where I'd met Vita.

"Want a cuppa, Dad?"

"Your mum's in the kitchen making one," he said, eyes fixed on the remote control.

I made my way through the dining room to our tiny kitchen. My mum was dressed in colour-coordinated clothes, pouring porridge into two bowls.

"Hello, baby bear." She leaned across to peck me on the cheek and looked me over. "Do you want some porridge?"

"No thanks – I ate at work." I flicked on the kettle and folded my arms over my chest, waiting for the chastisement about my appearance I knew was sure to come.

"Did you wear that to work?" She eyed my garb: hoody over black jeans. The tag had read trousers when I'd bought them, but they really were jeans.

"Yeah. I don't need to dress up for work, Mum, it's a greasy spoon. Besides, I wasn't wearing the hoody."

"Hmm." Her sky-blue eyes surveyed me disapprovingly. She smoothed my wayward hair down. Unlike her straight, pale hair, mine had a habit of springing up and frizzing. "When you look scruffy, people think less of you. I know you're not interested, but you must look presentable in the working world, darling."

I sighed. I knew that any protests would fall on deaf ears. Anyway, I was happy to look scruffy. I believed that if you looked like you had nothing, people wouldn't try to take from you.

The kettle was steaming, so I poured the hot water into the teapot and brought down mugs from the cupboard. My mum's was the one I'd made her at school when I was twelve. It was supposed to have the face of a bear, but it didn't look much like anything. I'd painted MB on it for Mama Bear and told my classmates it meant 'Mum's the best'. My dad's was a bucket-sized 'World's Greatest Dad' mug, and mine said 'I love Barcelona'. I hadn't been to Spain or anywhere abroad – Vita had brought it back for me when she'd visited there last year – but I longed to travel the world.

I poured hot tea into the cold mugs, the chill from the house seeping into my bones. "I'm putting the heating on, Mum; it's freezing in here."

"It's early – it'll warm up soon," she assured me, picking up the porridge for my dad.

The September morning was crisp, but the sun hadn't fully surrendered to total grey cloud coverage and would still peek out during the day. She was probably right.

"Bring the tea, Lori!" she called as she walked gracefully down the hall.

I looked nothing like my mum. She was five-foot-seven, willowy and still attractive at fifty-eight. I was five-one and sturdy, like my dad. Some people described me as 'curvy'. I was pretty sure my mum found my looks disappointing, regardless of what I was wearing – though with a small waist and full bosom, I wasn't devoid of all assets. But my bottom was more than ample. I couldn't deny that the best thing about a cup of tea was the accompanying biscuits, and it showed.

Tea made, I parked the mugs on the side table between my mum and dad. My mum's Highland cow and hare ornaments gazed at me from the shelves behind them, along with countless family pictures. I grabbed my own tea out of the kitchen and settled back in my spot, listening to my parents as they discussed the news.

Just then, a buzzing tone started almost imperceptibly in my ears. I studied the TV, wondering if it was feedback. The noise amplified into that blasted ringing. My breath came faster in realisation. *Crap, not again!*

My parents gave no sign they heard anything unusual and carried on talking, unhindered.

A disjointed voice replaced the ringing. It didn't belong to the news presenter or my parents. It came through like a whisper, unintelligible and thoroughly creepy. Ice snakes slithered down my spine. I gaped at my parents, waiting for them to mention the voice.

My mum must have felt my stare; she turned to me. I saw her mouth moving as the murmur faded.

"Are you alright, darling?" she asked for what must have been the second time, leaning towards me.

"Did you hear anything… a weird voice or something?"

"Yep, your dad telling me about the news, but I've already watched it, so I was ignoring him." Her eyes glinted mischievously at my dad. He pursed his lips and shook his head, inhaling and exhaling vigorously.

My mum eyed me closely. "I think you'd better get yourself to bed. You look ill."

"Aye, you look pale," my dad agreed.

I nodded, feeling wiped out. "Night. I'll see you in a few hours." Some sleep might get rid of these strange hallucinations.

"Have a good rest, baby bear," my mum chirped.

My dad chorused along with her. "Have a good sleep, daughter."

Dragging myself upstairs to my box room, I eyed my bed covetously. My skin felt a little sticky after my twelve-hour shift, so I should shower first. But my green-and-yellow-flowered duvet cover looked so welcoming… It made me feel like I was diving into a field of daisies whenever I went to bed.

As I contemplated giving the shower a miss, the high-pitched ringing ramped up from zero to full.

I sucked my head between my shoulders and covered my ears, panting at the onslaught. This time as the ringing subsided, a voice came through strong and clear.

"It is time. You are unbound... I will come for you."

An ocean of dread splintered through me. My knees buckled. I face-planted on my bed with a bounce. Heat tore from my inner core, filling me head to toe with a raging fever. Sweat broke out and clung to my skin; I squeezed my eyes shut.

Downstairs, the front door slammed. My mum had no doubt popped to the shop. My breath hitched. I tried to speak, but no sound passed my lips.

A wave of icy water washed through me, cooling and comforting. My heart slowed, my head clearing, the heat subsiding. Air rose up inside, buoyant and energetic. A light wind swirled in the room, reflecting the stir in my body, gently tickling my hair and fanning me. I shivered.

Then I felt a tremor under me, building from a gentle rocking to alarming intensity. My eyes flung open as the entire world shook, but it subsided as quickly as it came.

White light exploded from my back with such force that my top blew out from my prone body. I watched it from the corner of my eyes as the energy spread and arced, white and lucent.

I promptly lost consciousness.

CHAPTER TWO

I WRENCHED MY EYES open to the sound of my phone buzzing. Still in my clothes from work, I instantly recalled what happened before I'd sunk into darkness – and decided to ignore it. I had a busy day, meeting Vita and perhaps looking for a new job.

My mouth felt as dry as the sands of the Sahara. Smacking my lips together, I rolled onto my back and checked my phone. It was 1 p.m.

10.55

Vita: Hi Lor, I'm setting off into town now. Are you still alright for 3pm? Sorry if I woke you.

12.59

Vita: Hey-o, are you still sleeping? Are you going to stay at mine tonight for the party? What are you going to wear? What do you think of this outfit???

She'd attached a picture of her in a tight-fitting, split-to-the-thigh silver dress and stilettos. I messaged back.

13.04

Me: Hey-o Veets, just woke up. Love the outfit. Jake will rue the day!!! I'll bring my stuff with me just in case. See you at 3pm :)

My mum popped her head through the door. "I heard your phone buzzing. Just checking you're up?"

She walked into my bedroom. There was so little space that when she sat on the chair at my desk and swivelled round, it put her next to me as I lay on my bed.

"You didn't get changed for bed? You looked off-colour when you came home. How are you feeling?" she asked, holding a thermometer an inch from my head and handing me the pulse monitor to attach to my finger.

"I'm fine, Mum, I can do that myself. I'm eighteen you know." I waved it aside in feigned annoyance.

"Better to be sure. Thirty-six-point-six. You're ok." She smiled down at me, lifting her brows. "You're going out?"

I suppressed an eye-roll. She had three aims for me in life: to dress better, to eat less, and to go out more to meet boys. She would never understand ripped jeans or heavy boots. I could always eat fewer biscuits, I supposed, and I did meet plenty of boys at work. None of them inspired me.

"Yep, meeting Vita. I might stay at hers tonight. We might go out to a party before she goes back to uni. You know she's going to study in Italy for a year and I won't see her until she gets back... unless I fly out there for a visit." I flicked my gaze to hers.

My mum glanced to the corkboard map, pinned with my bucket-list of countries that I wanted to visit, on the wall at the foot of my bed and grinned.

"You should go," she said, standing up.

"To where? The party or Italy?"

"To both. Maybe you'll meet a nice boy at the party – or in Italy." She hovered at the door, eyes bright.

"You need help with Dad, so Italy is a no."

My mum sighed. "Your dad and I can manage for a week without you. Tell me when you want to go, and I'll book time off work." I opened my mouth to object, but she cut me off. "Think about it."

Her light steps descended the stairs, and I returned my attention to my phone. My parents' household budget was always tight, with no savings to speak of. They weren't spring chickens anymore, and it was worrying for people of their years. But now I'd finished my A-levels and worked full-time, I could support myself and help my parents paint the house, get a new boiler and fix the leaking bathroom. Next, we would replace our worn furniture.

I sighed heavily. I would have loved to go travelling, but even before my dad's poor health, we'd been a staycation family. Now, with a back injury and pins in his knees from a car accident – not to mention heart failure and angina – he couldn't be alone for too long. I contributed to the household bills and mortgage; my mum called it rent, and I was happy to help.

Could I really go abroad by myself and be so carefree?

Vita was a year older than me and starting her second year of university. Since she'd left a year ago to go to university in Wales, I'd barely gone out. Now she was going to Italy, I'd never see her.

I contemplated the journeys on my map. Travelling had always seemed like a mere fantasy to me. If it were to become reality I'd start with the closest countries, interrailing through Europe. Italy was definitely on my bucket-list, so it would be a good start for my first ever green pin outside Britain.

A brief flash of the Voice in my head and the strange events that had followed invaded my thoughts. A shiver coated my arms with goose-pimples. I shrugged the memory off and headed for the shower.

When I was ready, I looked in the mirror. I wore my usual checked shirt, vest top underneath, jeans, and leather boots. My hair looked smooth... for now. I applied a little makeup to cover the shadows under my eyes and to add colour to my pale face, then packed my backpack and tramped downstairs.

My dad was still in his recliner chair, but at least he was now dressed. A few years ago, he'd been stout with a potbelly; his shoulders were thick and broad. But since his health had declined, his burgundy jumper hung loose from his withered shoulders as if from a coat hanger. My heart squeezed for what had been.

"Laurel-Leah!" Dad exclaimed, eyes bright as crystals. "Did you feel the earthquake? I'm waiting for the report on the news."

My mum scolded him as if she was saying it for the hundredth time as she came into the lounge, a tea towel draped over her shoulder. "Dan, there was no earthquake. With all the medication you're on, you dreamed or hallucinated it."

She turned to me and whispered loudly. "I left the house for thirty minutes, and I came back to earthquake this, earthquake that. Sometimes your dad is—" She stuck her tongue to the side and averted her eyes. We both giggled.

"You're a cheeky bugger," Dad said, pursing his pale lips into a thin line, his green eyes alight with humour.

Mum ran a critical eye over me. "Are you wearing that to go out?"

I sighed and slumped my shoulders. "When or *if* I go to the party, I'll dress up. I'm meeting Vita for coffee first."

My dad leaned over to me and whispered loudly. "We're Fields, you know. Don't let the buggers get you down, even if that bugger is your mum!"

Mum flicked him with her tea towel and flung it back over her shoulder.

He wheezed with laughter. "I won't be like this forever. I'm not letting this ticker keep me down. Off with you, daughter, go out courting. I'll be courting the remote control for the rest of the day."

He smiled wickedly to himself, peering down at the remote-control buttons, no doubt ready to switch from watching news to sports or the worst B-movie about some war he could find. I would come back home to him recounting the plotline with animated enthusiasm. Thankfully, I would likely be tired and make a good listener.

I slipped into my coat, descended our front steps, and strode toward the alley to the main road, scanning the area for potential trouble. All clear. You could never be too careful in the Heights. I'd been in fights before.

On the way to the bus stop I thought of mentioning the Voice to my parents, but I was sure all of it had been brought on by sleep deprivation. But my dad had felt an earthquake too. Or was that coincidental? If it happened again, maybe I would tell them... or maybe they'd have me sectioned.

The swathes of grey clouds overhead started spitting rain. I hooked my coat hood over my head. No doubt my hair would be an irredeemable mess by the end of this journey. I blew out a breath at that and glanced over my shoulder on instinct and habit as I reached the alley.

Someone wearing a long, dark hooded coat – or was it a cloak? – flickered in my peripheral vision. I about-turned. There was no one there. I stood squinting at where I'd seen them, outside my house. I blinked and frowned. Nothing.

With one last glance, I took off down the alleyway to the bus stop.

"I'm losing the plot," I muttered under my breath.

The rain stopped during my bus journey, and I picked my way through the throng of people in the city centre to my and Vita's favourite café, Bean is Believing.

It was three o'clock, but Vita was rarely on time. I entered the café, smoothed down my hair and glanced around, getting my phone out in case I needed it. To my astonishment, she was sitting at a booth, surrounded by paper shopping bags. She waved me over, taking me into a big bear hug.

I felt a strong sensation of happiness, but then an underlying feeling of sadness, followed by a spike of uncertainty, confusion, and fear. I jerked back in surprise as the emotions washed over me, and Vita tensed in response.

It was a delight to see my best friend, and I'd miss her while she was away. But those emotions... weren't mine.

"How are you, gorgeous? You look amazing!" Vita said.

I relaxed a little and smiled, remembering why she was my best friend. Any positive comments about my looks, rather than the constant tirade of critique from my mother, were appreciated.

"So do you – stunning as you've always been," I replied, dropping my bag down on the bench of the booth and trying to act like nothing strange had just happened.

She looked like she'd had her hair, makeup, and nails done at the salon, blonde hair up in the most perfect messy bun I'd ever seen. Her blue eyes vibrant in smoky eye make-up, and she wore skinny jeans, a striped shirt, and a navy-blue blazer.

I searched for my purse in my backpack. "What are you having – hot chocolate with marshmallows and a slice of carrot cake? My treat before you leave." I was excited to actually have money in the bank for the first time since our six-year relationship as best friends had begun. Vita didn't have that problem; her family was disgustingly wealthy.

"We should get it to go and head to mine. I'm sure you'd like a rest after all the hours you've done this week," Vita suggested, to my surprise. This was our favourite hangout, and I was starving.

I explained to her in no uncertain terms that I must eat immediately, and she conceded.

"But if you're ordering, then I'm paying," she added, handing me some cash.

"My treat this time, Veets." I lifted my chin dramatically, held my purse to my chest, and stalked away. I heard her giggling behind me and smiled.

I wondered why Vita wanted to go home. She was a stay-out-all-hours, shop-till-you-drop kind of girl. She wasn't spoilt, not exactly, but like her mum, she loved fashion, cosmetics, and all that went with them, and would buy anything she pleased with price tags worth months of my payslips. Her mum was a fashion designer and worked all the time, and her dad had mostly ignored her even before he'd moved to Italy, seven years ago when her parents had got divorced.

He'd asked Vita to move there this year for university so she could spend time with him. She said her mum suspected the sudden attention was caused by a reversed midlife crisis. Vita had agreed to go, but I thought she felt conflicted about it. I might be slipping into madness, but if I really was sensing her emotions, then maybe that was why she was feeling confusion and fear.

There was someone in front of me at the counter, so I inspected the desserts on display. I'd probably have a brownie slice. I always had a brownie. But the Bakewell tarts looked intriguing... delectable, even.

An odd feeling prickled across my back and up my neck. I stiffened and glanced around, certain that someone was behind me. There was no one there. Everyone seated behind me was engrossed in conversation, or their phones, or both.

"What's your order, please?" the bearded barista asked, leaning over the counter as if to see what I was looking at. I snapped my attention to the choices on the board.

The barista, who looked a few years older than me, drummed his fingers impatiently on the top of the till. "Do you need some time?"

"No. I'll get a large skinny latte and a large hot chocolate with marshmallows, a brownie, and a slice of carrot cake, please."

I still felt someone's eyes on me. It caused my neck hairs to rise, like hackles on a dog. I hunched my shoulders to my ears to shake off that uncomfortable feeling, throwing another quick glance behind me. The barista flicked his eyes between me and the empty space and raised his brows. Then a dawning realisation lit his eyes, after his gaze floated to Vita, and returned to mine, like he now had me pegged. Bat shit crazy and out for the day from the local asylum, under supervision.

After I paid, I thanked him and scampered back to my seat, face ablaze with heat. At times like these, I was happy to live in a big city. Anonymity was a blessing.

As I sat in the booth, Vita looked up from her phone. Her expression changed to one of concern. "Is everything alright?"

I didn't want to talk about it. I wanted to have a good chinwag, like we used to. "Of course it is – why wouldn't it be?"

Vita eyed the barista as if looking for a clue, but he was busy making coffees. Then she scanned the café briefly, like she was searching for someone. Just as I was about to glance over my shoulder to follow her gaze, she told me I'd finally get to meet her boyfriend, Karl, at the party tonight... but they might be breaking up because she was going to Italy. Her lips tilted up in a sad half-smile.

"Are you ok? What happened?" I asked.

She showed me a text message from him that said, 'We need to talk later.'

I tried not to grimace, but those words in that order weren't usually positive. When Vita had decided to move to Italy, she'd told me her worries about a long-distance relationship with Karl, especially after what had happened with her ex-boyfriend, Jake. He'd gone to uni and cheated on her on the very first day. So, understandably, she felt that it would be best to end things with Karl before she moved. I'd asked her if that was what she really wanted, and she'd said yes, but now she seemed upset that it might happen. I wasn't exactly an expert at relationships myself, and I'd never met Karl, but it was possible the text was about something else entirely.

Hoping to comfort her a little and give her that control back, I said, "You suggested a break-up first, so if he wants to break up, you instigated it... plus, he might just want to talk about something else important?" I finished, shrugging lamely.

"Maybe," she replied, looking unconvinced, then exchanged her sad smile for a genuine one. "And guess who else is coming!"

I opened my mouth to speak, but she cut me off.

"Rob Ellis!" she exclaimed, eyes glittering in anticipation. My heart somersaulted at his name. "Remember how you always used to talk about him and deny you liked him, then admitted you had a crush on him... for a while?"

"I remember *you* also developed a crush on him," I teased. It had mostly been because he was one of the very few guys who hadn't returned her interest. He was the only guy I'd ever had a relationship with – sort of. We'd started kind of secretly seeing each other. Then he'd moved away... far away.

"It was only because of your constant gabbing about him." She laughed, and I joined her; her crush had been very brief, and I knew she'd never actually go for someone I liked.

"Last I heard, he was living in the Maldives. Is he permanently back in England now?" I tried not to sound too excited.

"I don't know. It's something we'll have to find out tonight!"

We talked and laughed, and I was aware of a distinct sinking feeling, knowing she was going away again. But I would definitely go to the party, despite feeling out of sorts – and I was more than excited about it now that I knew Rob was going. Vita persuaded me to wear a top she'd bought, which I was sure she'd purchased with me in mind. It was green, which she'd always told me wasn't her colour, and it matched my eyes. I checked the price tag, but it had already been removed. She knew I wouldn't accept a direct gift – not at the prices she paid for them. Trust Vita to find another way to be generous.

But she seemed on edge. When I asked if she was ok, she brushed me off, saying she was always ok. Since we both knew that was a lie, I'd ask her about it when we got back to her house.

After our drinks and cake, I went to the toilets at the back of the café. Opening the door, I entered a dimly lit hallway; a fire exit was straight ahead, the toilet doors to my right. I tried the door to the ladies'. It was occupied, so I waited.

The door I'd walked through from the café opened, then closed itself, but no one came in. I frowned. It was *strange.* The same feeling I'd had in the queue suddenly prickled on my face.

I swallowed hard and reached out beside me. My hand met something solid, smooth, and invisible. Pushing against it, palms sweeping across; There was no way around it. The route to the café was blocked off.

A soft, low laugh sounded.

My heart hammering, I backed away towards the fire exit. My eyes darted around, landing on nothing. Was I going mental, hearing voices and feeling things that weren't there?

Hoping an alarm would sound, I pushed down the fire door lever, but it didn't go off. I backed into a grubby, reeking alleyway that led to side streets on either end. Giant wheelie bins lined the wall to my right, and litter was scattered across the cobblestones.

I stumbled against the bins, pulse racing, breath coming fast. Everything felt wrong. Instinct told me to run. I turned to flee, but someone yanked me back by the scruff of my shirt and hurled me down.

My knees crunched on the wet cobblestones as my hands shot out to break my fall. I blindly kicked out behind me and connected with something. There was a cry of pain. I whipped my head around.

My eyes, sharp with adrenaline, registered the now revealed stalker: the hooded figure who'd been outside my house. I raced away from him, past the wheelie bins, toward the side street, ignoring the pain in my knees and recalling martial arts moves.

As I neared the side road, a blast of wind stormed into me and scooped me up. A stirring sparked within; Light buoyancy whirled inside me as I was dropped at the hooded man's feet.

I bit back a whimper of pain and shuffled back to put some space between us. I hit something solid – an invisible barrier at my back. The man stood in front of me, blocking my route to the café and to the other end of the alley. I was trapped.

"What do you want?" I heard myself say, my voice trembling and too high.

He laughed, a deep, cruel rumble. His features were mostly cast in shadow; I could see three braids in a blonde beard surrounding a thick-lipped wide mouth. His lips had a grey tinge to them.

My attention snapped to a broken beer bottle to my left. The thought of stabbing him with the jagged edges gave me a shiver of revulsion. He wore no visible weapons, though invisibility and control of the wind seemed weapon enough.

Ignoring the bottle, I lunged forward and barrelled into him. He went down, kneeing me in the stomach. My adrenaline was so high I barely felt the blow, but I woofed and wheezed as he knocked the wind from my lungs. I crawled off him to get away, and he grasped my shirt sleeve.

I clenched my free fist and smashed him in the face – once, twice. He released me, and I sprang up to start in a sprint. He grabbed my leg and pulled me down. I kicked out wildly, snapping some of his fingers back the wrong way.

He sucked in air through his teeth and pulled back, cradling his hand. I side-rolled up and sped toward the other end of the alley.

Something whipped around my ankles, forcing them together. My chin rebounded off the cobbles, pinpricks of light, burst across my vision, as I was dragged back to his feet.

Dazed, I blinked up at him. Something coiled from his right hand, linking him to me. As I studied my ankle binding, a translucent, silvery snake head flicked its forked, transparent tongue at me. I shrieked and tried to shuffle back, attempting to kick out, to no avail. The same light buoyancy that stirred in my chest reacted to this snake, as before, when the wind had blasted me into a heap at his feet.

The air snake vanished, and red fire snakes leapt from each of his palms. One snared me at my throat, and the other pinned my arms to my side. I opened my mouth to scream, but the fire snake tightened around my neck. It was solid, hot – not burning, but squeezing off my oxygen.

"You are not burning." His voice sounded gravelly; his accent was unfamiliar. "Fire Lakoliin." His thick, greyish lips curled up into a cruel sneer. I felt excitement, euphoria, greed and hunger all at once. They weren't my emotions. They were coming from him. Blending with my feelings of confusion and fear.

A stirring of heat ignited, not from his fire but from within me – fire and dancing flames. Above it, a swirl of air, eager and ready to go. Beneath the fire, a cool, icy fluid flowed in the depths. I didn't know how I did it, but I felt my air rise and expand outward, loosening his fire noose. I wheezed oxygen back into my lungs.

Suddenly I was drained, sleepy – not only from lack of oxygen, but something else, as if my energy was being leached away. His surprise now mixed with my cauldron of emotions. The snake's coil tightened once more.

"As you can see, you cannot overcome me. I will loosen your noose. You can scream, but no one can see you or hear you."

As a chill raced up my spine, my phone started bleating out a calypso tune from my jeans' front pocket. *Vita.* The man's nostrils flared in irritation.

The café exit door opened, and the barista who'd served me in the café dropped rubbish-filled bin liners on the cobblestones and lit a cigarette. I stared at him as he scraped his hand through his dark beard, entirely oblivious to me and the fire snake wrapped around my neck. A series of knots tightened in my roiling stomach.

"Now, girl, what is your name, and who are your people?" the hooded man growled, ignoring the café worker and my ringtone.

I looked up at him in confusion. He wanted to know who my parents were? Hadn't he been outside my house earlier? Panic reared up. The strangulation cases on the news. My parents – had he got them too?

"I don't know what you mean." My voice came out strained. If he hadn't got my parents, I didn't want to draw his attention to them.

He tightened the fire snake, his anger and frustration merged with my own.

I choked out a laugh. This was plain INSANE. A solid fire snake was coming out of this plaited bearded dude's palms, and no one else could see or help. *What. The. Hell?*

Icy waters flowing within me rose. I shivered. My life was being gently leached away... by him, like a parasite. My vision blurred and blackened. My face felt hot, too hot. Was it the heat from his fire, or strangulation, or both? Was this it? Would I die today?

The barista flicked his cigarette. It bounced off the invisible wall. He stopped to inspect it, shrugged, and hurled the rubbish away into the nearest wheelie bin, and stepped back inside. I thrashed, trying to scream for help, but I was weakening.

"You're a strong one, but it will not be long now. Easier if you don't fight it, no?" the hooded man crooned.

Despite the blurriness, I pinned him with my most poisonous glare and envisioned him being encased in ice. If I didn't at least try to fight him, I'd end up another victim on the evening news. *Eighteen-year-old female, another in a series of victims of the Seddingham Strangler.*

Somehow, I pushed his fire snakes out with the buoyant air from within. At the release, I coughed and sputtered, so hard I felt like I might vomit. Eyes tearing and snatching in air, I took hold of the snakes. Their flames licked around my hands, as their tongues flicked at me.

An icy coolness sluggishly crept from my palms. The man stared at me, puzzlement on his face. His eyes widened as ice crackled up and engulfed the fire snake. His panic and fear, swarmed into me, and he released his hold on me.

I pitched forward on all fours. Ice travelled from my hands and darted towards him, entombing his legs to the knee. Staggering to my feet, sapped of strength, shaking away the dizziness, I turned and moved as fast as my legs could propel me toward the side street.

Fire burned bright in my peripheral vision. He was already working to break free.

A silvery liquid oval appeared in front of me, and my heart plummeted. What the hell was that?! I side-stepped it and willed myself to go faster, snatching a glance over my shoulder.

Figures emerged from the oval, dressed in strange attire and carrying weapons – fearsome weapons of the medieval kind. I tried to dial up my speed, but stumbled and tripped in my clumsy, drained state. What I really needed was a good long nap.

A male voice, musical and rumbling, spoke behind me. "You, girl! In the checked shirt. Stop running and do not move!"

Like in a nightmare, I slowed to a standstill. I couldn't budge from my position. My breathing was laboured; my throat was swollen. I couldn't even turn to see what was happening.

There were flashes of light, the glow of fire, and people shouting behind me. I struggled against myself, but just stood there, entirely vulnerable, at the mercy of someone's words. This was worse than the fire snakes. Unable to do anything else, I listened to the shouts and picked out the names 'Art' and 'Rhode'.

There was a gravelly cry of pain, followed by a series of curses. Then silence. All I heard was the traffic of the city.

People were walking down the road at the end of the alley. None of them acknowledged me or anything going on behind me. I struggled again to move, but nothing happened. My hands shook. My neck throbbed; breathing was becoming progressively more difficult.

The musical voice addressed me once again. "You! Checked-shirt girl, turn around and face me."

I obeyed with zero resistance to his command.

Two men stood before me. The dark-haired man was young, slightly older than me. He wore a long black trench coat and black combats, and carried an enormous, flaming, razor-sharp sword. The other was older, maybe mid-twenties, and in a long, green cloak. His skin was light-copper toned and pearlescent, his ears pointy, his eyes fierce, and his long blonde hair tied back from his face. He aimed his bow and arrow at me.

My whole body started shaking. I felt my lower lip wobble and bit down on it, fisting my hands to hide the trembling.

The dark-haired man sheathed his sword in the scabbard at his back. He put his palms out to me; they had dark marks all over them. Was that henna? He gently shushed me, as if he was coaxing a spirited mare. His expression was soft, with kind, curious, determined eyes.

"You're hurt. You must be in pain, no? We can help you." He spoke softly, his accent just like the hooded man's.

I eyed the pointy-eared one, arrow ready to fire on me. I couldn't move to dodge it if he did. He lowered his weapon and returned his arrow to his quiver.

"We will not harm you. You're safe now," the dark-haired man said as his eyes scanned my body and landed on my neck.

"I can't move. What did you do to me?" My voice came out thin and rasping.

"When you answer our questions, I will release you," Pointy-Ears said, his strong, musical voice incongruent with the murderous gleam in his eye.

"You've asked no questions. I've done nothing wrong. Why can't I move? What... who are you and what was that man?" My voice trailed off in a croak, and my heart thundered in my chest at my boldness, but I was tired of being hunted and trapped like an animal.

"We don't have time for this. More may come," Pointy-Ears said to Dark-Hair.

Dark-Hair nodded. He held his hand up to a space behind them, and silver wisps shot out in the form of the oval symbol on his palm.

"You will walk through the apporting gate now and make no fuss about it," Pointy-Ears commanded me. As he spoke, bright green, glimmering spots issued from his breath, like dust sparkles in a shaft of light.

I opened my mouth to protest, then closed it and limped stiffly through the swirls, a slave to his words. The dark-haired man took hold of my arm. I snatched it away. He grabbed hold of my arm firmly this time, looking down at me with steady, ocean-blue eyes. I felt compassion and suspicion coming from him.

As I walked through the silvery liquid, there was a distinctly warm, numbing sensation. I heard the rushing sound of water and smelled the earthy scent of loam.

We were standing on a muddy road. Forest lay behind us, and a river rushed across our path. A huge stone curtain wall towered beyond the river and an arched barbican, was positioned directly ahead. Gargoyles stared menacingly out at us from atop the gate towers.

Bile churned in my stomach. It hurt to swallow, and I was wheezing in air. I swayed a little; the gargoyles trained their stony glare on me. The dark-haired man was holding me around the waist. I felt a hint of worry from him and anxiousness. He smelled of bergamot and vanilla.

Then the darkness consumed me.

CHAPTER THREE

I WOKE TO FIND myself lying on a wooden-framed bed in a long, rectangular, wood-panelled room, filled with similar single beds. A bookshelf stood opposite me, and a mirror hung above it. It was day. Large windows covered the wall to the left, and a door led out to the right.

Inhaling deeply through my nose, I remembered what had happened. My hand went to my throat. The pain had gone.

Shifting my weight back, I sat up to discover I was wearing a nightgown. I cast my mind back. I'd passed out by a river. Panic and disgust rose up at the thought of some stranger seeing me undressed. Scanning around for my clothes, I found them folded neatly on a chair beside my bed. I rooted through the pile, looking for my phone. Yes – found it! I pressed the power button, but it was dead. I swore violently under my breath.

I *had* to get hold of my parents to see if they were safe. The hooded man had been outside my house. What if he'd done something to them?

My attention snapped to my right as I heard a rustling sound. There was movement from the two potted plants on the bookshelf.

They appeared to be having a scuffle, one swiping its long vines at the other. I blinked and quietly crept barefoot across the polished floorboards to inspect them more closely, not quite believing my eyes.

The recipient of the swipe lifted all its vines and wrapped them around the other's pot. It started edging the other pot off the bookshelf, while the instigator plant swiped at its white flower-heads.

I moved to rescue the distressed plant, but the door opened.

"If there is any more of this nonsense, I will separate you both! Understood?" A stout lady with dark hair marched over to the plants and perched her fists on her hips, glaring at them with intense dark eyes. They both drooped their flower heads and nodded slowly. The plant that was pushing the other off the shelf scraped the pot back to its original position.

"What's one to do about misbehaving Prickly Snowdrops? It's their nature, I suppose." The woman sighed, looking at the floor and scratching the side of her nose. Then she blinked up at me, as if remembering I was there. She was probably in her mid-fifties, dressed in a long blue robe. "Hello, my dear. Good to see you're awake! I'm Healer Gale, and I wanted to check how you're healing. May I?" She gestured for me to sit on the chair.

I shoved my clothes aside silently. As I sat down, she rubbed her hands together.

"I don't want to touch you with chilly hands," she explained, then gently felt around my throat and inspected my chin, hands, and knees. I felt calm coming from her industriousness, and total joy in her occupation, as she looked into my eyes. "How is your breathing now?" she asked.

On her robes, she was wearing a badge of what appeared to be a cauldron. What was she – a witch? I cleared my throat nervously. "Good, thanks."

I felt delight and satisfaction coming from her. My gaze settled on her face; her expressions reflected her emotions transparently. I didn't feel anything dark or foreboding from her at all.

She dropped her hands and sucked her cheeks in. Her eyes narrowed and took on a disconcerting look of scrutiny.

"That's an interesting badge," I breathed.

She brushed a thumb over it almost lovingly. "Yes, it shows that I am of Healing House, but all will be explained in good time."

I had so many questions in my head, but the most burning one was: "Was it you who changed my clothes?"

"Of course, my dear. Your clothes were damaged and filthy, but they're all clean for you now."

I breathed a sigh of relief inwardly and cleared my throat. "Can you tell me how long I've been here?" I needed information – and to get away from here, immediately.

"They brought you to me yesterday. I'm going to bring you a potion. It should perk you up more than adequately," she replied, standing up and smoothing her robes.

"A potion?" I asked, now on red alert.

She beamed at me and stepped out the door. I heard a male voice speak. It belonged to the dark-haired man from the alley.

"Healer Gale, how is she? Is she fully recovered?"

My pulse raced as I looked down at my nightgown. I didn't want him coming in when I wasn't properly dressed, and I didn't want any potion either. These people were most likely lunatics, or part of a supernatural cult. They'd held me against my will, kidnapped me, then... yes, I supposed they'd healed me too. Why would they do that? Maybe they were healing me to offer me up in some kind of ritual sacrifice.

I started tugging my jeans on, then hop-dashed to the door with one leg on, pushing it shut and pulling on my clothes and boots as quickly as possible.

Healer Gale returned to the room and gasped in surprise. "Ah, you're dressed! They wish to speak to you, but I've told them you will first have a potion."

I asked, more shrilly than I intended, "Who are *they*... and where are we? I don't have time to speak to anyone. I need to get home!"

"Of course you do. They will explain it all to you, but not until you have your potion." She wagged her finger at me. Her eyes held a determined glint.

When she left the room and closed the door, I edged towards the windows. The flower heads followed my path across the room. There were no latches to open the windows, but when I looked out, a few hundred feet away were the same curtain wall and gate I'd seen before I passed out. Or it looked the same. There was my exit... maybe. I wondered briefly if this was a fortress. Curtain walls were built around fortresses or even cities, weren't they?

Below the windows lay a gravelled car park containing a few regular vehicles, but my gaze was drawn to the shiny contraptions hovering in the air. They looked to be made of silvery crystal and shaped like the top half of a racing motorbike, complete with seat, foot pegs, and handlebars. The front end was elongated and covered by a shield. They were leashed with chains to buried iron loops. Some spaces contained rolled-up rugs, which were triple-chained to the ground. What *was* this place?

I heard the handle of the door turning and darted to my bed. Healer Gale was carrying a glass goblet of purple, bubbling liquid. It smelt bitter and slightly burnt.

"It tastes far better than its odour," she said confidently, handing it to me.

"I feel fine. Thanks for this, but I'm not thirsty."

It was a lie. I could have downed the contents of the Thames and all its tributaries.

"I must insist. You are my patient, and I wouldn't be doing my job as healer if you didn't take it," she said, eyes boring into me. "It's simply an energiser."

"An energiser. Like caffeine pills?"

"More like a smoothie – rich in vitamins. You will feel wonderful afterwards, I promise. I healed your neck and other injuries, did I not? Why then would I give you something that would harm you?" She arched her brows.

"Well—" She had a point. But what if it was a sedative to stupefy me for the sacrifice? I'd watched movies, and if my life was a movie, the past twenty-four hours would have been a horror – or at the very least, a nail-biting thriller. But I was dying of thirst.

She raised a finger suddenly, and I shrank back at her sudden movement. She took an upturned goblet from the next bedside table along and dribbled some bubbling, thick potion into the glass, then drank it. Her dark eyes brightened.

I watched her closely for a few moments.

"Well? As you see, I haven't sprouted horns," she quipped as she handed me the goblet.

I had also seen movies and read books where people had ingested tiny amounts of poison to build up an immunity. My lips pulled down at the corners in distaste, but I took a reluctant sip.

It tasted like chocolate sherbet mixed with almonds, a hint of garlic, and something smoky and salty, like smoked kippers. I knocked it back. The last of the dregs included what felt like chopped-up fish bones, so I ended up chewing rather than drinking. Chocolate, nuts, garlic, and fish: sweet, nutty, garlicky, smoky and salty. Who would have known that combination would work? *Not too shabby.*

"Feeling better – more energised?" the healer asked with a knowing smirk.

I nodded. "Thank you." Energised was an understatement. I felt like I could climb, descend, and throw mountains. I set the goblet down on the side table.

"I'm famous for my rejuvenation brews," she said, more to herself than to me. "Right, young lady." She snapped her eyes to mine, taking a deep breath. "My work here is done. If you feel ill at all, come straight back here to me." She smiled, her eyes crinkling at the corners, then her gaze became focused and curious. "You're an empath, aren't you? A rare gift… You should do well at healing."

"Erm. Healing... an empath?"

"Ah, that's right. You're new to the alius world. I have a gift for sensing powers in others." She grasped my hand, and I felt her compassion. "As I hold your hand, do you feel emotions besides your own?"

I nodded.

"Then you're feeling my emotions, which means you're an empath."

"Riiight." I decided it wouldn't hurt to try with my fact-finding again. "So, could you tell me exactly where we are? Perhaps there's a map?" I studied the bookshelf for clues, trying to gain more of an insight into our whereabouts. It would be great to escape from this place, but where were we?

"Explaining is not my department; my department is healing. And now you're healed and rejuvenated. I'll call for the chancellor, and she will be the one who explains it." The healer marched out of the room as if on a mission.

What the hell is a chancellor? It sounded very official. And why hadn't they brought me to a hospital? Although Healer Gale's method of healing appeared to be more than effective... Still, after nearly dying and being trapped against my will by a pointy-eared git, all I wanted was out of this place.

The memory of the shiny giant sword, the swirly magical door, and an arrow pointed at me sealed my decision. I checked myself in the mirror. My eyes looked brighter than usual, my hair appeared smooth, and my skin held a healthy, rosy glow. I wondered if her famous brew improved looks, too.

Creeping over to the door, I tried the handle. It opened into a dimly lit hallway.

I tiptoed through it quietly. Healer Gale was in an office to the right, her door ajar. She was talking to what looked like a hologram of a lady. I blinked at that and sneaked past her office to the door at the far end. Holding my breath, I grasped the door handle. Was it locked? I cheered inwardly as I swung it open.

Silence filled the widest corridor I had ever seen, leading both left and right. I chose right and made my way to the other end, impressed with my covertness until I collided with a bench that scraped loudly against the parquet flooring. *Ow!* I slid down beside the bench and crouched to hide myself, rubbing my injured knee, feeling sure someone would come out to investigate.

Movement opposite me attracted my attention. The marble busts lining the wall were all sternly glaring down at me.

"Pathetic excuse for a warrior," a bust with a moustache and a large set of fangs snidely commented. I stared blankly at him.

Footsteps came from the direction I'd been creeping in. The lady I'd seen as a hologram now appeared in the flesh, stalking by in her clacking heels and turning down the passageway I'd just escaped from.

I ducked my head, still in my hiding spot at the side of the bench. The smell of lilies and ginger hung in the air in her wake. I hurried in the direction she'd come from, flinging a dirty look at the rude bust before I left.

The hall I entered was flooded with natural light by a ring of windows in a domed ceiling. Two hulking boys who looked to be my age – wearing T-shirts that were far too tight for their broad frames – were reading newspapers on book stands that lined the lower walls. Neither of them looked up as I entered.

To my right was a colossal double oak door. One side stood ajar. This must be the front door. *Please be the front door.*

I pushed it open, and the wall was in view. My heart soared.

"Who's that?" one of the hulking boys said from behind me.

I didn't stop to hear the rest of that conversation. I sprinted past the car park with the hovering crystal bikes and down the gravelled road to the barbican. It was further than I'd first thought, at least half a mile, but that potion had given me some juice. I was running faster than an Olympian. I just hoped no one stood guard at the gate.

The wall was taller than I had expected. It was twice the height of my terraced house back home, and gargoyles haunted both sides of the barbican. Four sets of angry, stony eyes swivelled audibly down to glare at me accusingly as I approached the gate. Why were all inanimate objects animated here? I ignored them and inspected the gate doors. They had no keyhole – not even any visible sign of how it could open.

Suddenly, the gate doors blinked out of existence. My heart quickened. A coach was revealed on the other side of the river, and a stone bridge shimmered into being. The coach rolled forward across it, and I quickly shuffled to the side.

It was midnight-blue with *AA* written in curly, swirled gold letters on the front and side. AA breakdown cover for automobiles or the Alcoholics Anonymous sprung to mind, although the logos looked entirely different to them.

I stepped toward the gate, but another vehicle followed behind it, and another. It was a convoy of coaches, packed with kids my age, some of whom stared out at me. On the last coach, a handsome, dark-blonde-haired boy gazed at me from the window. I locked eyes with him. His face appeared again from the back window as the coach passed, accompanied by a red-headed boy. I stared after them, then turned and promptly exited the gate.

The bridge in front of me blinked out from existence.

Edging to where it had been, I toed the space with my boot; but there was nothing. The gate remained open behind me. There were seven scruffy-looking boats on the riverbank to my left. They were round and the smallest boats I had ever seen.

I considered my options. Swimming across the river and drowning; using one of those half-boats, capsizing and drowning; returning home to find my parents strangled and the hooded man awaiting me in my lounge. My chest felt tight. I needed to contact my parents to see if they were safe. If they *were* alive and well, they'd be worried about me.

Who was the hooded man? Who were these people, and what did they want with me? The healer had called them 'alius' and me an empath. The AA logo... was that an acronym for Alius something? I walked over to the half boats and checked the nearest one for holes, then realising I'd need an oar, I scanned around for one.

A melodic voice called out to me. "Hey, checked-shirt girl. You need some help?"

I would have betted a week's earnings that he had pointy ears.

"Why is everyone calling me checked-shirt girl?!" I hissed as I spun around, looking for the source of that beautiful voice with a smooth, deep timbre.

It came from a bare-chested guy roughly my age, in the middle of the turbulent river rapids. I blinked. How was he floating there like the rapids weren't trying to pull him downstream?

He swam closer to the riverbank, apparently encompassed by a haze of shimmering, palest blue. His shoulders were broad and roped with muscle, his dark copper skin perfection. High cheekbones; pointed, elfin chin; stunning, pointed ears.

"Do you require aid?" he asked with a grin as I ogled him shamelessly.

What the hell was wrong with me?! I gulped. "Just looking for a way to cross. Do you know where the bridge went?"

"You'd need a spelled token or to know the magic-word of the day, before it emerges once again. If you join me in the river or use a coracle, I can help swim you across." His voice sent a thrill up my spine.

I would go anywhere with you, I thought yearningly. I blinked, feeling an urge to do just that. I glanced doubtfully at the water, then stared back at him in rapture, moving closer to the river's edge.

"Zale, stop that immediately!" a commanding voice that sounded vaguely familiar bellowed from behind me.

I whipped around. A tall, slim woman with smooth, bobbed, chestnut hair, wearing a grey designer trouser suit and lilac top – complete with a diamond necklace and earrings – stood in front of me. She looked to be in her fifties. It was the hologram lady.

I looked back at Zale. The blue haze surrounding him had disappeared.

"It's Laurel-Leah Fields, isn't it?" the woman said, holding out her hand for me to shake.

I took it hesitantly and detected a flare of irritation, suspicion, and determination from her, but I was quite certain she had saved me from another pointy-eared person. His magic felt different from the former. He hadn't been commanding me; it was more that he'd been dazzling me with his insanely breath-taking looks.

"I'm Gertrude Wutterhorn, Chancellor, or better known as the head of the Alius Academy," the woman went on, gesturing toward the building I just escaped from... sort of.

"This is a school?" I asked, then my head snapped up, immediately on my guard. "Hold on... how do you know my name?"

She chuckled. "Indeed. It's an academy for young alius – young magicals – who've either been recently unbound or whose magics have emerged for the first time. We discovered your name by pinpointing where your magic emerged. At your home." She started back toward the academy building as if expecting me to follow.

I hesitated. The gate remained open, and my chance of escape had likely disappeared, but there was a lingering sliver of hope. I scanned my surroundings, desperately searching for a way out; my feet flipped from pointing towards the river and escape, and back towards the academy and my captors. Escape. Captors. Escape. Captors. Perhaps I could just ask her what I needed to know.

"Did you go to my house?"

She halted and turned. "I didn't go in person, but yes, we have spoken to your parents."

"Are they alright?" I asked. "Do you have a phone I could use? I need to speak to them; I need to get home."

She looked into my eyes appraisingly. "I understand your concern for your parents. And in light of your recent emergent magic, and the attack you suffered... you must have some questions?" She raised her eyebrows slightly.

I nodded.

"And I will answer your questions, then present some options for you – but we will do so in the privacy of my office," she concluded, eyes shifting around as she spoke, as if someone might be listening, then settling back onto me. My gaze darted around; I half expected an attack. When none came, I considered her words.

What options? I didn't like the sound of that – I'd much rather just go home. But she had a point. How would I handle the murderous hooded man when I returned home? How would I learn to use the powers I could feel swirling around within me?

Rock... hard place. But I needed answers and solutions.

With some reluctance, I nodded in agreement. "Ok."

CHAPTER FOUR

WE AMBLED SILENTLY SIDE-BY-SIDE back to the school. The façade of the building was pale stucco, punctuated at the window ledges with the darker stone used to build the curtain wall. It was really more of a mansion than a fortress.

A shield was buried in the dark stone above the entrance door, divided into four sections. In each section was a different symbol: a cauldron, a pegasus, a fox, and a spider on its web. *Alius Academy* was written in script above it, and a motto written in Latin below.

I followed the chancellor to her office, which was next to the domed hall.

The door ahead of us read *Chancellor's Secretary*. A long-nosed, middle-aged man with voluminous red hair greeted us from behind his desk. We walked through his office, to another door marked *Chancellor Wutterhorn*.

Her office was enormous and furnished elegantly. There was a spotless, smooth walnut desk, parquet flooring, plush Persian rugs, bookshelves lined with alphabetically arranged tomes on two walls of the room and filing cabinets covering another. Another door led to somewhere unknown.

In front of her ample desk were four Chesterfield couches arranged in a square with a large glass coffee table nestled in the centre of them. The chancellor gestured for me to sit down. I sat facing the office door, and she perched on the adjacent couch.

"Would you like a drink?" she asked.

"Yes, please." I decided to extract as much information as possible and hope they weren't trying to drug me.

"Clarence!" she yelled.

The red-headed secretary appeared at the door. He wore a white button-down shirt, a tie, and a brown suit with waistcoat. A pin of a red fox was attached to his lapel. "You called Chancellor Wutterhorn?"

"A coffee for me, please – and for you?" she asked me.

"White tea. Four sugars, please." I needed my energy.

His lips parted for a moment, then clamped shut. He left the room as silently as he'd entered.

"I realise it may have been frightening to wake up in a strange place, particularly in view of recent events. For that, I apologise. I came as soon as Healer Gale alerted me that you had awakened."

"No harm done. I'm fine now. Thank you for having me healed." I aimed to be cordial so I could get the information I needed and get away as soon as possible. A trick Vita used frequently – though diplomacy wasn't usually a strength of mine.

"Healer Gale is a highly skilled and exceptional healer, one of the best. You have mended well." She smiled, but her eyes lacked the warmth of the healer's.

I gave her a wide smile in return. *Diplomacy.*

"Now that I'm in your office, can you tell me about my parents? You said some of your people spoke to them?" I didn't mention Vita. Hopefully she was ok after the pointy-eared and dark-haired ones had chased the fire snake man away. I didn't want these people to know about my life and the people I loved any more than what was necessary.

"Your parents are safe, as is your friend, Vita."

My fingers tightened around my knees. Bugger! They knew more than I wanted them to.

"I will explain in more detail shortly, but it's of the utmost importance that I learn about the man who attacked you. Had you seen this man before?" the chancellor asked.

I crossed my arms. "I think I saw a glimpse of him outside my house, before I set off to the cafe, but then he seemed to vanish. Other than that, no... What *is* he?"

How much to tell her? I pondered sharing the ice, air, and fiery feeling I'd had within. Something in me said to avoid saying anything about the Voice I'd heard in my head. Not because it sounded crazy – although no crazier than a fire snake man – but because it felt... wrong to mention it.

"He is a light-reaper, named so because they drain you of your light – your life, in essence – and absorb it into themselves." Chancellor Wutterhorn's eyes darkened.

I'd felt him draining my energy away. That was true.

She inhaled. "I have much to share and explain to you now. It will be difficult for you to understand. You've lived amongst the naries of this world as one of them, but now you'll learn the truth."

"What's a narie?"

"It's a word we use for non-magicals." She cleared her throat. "The man who attacked you hunts a particular type of magical-user."

My palms grew slick. I had a feeling she was going to tell me something I really didn't want to hear. I blinked and blinked again.

There was an insistent knock at the door.

"Come!" Chancellor Wutterhorn commanded, and the door swung open. Drinks and a plate of what looked like biscuits bobbed through the air toward us, Clarence-less. They arranged themselves on the coffee table as I gaped.

The chancellor took a sip of her coffee. Suddenly hungry, I leaned over to grab what looked to be a homemade chocolate-covered biscuit – yum, shortbread. I chased it with a sip of my tea.

"I will speak frankly with you. The light-reapers hunt their own people whom they consider to be traitors. You may have seen murders reported on the narie news, namely strangulations?" She quirked an eyebrow.

"I've seen the reports. Can I just ask about, er... traitors?"

"I will explain in due course. These murders are being committed openly, for all the world to see. Did he ask you questions during your attack?"

"Yes, he asked me who my people were. I thought it was strange, cos I'd seen him outside my house."

She pursed her lips and placed her coffee cup down. "When our people visited your home, your parents were unharmed and unaware of anything untoward. We did, however, discover that a protection arc had been placed around your house." She paused and eyed me for my reaction.

I shrugged. "Am I supposed to know what that is?"

She merely kept an even gaze on me.

I shuffled on the couch at her silence, then rephrased. "Are you saying someone protected us?" I wondered if the person who belonged to the Voice had done this.

"The protection arc matched *your* emergent magical signature. It was *your* powers that protected your home."

My jaw dropped, and my mouth started goldfishing. I gawped at her, entirely bewildered.

"I – I don't know how that's possible. I can feel the magic, and it reacted when the light-reaper—" I shivered. "When he used his fire and wind powers on me, I felt my magic react. Is it possible the magic does what it wants, without my knowing it?"

"Yes." The chancellor stared at the glass table, in thought, then raised her eyes to mine. "It's possible. It is a sophisticated form of magic for a recent emergent, but it's not impossible." She squared her shoulders, seeming to resolve to something.

I edged to the front of my seat in anticipation.

"We spoke to your parents, and we found that neither of them are alius." She tucked her chin toward her chest and narrowed her eyes.

I looked at her blankly.

"They don't have magical powers," she elaborated.

I clicked my tongue in understanding. "I can't imagine that was a simple conversation. Did you just ask them?"

"You have talked to two fae with influencing mind-magic: Rhode, who rescued you with Art, and Zale, whom you spoke to on the river. That magic is prevalent amongst other alius as well. We used mind-magic."

My heart leapt into a gallop. I gripped my cup tightly, and an insane feeling of rage mounted; my hands shook. Aside from her patronising tone, I couldn't believe they would use those subjugation methods on my elderly mother and frail father. Being bent to someone else's will was like torture, even if it didn't physically hurt you.

Biting my tongue, I closed my eyes to calm myself and shut out the chancellor before I did or said something I'd regret. My fire flared within. The contents of my mug suddenly boiled and fizzed.

I dropped it in shock, the tea spilling over her plush Persian rug. Her own mug shook on the coffee table like a kettle brought to the boil. So much for diplomacy.

I breathed slowly through my nose, not trusting myself to speak. Who the hell did they think they were, taking advantage of my parents? My tea continued to boil on the carpet. I closed my eyes and tried to meditate – remember my mindfulness app.

It worked... sort of. When I opened my eyes, the water had stopped boiling and reduced to a simmer. I cast around for a towel or tissue to clean up my mess. That rug looked expensive.

"Apologies, I dropped my drink. Do you have a towel or tissues?" I stated the obvious in an unapologetic tone and entirely ignored the simmering situation whilst trying to maintain my manners. That was what my mum had taught me, anyway. (Not the unapologetic part, but the manners.)

Chancellor Wutterhorn lifted a hand toward the stain. The silver ring on her right middle finger glowed white, and the stain vanished.

I stared at the ring in interest: two silver bands that linked at the top and bottom to form an oval shape. At the centre of the oval lay a sword with a white blade and pommel, a silver cross-guard that curved up at the ends, and a tan hilt.

Relaxing a little now that the stain was gone, I pressed my boot to the carpet to check for any remaining liquid. Nothing.

"Magic has its perks," the chancellor said with a smile, then went on more seriously. "Your parents were not harmed. Understand that the most important law for alius is to ensure the naries are unaware of our existence. That's how we have survived all these years. Using one's influencing mind-magic is the gentlest route to uncovering information."

I nodded begrudgingly. I'd rather they didn't use magic on my parents, but my mum would have banished them out of the house for sure if they hadn't. She was feisty when you got on her wrong side.

"Do you think you're ready to continue?"

"I'm as ready as I'll ever be," I said, nodding repeatedly as if trying to convince myself rather than her. "I apologise for the boiling drinks; I can't control it." I supposed I was getting the information I needed and asked for – it just wasn't what I wanted to hear.

She laughed. "That's why the academy exists – so we can teach our young emergents control. No harm done. I will call Regina; things tend to run smoothly in her presence."

She extracted from her suit pocket what looked like a silvery, translucent crystal ball the size of an orange; it reminded me of the crystal I'd seen on the floating half-motorbikes. She threw it in the air, where it hovered. It spun as if looking at me, then spun back round.

"Contact Regina Wyrmglas," Chancellor Wutterhorn said, and flashed a grin at me as she waited.

The crystal ball flashed green, then projected a live, three-dimensional image of a stunning woman with long, wavy blonde hair, who looked a few years younger than the chancellor. She was wearing a jewelled tiara.

"Regina, we could use your help. Can you make it to my office?"

"I certainly can." The woman glanced at me with a set of warm brown eyes. "Hello, Lori Fields. I will be with you shortly."

I opened my mouth to say hello, but she disappeared before I could respond. Still thirsty and hungry, I stared mournfully at my empty mug and selected another biscuit.

"Regina has a calming effect on us all. The information I'm sharing with you, as you've now realised, can cause... upsets," the chancellor said in explanation.

I crossed my legs at the knees and bounced my foot in nervous anticipation, the hard lace ends of my boots rattling. Some moments later, Regina entered the chancellor's office. She headed over to me, draped in golden jewellery and shook my hand. I felt nothing coming from her, no emotions. I stilled my foot in confusion.

"I'm Regina Roberta Wyrmglas. I'm a counsellor here at the academy, and the Dragon-Shifter Queen of the North." She gave me a dazzling smile, revealing sharp ivory teeth.

Instead of feeling panic and alarm at the words "dragon" and "shifter", a calm, peaceful sensation poured into me. My shoulders loosened, and I sat back.

Regina nodded to Chancellor Wutterhorn, who shifted her knees back towards me and steepled her fingers.

"When your magic emerged, you released a magical signature," she said. "We cannot detect what kind of magic it is until we test it, only that it's emergent. The light-reapers can sense when a similar magic to theirs is released; they only target people of their own kind, as I previously mentioned.

"Now... light-reapers are not of this world. They're from a world named Eassus, of the Lysalian galaxy."

I felt more positive emotions being pushed into me from the dragon-shifter queen, who stood at the chancellor's desk. I laughed, feeling thoroughly at leisure.

"Are you trying to indirectly tell me I'm an alien?" I laughed again, shaking my head. "Yeah, right – pull the other one." I giggled and continued to do so.

"Perhaps we should ease the feel-good factor," Chancellor Wutterhorn said sharply to the Dragon Queen of the North, her expression vinegary.

Some of the giddiness I felt was withdrawn from me; I stopped laughing and blinked.

Chancellor Wutterhorn leaned in toward me as she spoke. "We found you're partly an Earth mage, as I am, and part Eassusian Elemental."

I furrowed my brows. "You're telling me one of my parents is from a different world? Why didn't they tell me? I *really* need to speak to them. If you have a telephone, or a magical gateway home, or even just a charger for my phone, I would be soooo grateful." I used my best persuasive tone. If this news had come from my parents, I might be more inclined to believe it.

"We used a magical and a narie DNA test. You are not your parents' biological child. Both your parents were adamant you were. Unfortunately, their memories had been tampered with... as have yours."

I leaned back, feeling more feel-good factor being pushed into me. I flicked my gaze to Regina and gave her a nod of thanks. If not for her, I'd have been having a full-on breakdown by now.

I didn't believe anything the chancellor was telling me – except about the memories. I thought about what Regina Wyrmglas was doing now, and how I could feel people's emotions. Apparently, I could also manipulate air, water, and fire, to an extent. The pointy-eared people could influence me with words alone. Why not be able to tamper with people's memories?

Something occurred to me that made my heart skip a beat. "What did my parents say when you told them I wasn't theirs?" I didn't believe her, but what if *they* had?

The chancellor shifted in her seat and pursed her lips. "As you know, I wasn't there, so I can't relay their reactions or words, but your family cannot know about the alius. It is procedure that narie memories are wiped after they've witnessed alius using magic.

"The memory wipe is painless, and they will think nothing different about you than they did previously. We placed several safeguards around your house to protect them, in addition to your enormously powerful protective arc. They are safe and being monitored."

Despite the wonders of the calming magic being pushed into me, an immediate weight lifted at hearing they were safe and in no doubt that I was their child. Perhaps using magic *was* the best way forward in this delicate situation. "I think you're wrong about my parentage, but I'd like to thank you for protecting them."

She waved away my thanks and moved swiftly on, nodding to Counsellor Regina. I felt a boost of calm.

"Our main concern is you. All alius of Earth are registered at birth, and interplanetary visitors and refugees are registered on arrival. You are unregistered, and despite what you choose to believe, your true identity remains unknown. Your magic has emerged, and you must learn to control it." She pulled her suit jacket down at the cuffs and laced her fingers on her lap.

"It's a problem being unregistered. Is it like not having a narie birth certificate?" I asked.

"A suitable analogy, Lori, if naries wielded exceptional powers," she said, her eyes darkening. I repressed an eye roll. "As you are an unknown entity, you have two choices. The first is to complete and pass the Alius Trials, a set of trials used to measure your suitability to train here. If you passed the trials, you would be accepted as a student. This is the most prestigious combat academy in the world. Attending here will open many doors for you." She glanced at Regina Wyrmglas, who nodded.

"And if I fail?" I said.

"If you fail, you will be sent to the Alius Detention Facility, where you will learn basic control of your magic and remain there. This would be necessary due to your unregistered status, and to protect your narie parents from being attacked by light-reapers. If, however, your identity is uncovered and proves to be innocuous, you could be released from the facility and start in service in a low-paying job amongst the alius."

"What's the second option?"

"The second option is going directly to the detention facility."

I puffed out my cheeks and exhaled. The dragon-shifter filled me with a burst of positivity, and I had an idea. "In the same way my magic emerged, could it be taken away? If you can alter memories, you could make me forget I was ever here and I could return home, none the wiser!"

Even as I said it, I feared the light-reaper and all the alius. Would it be better to learn magic? I still hadn't figured out what path to take in my narie life, and the magic I could feel coursing through my blood felt good. It felt like... how it should be. But my parents – they needed me.

Chancellor Wutterhorn was shaking her head before I finished speaking.

"The light-reapers have identified you as Eassusian; they know where you live and what you look like. They rarely attack non-Eassusians, such as your parents – unless their work is interfered with."

"As in, 'killing people' type of work?" I asked, thinking it would be uncommon for a family member to sit aside quietly and watch their family being murdered without *interfering*.

"Precisely. If your magic were bound and memory wiped, you would have no defence against them whatsoever. Your presence amongst the naries would place you and your family in greater danger. The Alius High Council are considering relocation for your parents. Surely you want to keep them safe, if not yourself?"

She was doing a better job at persuasion than I had so far.

"As we don't know why you were not registered, who your biological parents are, and why you were placed amongst naries, we need to monitor you. As you're an emergent, we need to train you. This can be done in the detention facility, or you have the opportunity to complete the trials to train at the academy. Those are your options," she concluded.

I felt steady calm flowing into me from Regina Wyrmglas. It was a relief.

"Who would we be training to fight? Eassusians?"

"Domestic enemies, foreign enemies, and interplanetary enemies, both alius and narie."

I absorbed that. They had a lot of enemies. "What's involved in the trials?"

"The trial events are never revealed to invitees. You and your fellow prospectives are invited to complete them, and if you pass, you attend the academy. You should know that we only invite those whom we view as having great potential."

I shook my head, still grateful for the emotional manipulation and the ability to consider this calmly. "How much does it cost to study here?"

"We invite you; if you pass, we teach you. There is no monetary cost. Jobs are discouraged, courses and training are rigorous, and we expect you to give it one hundred percent of your attention. In fact, if you don't you are likely to fail and be sent to the detention facility."

"I need a job to help at home," I protested. "My mum also needs help with my dad – none of this can work!"

"We can help your parents indirectly. That is another benefit to magic; you need not worry."

"How?" I demanded.

"If your parents play the lottery, we could ensure a win, for example. There are many ways we could improve their situation. With more income, they can hire a healer or a carer," she said, folding her arms.

I stared at my hands, wondering if a healer could help my dad. The magical lottery win sounded unethical, but if it helped my parents and I couldn't return home, then... *Who gives a shit about ethics? With all that money floating around the universe, why not give it to my parents?*

The chancellor's gaze bored into me, waiting for a response. "I need to think about it," I said. I was never one to make hasty decisions. It seemed a simple choice on the surface, but I knew nothing about this world.

"Very well. I anticipated this and have arranged for someone to show you around the academy. We have unparalleled facilities here," she said smoothly. She flicked her hand toward the door; the crystal on her ring glowed white. "Clarence!" she yelled as the door opened.

Clarence appeared in the doorway. "He's been waiting in my office since the drinks flew in, Chancellor."

He stepped aside to reveal the young man with dark-hair and ocean-blue eyes from the alley, standing self-assuredly, relaxed, hands joined in front of him.

He no longer wore combat clothes; his loose, long-sleeved T-shirt clung to a set of thickly muscled, broad shoulders, his trousers tucked into his boots. His hair was short at the back and sides and slightly longer and tousled on top. When my eyes travelled back up to his, I saw a hint of amusement in them. He quickly swept his gaze to the chancellor.

"Art, thanks for coming so promptly. Would you be so kind as to give Lori the grand tour? I would have asked one of the other students, but these are complex circumstances. Perhaps you can tell her how it went at her parents' house," Chancellor Wutterhorn said to him, narrowing her eyes. Her gaze flicked to me. "Will two hours be sufficient time?"

I glanced at the cuckoo clock; it was five to one. "Yes, but is there a chance I could just call my parents... or even a friend?"

"We discuss that when you return." She turned to speak with Regina Wyrmglas. I took that as a dismissal.

"Thank you," I said to Regina. If she could bottle that emotional manipulation, she'd be a billionaire. Perhaps as a queen she already was.

"See you at three p.m.," Art said to the chancellor.

CHAPTER FIVE

Art about-turned and strode out of the chancellor's office. I followed his lead. As we stepped out from the secretary's office and into the corridor, he gestured to the left.

"The sanitorium is here on the left, as you are aware." He walked down the corridor to show me.

"Sanitorium?"

"Healer Gale, where you recovered. We call it the san."

"Isn't that for crazy people or something, or people with a terrible disease?"

"I believe you're thinking of an asylum, but yes, some of the people who require healing could be described as crazy, or even diseased." He looked sidelong at me with a glint to his eye and a twitch of his lips.

"Ha, bloody ha," I muttered under my breath. "So, any chance I could use your phone? You kidnapped me, so you owe me."

Art lowered his brows. "I would describe it as *rescuing*, healing, and securing you for your own safety, and there are no external calls permitted, not until the chancellor says so." He shoved his hands in his pocket forcefully.

I clicked my tongue and mimicked him under my breath, aware I was being childish. "'*Until the chancellor says so.*'"

"What was that?" he asked, his eyes sparkling.

"Nothing. Just clearing my throat." I flashed a broad grin.

I walked beside him, keeping my eyes peeled for anything that resembled a phone, as we approached the busts again. Queen Regina's emotional manipulation had clearly been severed, and now my emotions were all over the place.

"Simply ghastly," a bust with an impossibly long beard said through barely opened marble lips, glaring at me and Art with disdain.

"That's quite enough of that. I don't tolerate rudeness, Elias Philipus," chided another bust sporting a marble moustache and goatee and an excellent set of straight teeth.

I smiled at our defender. He gave me a wink in return. I stopped walking for a second as I thought I saw real human eyes flicker in his marble ones. I blinked... just a trick of the light.

We entered the domed entrance hall, the bust heads swivelling on their marble necks to follow our path.

"This is Dome Hall," Art stated as we entered the oak-panelled room.

"Imaginatively named," I quipped, but I took a moment to take in the grandeur of it. Galleried balconies revealed the upper floors. Individual heraldic shields studded the unpanelled portion of the upper walls, embossed with the symbols I'd seen before: a cauldron with an emblem of a snake emblazoned on its front, a pegasus, a fox, and a spider on its web. Wooden plaques with names engraved on silver badges covered the rest of the space, but they were too high to read. Newspaper stands clung to the walls, and in the centre of the room stood a hexagonal table.

Five arched doorways led off from the hall. One was the entrance from which I'd made my failed attempt at escape; two of them, Art explained, led to temporary student accommodation upstairs. The fourth was the corridor we'd just come from, and the fifth led to a bisecting hallway, similarly oak-panelled.

Art led me down that one, telling me that the hallway led left to the main hall, right to the grand library, and straight on to the dining hall. He marched ahead, passing several doors and rooms whose functions didn't seem worth an explanation. He did, however, explain that the library was off limits during the trials.

We reached another area with a high domed ceiling named North Hall. There was a sweeping staircase to our left, then corridors beyond it that branched left and right.

"Most rooms in this building are reserved for the teaching staff and meetings. If you decide to attempt the trials, you will stay in this building until you have completed them, then you will move to your selected house: Combat, Healing, Creative or Intelligence," he elucidated.

In front of us was another massive arched doorway. I could smell an assortment of food and hear a murmur of voices echoing inside, drifting out to us.

"Dining hall," Art said as he led me in.

There was a food service area to the right. To the left were long oak tables with benches, and round tables with chairs filled both ends of the room. The ceiling was beamed and vaulted, pulling your gaze ever up to appreciate its grandeur.

On the opposite wall was a set of large French doors leading to a gravelled outside eating area. Round patio tables and chairs overlooked a fountain and a vast expanse of green. The green was lined with trees, thickets, and buildings. Beyond them was a view you'd see on a postcard – woods nestled around a mountain, that stood directly opposite.

Students sat in groups, both inside and out. Many wore sunglasses, and most wore designer clothes. None of them wore a checked shirt.

"Do you want a drink?" Art asked.

He walked over to a long oak table lined with drink machines, leads trailing down to sockets. There was an array of hot and cold drinks; one machine offered twelve different milks! There must have been a hundred distinct types of teas and coffee blends. Art picked up a glass, his selection made.

I drifted over to another table of drink machines, wondering if they were any different, noting a distinct metallic odour in the air. My head snapped back in shock. The drink labels displayed blood types and varying temperatures – including one that said *Vegan Blood (Human-Free)*.

Art walked toward me, carrying a dark green drink with steam pouring off it. He gestured to the machine I was studying in horror. "For the vampires," he explained.

"Vampires are real?!" I blurted out.

A group of sunglasses-wearing people drifting into the dining hall, stopped walking, and looked my way. Art frowned and pursed his lips.

"Sorry." I lowered my voice to a loud whisper. "*Vampires are real?!*"

Art cracked a wry grin. "Yes," he replied, voice pitched low. "But first get yourself a drink. We'll sit down, and I'll answer your questions."

I gulped, but my mouth had gone dry. Trying not to think of all the human blood stored in those machines, I returned to the former drinks table and settled on apple juice and a bottle of water, eyes darting around for a cash till. There wasn't one.

I didn't have any money on me, so I turned to Art. "Do I need to pay?"

"No, everything is paid for by the academy. You can get anything you want."

That was a pro for the academy, but the choice of human blood groups was a con. So were the designer-clad students. Sure, Vita had designer wear, but she wasn't above my style of clothing... even if *her* checked shirt and jeans cost six times as much as mine.

Art sat in the outdoor patio area, next to the marble fountain and away from everyone else. I joined him, taking in the fountain's majesty. It was the height of three men; water spurted from a central sword into a series of six bowls, growing ever larger, and finally into the circular walled pool below. Six marble figures of different shapes and sizes gazed outward from pedestals sprouting from the circular wall at equidistant intervals. From where we sat, I could see a male in a pointed, hooded cloak holding a staff aloft; a tall, willowy female wearing an intricate tiara, a bow in her hand and a quiver strapped to her shoulder; and a man, two heads smaller than the other statues, with an impressively thick beard, wearing a helmet-type crown and wielding an axe. Water sprayed from their rocky pedestals into the fountain.

Despite the weaponry they were holding, the expressions of the figures were serene. The sun sparkled off the fountain water. I had to admit that this was the most beautiful place I had ever been in my entire life. That was another pro.

Art interrupted my thoughts as I cradled my apple juice glass in both hands. "So, you're not going to ask me anything? Have you already decided?"

I looked up, startled. He brushed his hands through rich brown hair.

"I was waiting for you to tell me about my parents, but I'm having a hard time controlling my... feelings about you going to see them. It won't bubble up if I don't hear about it," I confessed. I could do with no further uncontrolled outbursts, particularly as I was thirsty and didn't want to drink scorching hot apple juice.

He leaned toward me. His ocean-deep blue eyes were bright and clear in the sunshine. They were flecked with gold and utterly mesmerising. The scent of bergamot and vanilla lingered in the air around him.

"I can help you with your magic. It seems..." He trailed off, choosing his words carefully. "We are the same, in part. I am from Eassus."

"Are you? Your accent is like the light-reaper's, so I was wondering. Well, I'm still hoping this is all a nightmare and that I'll wake up sometime soon. If it isn't a bad dream, and if what the chancellor told me was true, then I don't understand – if I'm half from Ea... Eassus—" I stumbled over the unfamiliar word.

"*E-zzuews*," Art emphasised slowly, "not *Eass-us*, and the phrase would be half-Eassusian."

"Thanks so much for the correction." I exhaled deeply.

"Always a pleasure."

"Alright, smart-arse!" I snapped.

Art's eyes widened in surprise. My patience was fraying. Although he seemed like he was genuinely trying to help, the last thing I needed was a pronunciation lesson for the alien world half of me apparently belonged to. My negative emotions had come back with an unwelcome bang.

"If I'm half-alien, then why do I look human? Why do you?"

Art opened his mouth, but I went on.

"How can all this be? It just seems off-the-charts ludicrous – impossible. It just can't be. I can't believe it. I don't..." I trailed off, folding my arms. I didn't think I'd ever used the word *ludicrous* before in my life, but that was how it felt.

"If it's safe for me to speak, I'll explain," Art said sarcastically.

He paused, waiting for a further outburst. I remained silent.

"Of course, some aliens don't look human, but Earth resides in the Milky Way galaxy, no?" He continued without awaiting my confirmation as he raised his eyes to the sky. "This galaxy has billions of habitable planets alone. Is it surprising there would be other planets in the universe with similar beings, when there are countless trillion galaxies?" He leaned back in his chair.

"Erm... is that your whole answer?" I stared at him from across the table, expecting more.

He sat silently, gazing at me with wide eyes, then turned to watch the fountain, giving me time to absorb his words. I noticed his eyelashes were long.

I suddenly felt tiny as I looked up to the blinding, sun-filled sky. I was but a grain of sand on the beach. *Maybe it's not so ludicrous after all.*

"So how did you get here – in a spaceship? And why did you decide to come to Earth, and why attend this academy?" It sounded like I was being facetious, but I really couldn't get my head round what he was saying. As far as I understood, humans hadn't made it past the moon, never mind to the rest of our galaxy.

He leaned forward, planting his elbows on the table. "Many worlds have superior technology to Earth's. Regardless, each humanoid-habited world has two people who can traverse the universe in the blink of an eye. They are called ferans. There is always a Dark Feran and a Light Feran. I traversed to Earth with the Dark Feran of Kerrasus."

"Kerassus? Is that in Eassus, or did you mean to say Eassus?"

"Eassus is a planet, and the seat of power for the Eassusian Empire. There are twelve other planets within the Eassusian territories, including Kerassus. I was born on Eassus, but I escaped to Kerassus after the emperor ordered my execution," Art finished bitterly. His face darkened, and his hands curled into fists and covered his mouth.

I blinked. My mouth felt like it was filled with sand.

"Execution?" I quavered.

He gazed into my eyes. I saw a flash of pain and then sadness before he fixated on the pepper shaker on the table.

"Emperor Valeconiss seized control of Eassus eighty years ago. He's a tyrant and responsible for countless genocides and murders... including my family." The lines of his jaw tightened. He'd gone pale. "People have fled as refugees or exiles over the years to different worlds, and some here to Earth."

"How old was he when he seized the throne? I mean eighty years is a long time. He must be a dinosaur now, and near the end of his reign?" I took a sip of my apple juice.

"Eassusians live for an average of a hundred and eighty years."

I half drank, half spat my juice out. Some of it went down the wrong way. I coughed and thumped my chest, eyes watering.

"Are you alright?" Art asked, concerned.

I nodded, scrubbing my hand across my face, catching the apple juice that – mortifyingly – dripped out my nose. Heat travelled up my neck and flared in my cheeks.

"So... he may live a while yet," I croaked.

Art laughed softly, but it didn't reach his eyes. "Some people believe Valeconiss has gained immortality. The powers of the gods. Rebellions are annihilated as soon as they arise. The result: refugees and exiles."

"Are the light-reapers refugees too? The chancellor mentioned they were hunting traitors."

He shook his head. "They have been sent here by Valeconiss to hunt us, kill us, and finish the job." His eyes sparked with anger.

"Oh," I said, blinking. "I understand why you escaped to come here."

The back of my eyes was burning with tears as I turned away from him. I didn't really understand why it upset me so much, but to have to go so far to escape and still be hunted... I had to process the concept.

If all this was true – and it was getting harder to deny, unless I was the victim of a seriously screwed-up game show – then my whole life up until now was a lie. Maybe I was hidden and unregistered because I had always been hunted. The reality was that if the academy hadn't healed me, the light-reaper would have killed me.

No matter how I wanted to deny it, I had been attacked by something I'd never seen or heard of before. Mages and vampires existed in mythology. Men wielding fire-snakes that drained your magic and life did not.

I felt unsettled... bewildered. It was like falling in a dream, down that sheer cliff, but never waking up and smashing on those rocks below. I'd thought I knew who I was, but all those beliefs were crumbling to my core, everything I was. Who was I if not Lori Fields?

We were quiet for a while. My eyes were fixed on the fountain, my mind submerged in thought. The susurration of the water soothed my nerves.

It was Art who broke the silence. "To answer your question, I didn't choose Earth, in particular..."

He inspected his glass between two large hands. I swung my chair around from the fountain to face him full-on.

"When I finally found him, the Dark Feran chose the destination." His lashes swept up, and he held my gaze. "In truth, I was relieved to go to any destination that took me away from the territories." He took a swig of his drink.

"So how long ago did you arrive?"

He raised his eyes to the sky in memory and ran his hand across the back of his neck. "I arrived here from Kerrasus three years ago. I was already advanced in combat, so naturally I chose the best magical combat academy in the world rather than, for example, a business academy." He paused, and a grim expression took hold of his features. "There were maesters here that I could learn from. I wanted the opportunity to improve my skills and learn other things."

He brushed his chin with thumb and forefinger, eyes taking on a gleam of light, of hope, before folding his arms across his broad chest and leaning back. "That's why I applied for an assistant teaching role in combat. They offered me the role and a place as a student. I had to complete the trials, but I passed."

My shoulders tensed. "You're a teacher here?" I asked nervously – and not just because he was attractive. I'd just yelled at him and called him a smart-arse.

"More of a coach, mentor, assistant, and a student," he clarified with a smile.

"I'm ready to ask now..." I shuffled in my chair, steeling myself and trying to harness my control. "How were my parents? How did they look when you told them I wasn't their daughter? What did they say when they found out? Did they deny it?" I looked up at him in a flinch, readying myself for a blow from the news I dreaded to hear.

Art raised his hands in surrender. "Woah, hold your horses," he said, eyes twinkling. I smiled at the very colloquial expression, wondering if they had horses in Eassus too.

He explained that there had been no signatures of magic in my house other than mine. This alone indicated my parents were non-magical. He'd misted them with a feel-good calming spray and used influencing magic, so they'd handled all news and information regarding who the alius were, and what they were trying to establish during the visit, incredibly well. I asked if the feel-good calming spray had been made by Queen Regina. He simply grunted.

He said that yes, my parents had been adamant that I was their child. He'd asked their permission to take blood to determine DNA and an alius test to detect magic. These had been analysed against my own blood, taken from me whilst I was unconscious.

I drew back from him and sucked air through my teeth at that news, but remained silent; I wanted him to tell me everything thick and fast. But these bloody alius needed to learn about human rights.

Art stressed again that influencing magic and calming spray had been used. My parents had not been harmed in any way, and the results for parentage and magical ability had been negative. I glanced away from him at that.

My parents' memories had been searched by a mind-mage, whom Art informed me was adept, highly experienced, and professional. It had been carried out with precision and without pain. I wondered briefly what exactly a mind-mage was, but I had a feeling the clue was in the name. I didn't want to interrupt him, so I let him continue.

Once the mind-mage had found my parents' memories had been tampered with, they'd erased any memories of the alius visit entirely. They'd fortified magical wards and alarms around the house and placed protection charms on my parents' clothes and car, and at my mother's work. They'd told my parents that I was at a friend's house and not to worry; I was fine. Art assured me they were unlikely to be attacked without my presence, but our house was being monitored around the clock.

I knew the influencing magic was painless, but it was frightening. The calming spray would have helped their nerves. I could see Art was gentle in how he approached people, so at least the academy had been good enough to send him. I breathed a sigh of relief that my parents didn't know I wasn't their child; maybe they wouldn't want me anymore if they did. At eighteen, having no adoptive parents as well as parents who'd given me away was not something I wanted to deal with.

After his monologue, which did comfort me to a point, there were some things I wanted to clarify.

"The chancellor said that whether I'm sent to the detention facility or attend the academy, I can't see or contact my parents or narie friends, because I'd put them in danger. Is that true?" I asked.

"The light-reapers are likely to be monitoring your house and all known friends. It's too much of a risk," Art said, eyes hard and determined.

"How do we explain that to them? I mean, sure, telling them I'm at a friend's for a few days they may believe, but any longer than that and they'll want a feasible explanation."

"We can alter their memories and use influencing magic to convince them you're safe and well. And they have no need to worry about you," he said simply.

I gulped at that. These people could run the world with their powers.

"The chancellor mentioned my memories had been altered as well. Who looked inside *my* mind... without my permission?"

"The same person who looked into your parents' minds."

I took a more direct approach. "And their name would be?"

He folded his arms. His jaw tightened again. "Do you have any other questions?" he asked quietly.

I decided to leave it. I would ask him about this again some other time. If people were looking inside my mind, I wanted their name and address. I would concentrate on more pertinent questions for now.

"How many years do you have to attend here?" If I was going to commit to this thing, I needed to know more.

"It's three to five years of study, depending on what field you decide on. Usually after that you'll apprentice wherever you go." He drained the rest of his green drink. It smelled floral and minty and it reminded me of something, but I didn't know what.

"What is that drink?"

He wiped his mouth with the back of his hand. When he dropped it, a wide grin emerged. "My favourite brew from the Eye of Eassus

– crushed rosemarian mint." A lightness had enveloped him. Home comforts... what wouldn't I give to be back at home myself.

Behind us, people emerged from the dining hall with food. They came out in as many different shapes and sizes as the figures on the fountain. There was a group of tall willowy people with long, flowing, silky hair, pointy ears and the ever-popular sunglasses. On another table sat little people, shorter than me and stout; even the males appeared smaller than me, and most had some form of facial hair – generally long, bushy beards. On a different table sat huge, bodybuilder-like men, like the guys reading the newspapers earlier. My stomach growled at the scent of the food.

"Shall we eat?" Art asked with brows raised, his lips curling up slightly at the corners.

"Yes, I'm starving," I said, returning his smile. "My mum told me to never make a big decision on an empty stomach."

His eyes lit up. "Ah. My father taught me, *Never take orders from a man who does not eat his fill.*"

It wasn't exactly the same thing, but I nodded and laughed. He was trying to find common ground with me, and I wasn't about to tell him we didn't have any.

He stood and waited for me to join him, and we made our way back into the dining hall to join the lunch queue. I picked up a tray and eyed the food choices ahead.

"Art, you are needed urgently by Maester Imod and the chancellor," Clarence declared, standing at my elbow. I jumped at his sudden appearance.

A tall, dark-haired girl with a pixie haircut stood at his side. Clarence turned to me and gestured to her. "This is Charlie. She will be showing you around until three p.m."

"Welcome to the academy. I hope to convince you to stay and take the trials," Charlie said, her light grey eyes steely and determined. She was wearing a tan leather blazer over black clothes. I took her outstretched hand in a warm, dry, sturdy handshake and felt curiosity and determination coming from her.

"Maester Imod sends his apologies for the interruption of your tour," Clarence added, glancing between me and Art. He looked around, as if belatedly realising we were not touring. His eyes flicked up to the cuckoo clock that hung on the wall behind the food counter. "Enjoy; must be off." He held a narrow, long-fingered hand up in a wave and sped off in the direction of his office.

"I'm sorry too," Art said to me as he picked up a sandwich. "I'll see you around... I hope Charlie can convince you." He gave her a nod and smiled at me with an incline of his head.

"Thanks for showing me—" I started, but he'd already stridden off in the same direction as Clarence.

Charlie stood next to me, watching me watch Art leave. I suddenly felt very alone.

CHAPTER SIX

"You've already got a crush on teacher, eh?" Charlie said. She glanced sideways at me, then back to eye Art up and down appreciatively as he disappeared out the dining hall. "He doesn't think you're too bad either, if you were wondering," she added with a smirk.

I felt myself trying to scowl but lost the battle against my smile. "I don't know if *that's* true. But he told me he was a teaching assistant and a student, so I don't know if whether he thinks me not being too bad is relevant. It might not even be legal."

"He hasn't dated any students in the two years I've studied with him. I think dating a student he teaches would be frowned upon. He's only twenty, but Eassusians start their magical education from age seven over there. They come into their powers early." She turned to face me.

"So, when do other alius start their magical education?" I asked.

"Let's get table service. We can sit and enjoy the sunshine – we may as well enjoy the perks, yeah?" she said, changing the subject and reminding me a little of the chancellor. She stalked out the queue and glanced over her shoulder, waiting for me to follow.

I stepped out and she swaggered off outside with long strides that matched her long legs. I scurried along after her, remembering my first day at my new school in Seddingham, when I had met Vita. She'd looped her arm around mine and dragged me all over the school.

Charlie chose a table outside, near to where Art and I had been sitting. I decided to stop scurrying and walk at my own pace, tray still in hand. I sat down and closed my eyes as the sun warmed my face.

Charlie answered the question I had asked back in the queue. "It differs amongst species. Most of us start at the academy at eighteen. Some mages emerge earlier, the earliest around fifteen years old, and may with special permissions be allowed to train at home until they're eighteen. Fae and dwarf powers emerge at puberty; that lot have their own rules. The powers of shifters, Eassusians, and vampires are bound, normally by the alius authorities, until they reach eighteen, regardless of when they emerge."

That information caused me to frown. It didn't seem fair. "Why the different rules?"

"It's safer that way. For example, the wolf-shifters' primary change occurs on the full moon during puberty. Puberty is not the best age for emotional control. Apparently, there were a lot of narie deaths caused by wolf-shifters back in the day, followed by narie-led wolf-hunts and wolf-shifter deaths. So... them's the rules."

"Ok, the bindings protect wolf-shifters, and what about Eassusians?"

"I've heard you were subject to a light-reaper attack as soon as your powers emerged. Need I say more? But I also hear you're half-mage, half-Eassusian. That's interesting. Your powers emerged later, like a mage?" She said it half as a statement, half a question.

"I haven't thought about it, but I suppose so," I replied, not wanting to correct her assumption. The alius seemed to differentiate between magic being unbound and magic emerging. I hadn't emerged, as she said; the Voice had told me that I was *unbound*. So, perhaps because I was part-Eassusian, my magic had emerged a while ago, which meant someone had bound it. But who? Having to explain the Voice was just too weird. I still felt that no one should know about it. "So, how long have you studied here?"

"I'm in my third year now, same year as Art."

"Are you Eassusian too?"

She smiled at me, white teeth gleaming. I waited for an answer, but she remained silent.

She blinked. When her eyes opened again, her pupils were enlarged; the pale grey of her irises covered nearly the whole of her eyes, and they seemed to glow. Teeth grew to fangs. Her nose elongated to a snout and whiskers.

I pushed back hard from the table, my chair flipping back. My heart flapped like a caged bird in my ribs; my palms were slick, and my hands shook. I held my tray in front of me as a shield.

People laughed in the tables around me. I scanned blurred faces around the patio and flicked my gaze back to the hard lines of her normal, square, human face.

"Sorry," Charlie said, smirking. "Didn't mean to scare you. It was a test. So, you really are completely new to our world. You don't know magic, wolf-shifters – anything." She shook her head.

I remained a few metres away, eyeing her cautiously.

"It's ok, I don't bite." She sniggered. "Ok, that's a lie. I'll clarify. I won't bite you, outside of combat. If I did, I could be suspended, and if the bite was fatal, I could be expelled." Her eyebrows arched in a smug challenge.

I edged back to the upturned chair and turned it upright, all the while keeping my eye on her.

"I'm starting to think I'll take my chances at home, with only fire-snake-wielding, strangling lunatics up my arse," I said, finally dropping the tray to my side.

She gave a huge, barking, hearty laugh. I'd never heard a laugh like it – partway between a wheezing seal and a hyena, with spatters of pig snort punctuating the end of each breath. I heard titters around the courtyard. This had to be a lively regular source of amusement for everyone at this school. Charlie seemed like she was having some sort of fit; her body shook with it. I finally wedged myself back into the chair and laughed, despite my scare.

"I like you, Lori – you've got big brass ones on you, and an interesting way with words."

Her words made me feel slightly more at ease, but I kept my eyes peeled on her all the same.

"Now... let's order." Her stomach growled. I wondered if that happened often when she was toying with her prey.

"How do we order then? Does someone come over?" I asked, casting around for a menu and a waitress.

She pressed her finger to what at first glance I thought were large round nail heads on the wooden patio table. Then she said to the void in front of her, "What are today's lunch choices?"

Bright orange letters appeared in the space at the centre of the table, as if someone had lit a sparkler and was writing with it in mid-air. The words lingered and formed into a menu.

Charlie ordered a steak with mashed potatoes and a ginger beer. Starving; I ordered a full chicken roast, with Yorkshire pudding, gravy, and a cola.

"Are the silver buttons linked to a bell or something?" I asked.

"I'm not sure how it works. You press it, ask for the menu, order what you want, and the food and drink fly over to you." Charlie shrugged. "Wolf-shifter magic is our ability to transform from human form to wolf form and all that goes with it, so I can't tell you how this works."

"So, what else goes with it – your wolf-shifter magic?"

She smiled a wolfish, toothy grin at me. "Our senses are enhanced. We're the second strongest alius, level-pegging with vampires in speed. We're hard to kill, but you'll learn all that once you've passed the trials... or more likely *during* the trials."

I gaped at her.

"We're taught how to *kill* other alius?" I asked in disbelief. Although... perhaps it would make me feel safer if I knew how to defend myself.

"We're taught one another's weaknesses and strengths, yes," Charlie said, nodding. "Ultimately to defend ourselves, if necessary, from other alius. If we fight light-reapers, for example, we need to know how to beat them."

"And what are the trials like? Are they hard?"

She chuckled. "Nice try, but my lips are sealed." Leaning over to me, she lowered her voice. "It can't hurt to ask other trial invitees what they've heard." She gave an exaggerated wink.

I giggled. "Thanks for the tip – I will do. So, do you enjoy it here?"

"Yes. Wolves need a pack. I have one back home, but when we come here, we form new packs. So yeah, I love it."

A group of people came to sit at the table behind Charlie. They were dressed in designer gear, they all wore sunglasses, and they all had the pointy-tipped ears I was now becoming accustomed to.

Charlie stole a glance at them over her shoulder. "Fae," she said, too loudly. She gestured to her ears and mouthed *pointy ears,* planting a forefinger to each side of her head. I bit back a laugh, shuffling down in my seat as all the sunglasses turned in my direction.

One of the girls, with long, sleek, black hair, squared her shoulders at me, red lips clamped into a tight line. Her head turned between me and Charlie, and she leaned forward, speaking to a blonde-haired, fresh-faced girl to her left and a fae boy dressed in a sharp suit to her right who had half his shoulder-length chocolate-brown hair tied back in a top-knot. They spoke in hushed tones. The buzz of other voices around the patio were too loud to catch her words.

"Priscilla Evervale, you now have four hours doing combat drills with me!" Charlie boomed, and everyone in the patio went silent.

"I beg your pardon?" the black-haired girl, who I presumed was Priscilla Evervale, demanded in an equally commanding tone. "Who are *you* to give me such orders?!" She jerked her chin and curled her lip back in disgust.

"I am Charlie Savage, House Captain and Head Prefect of Combat House," Charlie said, without turning around.

Priscilla stayed silent, folding her arms and turning away. Her nostrils flared.

"The reason for your detention is that you called me a snivelling mongrel." Charlie's tone was dispassionate. "I was simply explaining the differences between our kinds to someone who knows nothing about the alius. I was not making fun of you or calling you derogatory names." She finally turned to face Priscilla. "We start at six a.m. on Monday morning – that's *if* you pass the trials. There are *many* royals and ancient lineages here at Alius Academy; we do not tolerate derogatory comments between species. Understand?"

Priscilla looked like she was going to argue at first, but her expression changed, like she thought better of it, and she finally blurted, "Yes!"

Charlie eyed her with a predatory tilt to her head, and spoke in a threatening tone, "Was there something else, you wanted to add?"

Priscilla's eyes darted to her friends; Her male friend shook his head. Her shoulders lowered. She dipped her chin, as if in defeat. "No, Prefect Savage."

"Next Monday, six a.m., combat field," Charlie reiterated coolly. She was clearly used to giving orders and having them obeyed. Priscilla, on the other hand, was clearly not used to following them.

I was impressed and cowed by Charlie's commanding presence; she was a natural leader. I would just sound like a blithering idiot if I did the same – although I couldn't help suspecting that she had laid out bait for Priscilla. Even I'd been embarrassed by her pointy-eared gesture. Maybe she used the nobles and leaders of the school as an example to whip everyone into line, letting them know that this wolf was top dog – no pun intended.

"So... you can hear what people say in a crowded space full of voices?" I asked.

"Yep, I can hear from over a mile away. I'm also immune to certain magic, and I can detect emotional and physical changes through scent. That's why I could tell that Art likes you." She cocked an eyebrow. "And that you like him."

She cast her eyes down in the vicinity of my nethers. Horrified, I folded my hands in my lap, heat creeping up my neck.

Charlie snorted. "I'm kidding! I can smell your pheromones and see auras."

"You're telling me that every wolf-shifter in this academy can smell and see physical attraction?"

She nodded. Her eyes seemed to focus on a larger space above and around me. "For example, your aura has a reddish hue at the moment." One side of her mouth curled up, like she was happy to watch me squirm. Hanging out with her gave me the sweats.

"Can other magic species see auras? How do you do it?" I asked. It was something I'd love to learn.

"I don't know, wolf-shifters can just... do it. It's one of our powers." She shrugged.

I studied my hands, trying to see if I could detect an aura, then stared hard at Charlie, squinting my eyes a bit. Nothing. She gave me a self-satisfied smile and chuckled, shaking her head, as our food and drinks came floating through the air, artfully weaving between students. It looked and smelled delicious.

We devoured it silently and quickly. The food was glorious – every drool-inducing bite. Even the homemade biscuits I'd had in the chancellor's office had been to die for. *That's another pro*, I thought.

After lunch, Charlie took out a crystal ball and threw it out in front of her. It hovered in the air as the chancellor's had.

"This is a globe. It's akin to a mobile phone in the narie world. Globe, map of the academy," she ordered, and a detailed hologram map appeared in a projection in front of us.

She explained what the different quadrants and buildings were and what they were for. She pressed her fingers on the Pegasus House, the accommodation for Combat House. The map zoomed into the building and showed the plan of it, so you knew where the rooms were. Then she asked if I wanted a quick walk around. It was now 2.15 p.m., so we had time to kill. I agreed.

She led me towards the right side of the green.

"Here on the right is the mage quadrant. We generally don't go into each other's quadrants, except for parties," Charlie told me, lowering her voice and peering around. "The quadrants are more for training, so it's not relevant to alius who don't have those particular powers. On the left here is Fox House, the student accommodation for the Intelligence House. Up here is the—"

I had stopped walking. Charlie halted alongside me. I'd been concentrating on what I could see, which so far was amazing, but I hadn't considered what I *couldn't* see. "Charlie, do you know anything about the detention facility?"

"Detention facility... urgh." Charlie shivered.

My chest tightened. My choices were to go there directly, or attempt the trials... and if I failed, to go there anyway.

"There's not much to say. A few large buildings on a site. A large wall surrounds it."

"Like here?"

"No, we have a wall at the entrance; the rest of the barriers are magical and natural, such as the sea, the river and Dwarf Peak." She pointed at the mountain ahead of us. "The other difference is that we can leave the academy, and our walls are to keep unwelcome visitors out. The walls of the detention facility are to keep you in."

"Like a prison?"

"As far as I'm aware, it's similar to a prison. It's patrolled, and magical security systems are in place. I've heard there are alius refugees from different countries, or different worlds, in there waiting to be registered. Or alius who have been detained. They might be waiting to be sent to other countries or worlds."

I didn't like the sound of that. I'd made up my mind; there was only one main concern I had about this whole situation. Smacking my lips together, I realised I was still thirsty. "I think you can probably explain more about the academy while we have an after-lunch drink. What do you think?"

"Have you learned enough? Have you decided?" Charlie asked, her grin slowly broadening, and her grey eyes lit up like lanterns. She tilted her head back and sniffed. "Your odour has changed – the bitter scent of indecision has disappeared. You've decided, haven't you?"

"Yes, but I'd like to learn more."

"I knew I'd get you on side!" She looked thoroughly pleased with herself as we ambled slowly back to the refreshments and she went on with her explanations.

There were combined lessons for all alius, but most were specific to your individual alius powers. Cross-species socialisation mainly occurred in the houses, during events and in the social centre imaginatively named 'The Centre'. Alius Academy prided itself on the species mixing and integrating, but unfortunately, the alius community had a social hierarchy that filtered down into all areas, including here. Species were, in order of power and importance: mages, fae, vampires, dwarves, shifters... and Eassusians. As half-mage and half-Eassusian, I wondered where I would stand.

Lessons generally occurred in the outbuildings or the quadrants. Charlie showed me her favourite hotspot on the map of the academy, the Zeus Ring Stadium, and told me to never enter the area named the Garden of Statues, located between the mage and shifter quadrants. She swore it was evil. All shifters stayed away from there. Of course, after hearing that, it was the first place I wanted to go.

Just before 3 p.m., we started walking back to the chancellor's office. I liked and feared Charlie. I never wanted to get on her bad side, and I had a feeling that might be the case for most the alius.

I would miss my parents badly. I'd never been away from home for more than a few nights. Vita was away from home constantly, but she had the option to return; that was being taken away from me. Then again, seeing my parents might endanger them, so it was more the light-reapers that were the problem rather than the academy. But I needed assurance that my parents would be safe, and they'd have enough income. I needed a guarantee.

The detention facility sounded like nothing more than a prison for non-criminals. If I was to survive and see my family again, I'd need to learn more than basic magic to defend myself and them. The trials would give me an opportunity to learn that. My narie life did lack direction; I had been thinking of leaving Murray's anyway – why not learn at the academy instead?

And although I was one of them, if I was to ever stop fearing these alius people, exposure therapy might do the trick.

CHAPTER SEVEN

Back at Chancellor Wutterhorn's office, Clarence waved me to a couch opposite his desk, and Charlie spoke to the chancellor alone. I couldn't imagine Charlie being anyone's creature, but I felt uncomfortable that she was probably relaying all we'd spoken about to the chancellor.

Finally, Charlie exited her office and told me with a beaming smile that she'd see me around.

Chancellor Wutterhorn was standing at the door. She ushered me towards the chair in front of her desk as she settled into hers. There was a file spread out on the surface of her desk – my file. I attempted to read it upside down.

"Well, what is your decision?" she asked me, as if she already knew the answer.

"You mentioned that you're protecting my parents, and that you can help them financially. Is that guaranteed?"

The chancellor pursed her lips and nodded. "Yes. Whether you choose the detention facility or the trials and attending the academy, we will ensure your parents are monitored for safety, supported financially, and given extra help for care. I have discussed this with the High Alius Council and they have agreed. It is our duty to help naries whose lives have been affected by the alius."

I nodded in relief, hoping that was she was saying was true. I steeled myself, injecting a confident, positive tone into my voice. "In that case, I've decided to take the trials and get a place in the academy."

"I'm happy to hear it. I have your file here; I'll need you to sign some paperwork. First of all, you will be issued with a globe." She rustled through her papers, then walked to one of the filing cabinets across the room.

She selected a key from a large bunch, with varied interesting bows, then unlocked and pulled out the middle drawer to a length of around seven feet from the wall. She pulled a set of steps to the cabinet, climbed up… and stepped into the drawer. She disappeared entirely, seeming to descend some steps.

"Where did he put them?" she muttered from the depths.

A bright flash emanated from the drawer, and the chancellor climbed back out, holding a globe. She threw it up; when it hung in the air, she tapped her glowing ring to it. A rainbow of colours cycloned around it.

"If you would just hold it in your hand as it identifies to you," she said, pushing it toward me.

It was the size of a tennis ball and started nudging at my hand, so I took it into my fist. It heated, then returned to its normal silvery colour with a sound akin to a single drop of water falling into a water-filled dish below.

"The globe has taken your magical signature and knows your identity; it will answer to no one else. It will be needed for the trials, so bring it with you, and please sign this form saying you've been issued with one."

I picked up a biro, scanned the form and signed it, and she moved on to the next document.

"The trials – and indeed learning magic and combat – are, as you can imagine, not always risk-free. All students must sign a death waiver to take part in the trials and lessons at the academy."

My heart thudded as I read it, but I'd rather risk death trying to learn magic than be hunted by the light-reapers with no knowledge of it. I signed it before I could change my mind.

Chancellor Wutterhorn took out her globe and scanned her papers. "You'll be rooming with Saffron Underhill during the trials. The globe will show you the location of your dorm."

She pressed her fingers to her own globe. It turned green, then a sort of interfacing occurred as it sped over to mine, which in turn flashed green.

"Charlie mentioned the globes were like a mobile phone. Is it possible to call the narie world using them?"

"The globes are solely used within the academy. If you pass the trials, I can arrange for you to speak with your parents. However, the more you contact them, the more likely it is that the light-reapers will find ways to intercept messages and learn of your location. That could endanger your parents. Would you like me to arrange this for you?" she asked, smoothing over a judgemental expression.

I shook my head and sighed.

"The last signature needed is for your attendance here. I'll summarise, then you may read. Meals, accommodation, learning, books, uniforms, and transport are funded by the academy. You will receive a small bursary for any additionals."

I read through it and signed. I had a nagging question but was trying to ignore it. If she suspected me to be a possible danger because I was unregistered, then why not send me directly to the detention facility? I had no doubt she could change her mind and do just that, so I pressed my lips together.

"Trials start at eight a.m. tomorrow morning. You can get settled in your room presently; just ask your globe the way."

"Ok. Thank you, Chancellor," I said as I flitted out of her office, the globe bobbing behind me.

Clarence flicked his eyes up at me from his desk and offered me a sharp-toothed smile. I wondered briefly what he was.

Walking out into the corridor, I recalled how Charlie had addressed the globe. "Globe, show me to my room."

It spun up and down as if nodding, then spun around and led the way. It took me to Dome Hall, then through the arched doorway to the left and up uncarpeted wooden stairs.

I climbed up to the first floor and peered down over the balcony – not too close. Heights were not my thing. The globe floated in front of me and zipped down the right-hand corridor.

It stopped at a door on my left and flashed green. The brass door handle and knocker flashed an answering green and opened. I looked at the globe. Maybe it was better than a mobile phone.

The room was about six times the size of my box room at home. It had two cabin beds at each end, with a desk and wardrobe underneath. There were two chests of drawers and a dressing table with a mirror on top, a sink in the corner, and a strange-looking cuckoo clock, like in the dining hall.

I inspected the contents of the wardrobes. Black combat uniforms hung up in there, the same as the one Art had been wearing yesterday. Footwear, my size, lined its bottom. In the drawers were casual clothes – jeans, tops – and pyjamas, dressing gowns, toiletries, towels, and even underwear. How would they even know my size?

Scooping up the toiletry bag, some towels, and a fresh set of clothes, I addressed my guide. "Globe, where are the shower rooms?"

My globe bobbed and led the way.

The shower room had a set of six showers in a row, facing sinks and mirrors, similar to what you would find at the swimming pool. There was a wet and dry area in each, so you could shower and change. I chose the one on the end. Once I'd finished and was towelling off, I heard the door open, and girls' voices filled the room.

I tried to make some noise to alert them to my presence, but they had turned on taps and the showers, which drowned out my throat-clearing. *They should check the stalls for eavesdroppers anyway.*

"What do you think the trials will be this year?" Anonymous Girl One said. My ears pricked up as I dressed.

"It's anyone's guess. There's usually physical tests, magical tests, there might be a written test, the Revealing, fighting other alius, the winnowing, fighting beasts..." Anonymous Girl Two listed off.

I stilled, being suffocated by the shower steam. I was pretty sure I would not fare well in anything they had just mentioned. What the hell was the Revealing? A written test about what? I knew nothing. And what beasts?

"Livia, how's Sebastian?" Anonymous Girl Three said, changing the subject. Silence followed. "Livia?"

There was a sob. I pulled on the rest of my clothes.

"What's the matter?" One said.

"Umm. He – he doesn't really say much. He won't talk to me. I w-went over to his mansion to see if he was ok. He k-kept me standing at the door... He just said, 'I can't do this anymore', and that w-was it!" Livia fully broke down into what I imagined was an ugly cry.

"Wait... you're no longer an item?" Three asked, as if that was tantalising news.

"Eugenia, he's just found out. Of course, he's not going to be in his right mind," One said.

"Honestly, I was just asking. A lot of people would be very interested to know he's back on the market – that's all I'm saying." Eugenia said it like she was the one who was interested.

There was a sharp intake of breath. "You wouldn't!" Livia snapped.

That was my cue to leave. I cracked the cubicle door open.

Unfortunately, Livia – who had long, caramel-coloured hair – wasn't having a shower like the other two. She was crying on the stall bench, facing the sinks and mirrors opposite the showers. She wore a black mini-skirt, a white silk blouse, and grey spike-heeled boots.

She looked up at me through the mirror's reflection, stopped crying, reddened, then scowled.

"Where the hell did you come from?" Her face twisted, and her overly large blue eyes bulged a bit. "You should make your presence known instead of eavesdropping!"

The two running showers abruptly turned off.

"I wasn't eavesdropping, I was having a shower and getting changed. Which is, for all intents and purposes, the function of a shower room. If you want a private conversation, have it privately, or at least check the other shower stalls." I shrugged, balancing my bundled towels, clothes, globe, and toiletries in my arms.

A head popped out from the stall to the left. "Oh!" said One's voice. Recognition flared in grey eyes. "You're the unregistered."

She was slight and brown-haired, with a pale oval face and freckles; her tone suggested clarification of identity rather than spite.

"I saw you at the gate when I was on the coach, coming into the academy. What were you doing? Trying to run away?" she asked, eyes wide and unblinking.

A head crowned with a twisted towel popped out from the stall to the right. She was the tallest of the group. I guessed that was Eugenia. She looked me up and down, waiting for a response. Heat flared in my face as I searched for a feasible explanation.

"First of all, I'm Lori, not *the unregistered*, and I was just looking around the grounds. I must be off now."

I turned to leave, but the small brown-haired girl was inclined to ignore my statement and continue the conversation.

"I'm Karina – Karina Amberpot. This is Livia Leer and Eugenia Egbert." She gestured to each in turn. "I heard you're part mage, and you've been living as a narie." Karina looked at me expectantly, awaiting confirmation, then ducked back into the stall.

I dropped my towel and toiletries on the sink countertop. She came back with a towel on her head and another loosely hung over her shoulders, openly drying herself off. She was clearly one of those people who didn't mind who saw what. I looked away.

"Word gets around quickly," I commented.

Just then, one of the little people I had seen in the dining hall, with wheat-coloured hair, entered the shower rooms. She was a head smaller than me.

"Hi! I'm Cassidy." She walked over to me to shake my hand, noticed Karina towelling off, and averted her indigo eyes, looking scandalised.

"Lori," I returned, shaking her hand.

She gave me a conspiratorial smile. "I don't know why the academy can't give us ensuites."

"I have to agree with you, *dwarf*, they shouldn't expect *all* species to share the same facilities. It's unsanitary," Livia hissed, narrowing her eyes at me and Cassidy.

Cassidy crossed her arms. Glaring at Livia, she snapped, "Yes, *mage*, they should consider cultural differences. Not all alius strip naked and dance under the full moon – dwarves value modesty." She swung her gaze over to Karina. "For the Mother's sake, cover up, will you!" She was formidable for someone who was only about four feet and six inches tall.

I remembered what Charlie had said about the academy priding itself on cross-species integration. Clearly it didn't come without its problems.

"Nice to meet you all. I'm off," I said, before this could turn into a full-blown cat-fight regarding inter-species characteristics of which I knew nothing. Once again, I turned to walk out the door.

Livia stormed up to me and grabbed my arm, putting herself between me and Cassidy and spinning me to face her. "You will not mention our private conversation to anyone," she said in a low voice through gritted teeth. "In the alius world, eavesdroppers are not tolerated, and nor are *unregistered, illegal refugees*."

I snatched my arm from her grip, squared my shoulders, and lifted my chin. If Cassidy could look intimidating, I could too. "I told you – you should have checked there was no one else around if you wanted your conversation to be private. But I'm not a gossip, and even if I were, your sad little story isn't worth gossiping about. And if I'm not tolerated, why have I, like you, been invited to the trials?"

"Lori's part mage. It seems more characteristic of a *mage* than an Eassusian refugee to flout the laws and not register their child," Cassidy said, in my defence... I thought.

I gave her a half-smile and a nod, picked up my things, then walked out.

CHAPTER EIGHT

I HALF-EXPECTED LIVIA TO follow, to reiterate. She didn't. Had I made the right decision in choosing to complete the trials? After all, I had only been conscious for five hours in the Alius Academy, and I was pretty sure Priscilla and Livia already had it in for me. Though I couldn't see Priscilla's full expression at the time, as she'd worn those sunglasses, I *had* laughed involuntarily when Charlie had done the finger thing for the ears – and Priscilla had definitely turned her head in my direction when I had.

My sobriquet of *checked-shirt girl* seemed to have changed to *the unregistered.* And it seemed being unregistered was a far bigger deal than I'd imagined.

I returned to the bedroom, searched for my globe – buried in the towels – to unlock the door, and sat at the desk beneath my bunk bed, wanting some time alone.

After a few seconds, noise came from the hallway outside my dorm. The doorknob flashed green, and the door sprang open. A globe hovered in from the hallway, and my globe rose from my desk to interface with it. Then a stunning tall, full-figured, fiery-red-haired girl walked in, sunglasses pushed up onto her crown.

Her hair was tied in a meticulously styled twist at the back of her head, and wisps fell around her pointed, elfin chin. The room filled with the scent of strawberries.

She wore a one-shoulder fitted blue-and-yellow mesh top, heels, and brown, cropped trousers, which were so tight they looked like they'd been painted on. At her elbow was a miniature black flying horse. No – from the looks of its gold horn, it was a winged unicorn. My jaw dropped in awe before a leather trunk floated in after her.

"Hello, Laurel-Leah Fields, prefers to be called Lori," she said, with a smile that didn't quite meet her light-purple eyes. "I'm Saffron Underhill, resident fae in our assigned hovel." She cast her gaze around the room as if the walls were closing in on her.

I opened my mouth to respond, but she cut me off.

"I asked for a master suite for the trials, and they put me in the servant's quarters. Where is the bathroom? There is not even a three-piece suite! How am I supposed to *breath*e in these cramped conditions?" Another trunk floated in behind her.

My moment of quiet and contemplation had truly crumbled off a cliff and was speeding to the bottom of the ocean. Saffron pushed some loose hair behind her ears, and there they were – the pointy buggers, though her ears were less sharp than those of the fae I had met before. I stopped myself from rolling my eyes and groaning.

Her winged unicorn was adorable, though. It swooped in front of her and dropped into her arms.

"This is my teacup alicorn, Lilliput," she said, bright purple eyes shining as she glanced from me to Lilliput. It gave a high-pitched whinny and relaxed in her arms. It was no more than ten inches high.

I opened my mouth to say hello, but another *two* trunks floated in, followed by a small brown furry creature about four feet tall, with large, pointed ears and pale yellow eyes. I stiffened.

The creature turned to me, taking hold of the front of her fine green velvet dress, which she wore over a white top, as she bobbed me a curtsy. I rigidly semi-bowed back, confused, not wanting to be rude. Perhaps that was the custom of these creatures.

"I'll speak to the chancellor. There must be a mistake," Saffron muttered to herself, as she dropped to the chair at her desk. Her creamy complexion had turned pink as she cradled her pet. "How do you feel about the accommodation, Lori Fields? If I asked to move rooms, would you be happy to move into larger quarters?" Her bright eyes darkened to violet as she pleaded hopefully. I was surprised that she'd want to move and still share with me.

"I'm happy with it," I said gently. "It's large compared to my bedroom at home, although it's new for me to share." She was clearly distressed, no matter what the reason, and I didn't want to stress her out any further. I had to admit, there had been a lot more space before three further bodies and four trunks had appeared, though it was true that it was still far bigger than what I was used to.

"I've never had to share either," she replied, not unkindly, sucking in a breath. "Well," she said, resigned. "I suppose I can weather it if you can." She eyed the space dubiously. "But I'm guessing we have to share the bathroom with others, wherever it might be, and I'm definitely not looking forward to that."

"I can agree with you on that. I've just come from having a shower, and the people there were having a heated debate about modesty and nudity. Having said that, I was told these rooms are only temporary. Perhaps if we pass the trials, we might get ensuites," I suggested, trying to soothe her worries.

"Was it dwarves and shifters?" Saffron asked, purple eyes brightening with curiosity. It took me a few seconds to grasp her meaning.

"A dwarf and three mages."

She nodded, rolling her eyes. "Yes, mages dance naked under the full moon and the dwarves can't bear open nudity."

I smiled, having witnessed the truth of it.

"If it's just for a few days, I suppose I can bear it," she added, hollowly. She gestured to the brown creature. "This is my lady's maid, Thistlebloom."

"Hello... I'm Lori." My voice came out a little high. I was hoping at some point I'd get used to seeing things I never had before, but it seemed it wouldn't happen today.

"I can tell you've never seen the likes of me. I am a brownie of the Court of Underhill in Fairieland," Thistlebloom piped up.

"Very pleased to meet you. I'm part mage, part Eassusian, and hail from Seddingham in England," I answered, feeling I should introduce myself with the same formality.

She curtsied again. I did another seated bow. Saffron glanced between us, smiling.

The furry creature clapped her hands together twice. The trunk lids flung agape, and their contents disappeared, manifesting neatly in the now open wardrobe doors and drawers. Somehow, everything fitted perfectly. Thistlebloom told the trunks to pack themselves away. They promptly broke down like flat-pack furniture and fluttered behind Saffron's cabin bed.

"Shall I call the spriggan?" Thistlebloom asked, glancing at the cuckoo clock.

"That won't be necessary. I will call him when I'm free. I must take Lilliput to get settled in; if *I'm* to be subjected to meagre living quarters, perhaps I can do better for him. Thank you for your help, Thistlebloom," Saffron said with a nod.

"As you say, my lady."

"Nice meeting you, Thistlebloom," I said, offering a wide grin. I hadn't seen a creature like her before, but really, she was quite cute.

She returned my grin, baring a fine jagged set of pearlies. I jerked back in shock, eyes like saucers.

"I'm sure I will meet you again, Lori Fields," the brownie said, in a warm, knowing tone. She bobbed a curtsy to us both before she left the room.

Saffron placed Lilliput on the desk, then began rifling through the base of her narrow wardrobe, taking more time than I would have thought possible.

"Oh, it's fun to look for things myself – I haven't seen these for a year!" She extracted a brown pair of leather boots, sat down on the chair at her desk, and removed her stilettos. "I'm going over to the animal enclosures before dining, to ensure Lilliput's lodgings are adequate. Do you wish to join me?"

"Yes, I'd love to!" I found myself replying, standing up. "Will there be many teacup alicorns, do you think?" I pressed my hands together, balancing on the balls of my feet in delighted anticipation.

"I'd imagine there will be a considerable number and variety of all magical creatures, even some from Eassus." She inclined her head with a half-grin.

"Yes!" I said, stopping myself from pumping my fist.

"See, Lilliput, everyone who sees you loves you and wants to meet more like you," she cooed, nudging him with her nose.

We made our way from the dorm, our globes guiding the way. Lilliput spread his wings, glided along the hall, and dropped over the balcony to Dome Hall's hexagonal table.

"Is it usual for maids to curtsy in Fairieland, or are you royalty?" I asked Saffron awkwardly. I'd never met royalty before. Well, not before today. I was pretty sure Priscilla was royalty… and the Dragon-shifter Queen of the North. The clue was in the name.

"I am Princess of the Court of Underhill, but Fairieland has a number of courts," she said casually as we descended the stairs. "Please don't address me as Princess; it's a pleasure to be at the academy, where such formalities do not matter and are discouraged."

"Okay." I shrugged and said nothing further about it. I didn't want to refer to all the royals by their titles anyway. They weren't my princesses or queens.

As we entered the dining hall, Art was making his way out, accompanied by an older man dressed in dark clothes and a long, black, hooded cloak. Art glanced at me with a smile, and my heart leapt. The other man looked between us.

"Lori Fields, no?" he asked in a gruff voice, as his dark eyes met mine.

"Yes, sir," I replied, observing him. He was a broad man probably in his late fifties, with light brown skin and black, silvered hair. He had two black tattoos running from beneath the centre of each eye and down his cheek and throat, the lines interrupted by burn marks which had puckered his skin. A deep scar marred his complexion, running from his lip to his ear.

He cleared his throat. "It's Maester – Maester Imod." He waved a hand to his face and neck. "Light-reapers have ways of hurting you that can't, in every instance, be healed with magic," he said gravely, in answer to my gaze.

I flushed. "I apologise, Maester Imod, I didn't realise I was staring."

"It's hard to ignore imperfections in others, particularly for the young." He raised a wayward silvery eyebrow at me. "We should have a discussion soon, you and I, after you pass the trials."

If I pass the trials.

As if reading my thoughts, he continued. "I have no doubts that after surviving a light-reaper attack alone, with no training, you will do very well."

"Maester Imod is a senior member of the Feran Council for the Dark Feran of Eassus," Art explained.

I didn't like the sound of *Dark* Feran, though Art had mentioned that it was the Dark Feran of Kerrasus who'd rescued him from Valeconiss.

"Yes, perhaps I can help you regain your memories," Maester Imod said in a kindly tone, narrowing his eyes as he searched my face.

A warning bell went off in the back of my mind at his words. "I – I see," I stammered. I didn't particularly want anyone poking around my head. As I groped for words to decline that offer, Saffron interjected.

"Hello, I'm Saffron. It's a pleasure to meet you both. I must get my alicorn settled in the animal enclosure. Lori promised she'd help me. We really must be going now; I do apologise, I feel terribly rude."

"We equally must be going, as you say. We have an imminent engagement. Best of luck in the trials to both of you." Maester Imod inclined his head.

"I'll see you both in the morning," Art said, glancing between us brightly, his gaze settling on me. "I'm happy we convinced you to stay." A glint sparked in his eyes.

"Thanks – see you in the morning." I felt hot, too hot, all of a sudden and wanted to get away as quickly as possible.

We said our goodbyes and followed our globes across the green toward the dwarf quadrant, to Dwarf Peak straight ahead of us.

The animal enclosure was bordered by a wooden fence fronted with a low hedge. It was a stable, roofed with slate and built of stone. As we advanced through the gate we approached a large, muscular, hairy creature, who had now stopped sweeping the cobblestones.

He was seven feet tall with unsettling black eyes, pointed ears, and a nose so long and sharp a bird could use it as a perch. He wore a spotless white shirt, sleeves rolled up, a green waistcoat, and brown corded trousers above bare, hairy, clawed feet the same length as my arm. He greeted us with a grin, revealing razor-sharp teeth.

"They call me Thwaite. Will you be wanting to stable this handsome alicorn?" He whistled through his teeth to Lilliput, raising a palm. His hand was the size of a bunch of bananas, fingers topped with black, pointed claws.

Lilliput fearlessly swooped up from Saffron's hold and alighted on Thwaite's open palm. I tensed, waiting for him to shove the alicorn down his throat.

"What's your name, boy?" he said instead, holding the alicorn up to his ear.

He whinnied.

"Lilliput, you say? That's a very fitting name. Let's find you the finest stall, young Lilliput."

He turned and led us into the stables, where the odour of horses, hay and manure I had detected from outside overwhelmed my nasal passage and burned the back of my throat. Ahead and to my right, stalls lined either side of a central passageway, containing beautiful, elegant horses. We walked straight ahead to a door leading outside.

As we followed Thwaite, I noticed that his trousers were tailored to allow for his short, furry tail to be on display. I watched it, ignoring the fine display of horses, as it swished from side to side. When we reached the open door leading out to the rest of the animal enclosure, I amended my initial observation. The animal enclosure was enormous. There were multiple large paddocks, buildings, and enclosures, like in a zoo.

We crossed a cobbled courtyard to another stone building, and I whispered to Saffron, darting my gaze over to the beast to be sure I was out of earshot. "What is he?"

She pitched her voice soft and low. "He's fae – a lubberkin, to be exact. They're excellent with animals, building work, and gardening, and there are more than a few fine chefs. We have them working for us on our estates at home. They do invaluable work." She watched his easy manner with Lilliput with an almost smug expression on her face.

Thwaite ducked down to enter the next door, stooping as he moved down the passage. I found miniature stalls occupied by a variety of teacup animals. There was more than enough space here when you were only ten inches tall.

Thwaite stopped at what I guessed was Lilliput's lodgings and whispered to him. Lilliput nodded his little head as the lubberkin opened the lower stall door and he flew in. He trotted up and down happily.

"We take them out so they can go out flying together daily, and let them graze in their own paddocks," Thwaite said, turning to Saffron.

"I'm more than satisfied with his lodgings, and maybe he'll make some friends." She glanced at the other stalls as if she was silently selecting those friends.

"He's a handsome fella – I have no doubt he will," Thwaite agreed.

I walked through the space, enamoured with the teacup alicorns, unicorns, winged horses, and regular horses. Well, regular was a matter of context – they came in all the wondrous colours of the rainbow. They crowded to the entrance of their stalls, hanging their noses over the closed bottom half of their doors in greeting. I ran my finger down their noses.

Saffron removed a silk purse from her boot and handed it to Thwaite. Extra gold to take good care of Lilliput? He shook his head and tried to hand it back. She insisted, and he shoved it into his back pocket, his little tail wagging furiously.

I waited for a pause in their dealings. "Do you mind if I have a look around the other enclosures?" I asked Thwaite.

"Not at all. There are a few hands scattered around – just shout if you need anything. Er... don't get too near the caged enclosures, and *feed nothing* unsupervised," he warned, his dark eyes almost burning with intensity.

I didn't stray very far after his warning but wandered into the adjacent building. Both walls were lined with glass enclosures – the kind filled with loads of plants, trees and foliage, with inadequate lighting so you couldn't see what was supposed to be in them.

Just as I was about to leave, I felt a strong tug to remain. I wandered past a few enclosures and stopped in front of the one labelled

Raziert of Eassus. There was a rustling in the leaves, and a small, fluffy creature the size of a cat emerged.

Large orange eyes peeked from a heart-shaped ruff of white fur, which ran down the length of the creature's chest along with a white strip lining its back, meeting its white fluffy tail. The rest of its fur was a golden yellow. Its ears were long, tapered to a point, with tufts on the end like a caracal. It had three fingers and a thumb, and three toes with an opposable thumb like an ape. It approached the glass on all fours.

It was the cutest thing I'd ever seen, gazing at me with wise, wide eyes. "Hello, little one, aren't you gorgeous," I cooed.

It stood up on two legs like a bear, then put its long fingers and palm up against the glass. I bent down on my knees and pressed my own palm to the glass, mirroring the raziert.

"Are you in there all alone? It must be lonely."

It nodded. I laughed out loud. Did It understand me?

"Well, I'm available for some company, if you need a visitor," I said, lowering my bottom to the heated floor and maintaining contact with the window.

It nodded again, mirroring me as it sat down on its rump with its legs askew in front of it, like a toddler would.

"That one is Talis. He will take all the hours the star sends, if you let him."

I jumped at the voice. I'd heard no one enter the building – that seemed to happen around the academy more than I was comfortable with. I glanced to my side and saw a pair of hooves.

My eyes travelled up and took in a furry set of goat legs, then the upper half of a boy, a bit older than me, complete with a large set of curved horns and pointed ears. A faun, like in a fairy tale. Unlike in a fairy tale, he was wearing a hoody.

"How do you do? I'm Filibert," he said as I met his milky eyes, complete with rectangular pupils. How could something with hooves for feet sneak up on anyone when trotting along hard stone flooring?

His eyes went round, and he glanced over his shoulder as if to escape as the silence and tension mounted. I snapped myself from my thoughts as I realised I hadn't answered him.

"Apologies. I'm Lori – pleased to meet you." I held my hand out for him to shake.

He squeezed my hand and let go; I felt nervousness and confusion coming from him. He stared at his hand for a moment as if hand-shaking wasn't a familiar custom for him. I smiled, hoping to make him feel more comfortable.

"He's so lovely, isn't he," I said, glancing back at the raziert. "I can't imagine it would be a chore spending some time with him." Talis opened his wide mouth, a pink tongue showing beneath his button nose as if in a smile. "Do you work here, or are you a student?"

"I work here – have done since I was a kid. Talis has been with us for six months; I've never seen him react so well to anyone he's just met." Filibert gazed between Talis and me, his lips curling up.

I blinked and beamed down at Talis. He fluttered his fingers at me, then pressed them together.

"It's his feeding time at seven p.m, if you want to come back and help. Some students do that, and they get paid for their time."

I quirked a brow at him. "And all you do is feed them? What's the pay?"

"I won't mislead you – feeding the animals can be a challenge at times. The pay is ten moons an hour," he finished, folding his arms across his broad chest.

How difficult could it be? I had no idea how much ten moons was and what they would get me, but to get paid for looking after this delight would be a treat. My gaze travelled back to Talis.

"I think you'll be seeing me again, if I make it past the trials."

Talis batted his long, thick, white lashes at me hopefully. My parents never had let me have a pet – not after I'd begged them to buy me a bird and found I was so terrified of its fluttering that I wouldn't go near it. My mum had had to return it to the pet shop. Maybe I could just adopt this one... and a few of the teacup alicorns...

Saffron entered the building and sauntered towards us.

"Is Lilliput happy with his new surroundings?" I asked her.

"He adores it, and he loves Thwaite, and... Who's this down here?" she said, ignoring Filibert entirely. She bent down to peer at Talis as he moved behind the glass towards her, eyes bright.

"This is Talis of Eassus. He's a raziert, and if you come down here to visit Lilliput in the future, I'm coming with you to visit this little one."

"I'm not surprised in the slightest – it's a precious little thing," she observed, straightening. Her stomach grumbled. "Shall we get some food? I could eat an entire goat," she said, eyeing the faun's legs.

His eyes widened, and he attempted to cover his white goat legs unsuccessfully with his human hands. Saffron's mouth gave a satisfied twist at his reaction, and I sucked my lips between my teeth to suppress a laugh. He, like Thwaite, towered over us at roughly seven feet – he couldn't possibly fear Saffron.

"But I'm more in the mood for partridge in a hedgerow sauce and rose tea," she added, holding her chin in thought.

Filibert the faun quickly took up on that preferred line of conversation. "I'm partial to my partridge in a pie, followed by a hefty glug of cognac." He released a nervous laugh and an uneasy smile, still bracing his legs protectively.

I didn't mention my hankering for baked beans on toast. I'd had a large roast for lunch and wasn't that hungry, but even if I had been, I'd probably never be in the mood for an entire goat, nor partridge, rose tea, or cognac.

I put my hand to Talis's enclosure glass, and he pressed his fingers towards mine. "I'll see you again!" His large eyes looked up at me, forlorn, and his long-tapered ears drooped low. My heart squeezed at leaving him. I returned my attention to the faun. "It was nice meeting you. Thanks for telling me about Talis, and if I stay, I think I'll take you up on that job offer," I said, hoping his obvious fear of Saffron hadn't made him want to withdraw his offer.

"Of course, glad of the help," he replied, backing away, his eyes rounding as they slid from me and anxiously back to Saffron.

We left the way we came in. I felt that tug back to Talis. In my heart of hearts, I was sure that Talis was my raziert – that he belonged to me.

CHAPTER NINE

ON THE WALK BACK to the main building, I thought of how Vita would love Talis and Lilliput and seeing all these animals and imagined what my parents would say if I could tell them about it. A lump came into my throat, and I pushed my thoughts of them out of my mind. I couldn't speak to them for now, and that was all there was to it. I had to concentrate on the trials. *Focus, Lori!*

Listening to Livia and her friends had given me some clues about what the trials might include, but I didn't know what any of them meant. I asked Saffron, "If there's a written exam for the trials, what questions could they ask? What creatures and magic might we face? I've heard beasts being mentioned..." I trailed off, waiting for a response.

"The trials ascertain your current magic level, knowledge, skills, and potential. When assigned to you as a dorm-mate, I was told you didn't know anything of the alius. I'm certain they will consider that throughout the trials. There are many magical creatures; you've seen some of them here this evening."

"So, did *you* have to sign a death waiver before starting?" I asked.

"Yes, we all do," she said casually. She stopped and turned to me; red brows raised. "I have books on the alius and magical creatures, if you want to study them after dinner?"

I breathed a sigh of relief. "Yes please! It's just so I have an idea. Thank you, thank you."

"Generally, there's a revealing at every trial. It reveals all your current powers and any you may have potential for in the future, so I am almost certain that will happen over the next few days."

"The trials last for days? I thought it was just tomorrow!"

Saffron offered me a sardonic grin. "It takes more than one day – usually three to five."

"I thought I might make it for a day, but three to five..." I shook my head. "Are you not worried about any of this at all?"

"Fae learn magic in Fairieland from when we come into our powers at puberty. We are far more prepared than other alius. But the trials measure your potential. They would not have offered you a place here if they didn't see potential in you, Laurel-Leah Fields. I have never faced a light-reaper, but I know it is no easy feat to overcome one. There have been deaths at the trials, but often we can work in groups. Like the motto of the academy says, 'Together we are stronger.'"

I'd had no idea that was the academy's motto, but the trials would be a lot easier if I could work with the more experienced alius and at least I wouldn't be alone.

Saffron put her arm around my shoulder. I felt compassion and happiness from her, mixed with worry and fear – fear of pain. This fae had a fantastic poker face; I'd never have guessed that she feared the trials. I, on the other hand, had been terrified for a full two days now, aside from my short reprieve with the dragon queen. I doubted it would stop any time soon.

The dining hall was busy, so Saffron and I sat in the patio area, where floating Chinese lanterns hovered above us – strange, as it was still light outside. Mood lighting?

"It's warm tonight. Are we even in Britain?" I asked.

"We're on an island. It was off the coast of Bristol when I arrived, but it moves location, so I couldn't tell you even if I wanted to. My guess would be the Mediterranean Sea – it's nice for the students to have a longer summer season."

I gaped in surprise.

"And I know what you're thinking, Laurel-Leah Fields," she went on.

If it was *OMG! I'm on a frickin' travelling magical island,* then she would be right.

"What about a white Yule?"

I crinkled my brows in confusion.

"Don't worry – I've been told we always have a white Yule," she reassured me.

It seemed that one power my fae friend did not have, was mind reading. *Who even uses the term Yule anymore? What's wrong with 'Christmas'?* My first instinct was to call her liar, but with everything else I'd seen today, who was I to deny the possibility of a moving island?

"Did I get it right? Is that what you were thinking?" She smiled in anticipation.

I didn't have the heart to tell her how wrong she'd got it. "One hundred percent correct!" I plastered on a smile.

"Really? You don't seem sure."

I wondered briefly if she actually could *read* my mind. "Well... it wasn't *exactly* what I thought."

"So, what were you thinking?"

"I was thinking it's amazing that we're on a travelling island!"

"Oh. I'll have to learn your ways, Laurel-Leah Fields. And travelling islands... they're more common than one would think," she told me with a shrug, as she brought up the evening menu.

I stared at her for a moment, open-mouthed and speechless, as she talked about the menu choices. Our previous hankerings were not available, so Saffron ordered a truffle-stuffed roasted quail with her rose tea, and I ordered the chicken and bacon pasta and a pineapple juice.

Our drinks flew over, and as we waited for the food, Charlie came over to say hello. She pulled up a chair uninvited and made herself comfortable, asking if I had found out anything about the trials from other invitees.

I told her I had and thanked her again for the tip. I introduced her to Saffron and was pleasantly surprised that she was nice to my roommate and didn't try to intimidate her. Then again, even having only known Saffron briefly, she seemed lovely – aside from that exchange with Filibert – and I couldn't imagine anyone having a problem with her.

Charlie returned to her seat across the patio, near the entrance to the main building. I stared after her and tried to work out if the people she was sitting with were all wolf-shifters and tried to envisage the array of colours they must be seeing around people. I found myself scanning around for Art, but he was nowhere to be seen. I thought of Rhode and Zale and their powers.

"So, can all fae control people just by talking and telling them what to do?" I asked Saffron.

Priscilla's group was gathering at their usual table, in front of where I was sitting. Priscilla didn't sit down; instead, she stalked toward us in stiletto heels, sneering, before Saffron could answer my question.

"Shit," I muttered under my breath.

"Can't get a better dorm-mate than this pathetic creature, Underhill?" Priscilla said, addressing Saffron but indicating me. "So pathetic, her own *alius* parents wanted nothing to do with her! I heard you're unregistered," she said directly to me. "Are you a spy sent to the academy – biding your time to kill off your own people?" She looked over at a group of people to my right, sitting near the main building. I followed her gaze. They must be Eassusians too. So *that* was why people kept mentioning being unregistered – they feared I was a spy, a killer.

Everyone in the patio area had gone quiet. Charlie and the people she was sitting with, stood up and headed our way.

The Eassusians were now all focused on me, some glaring, some evaluating. They looked human – all except one of them. One male had too much facial hair where he shouldn't; it grew in lines from his forehead and across his cheeks. His ears were pointed and furry, his eyebrows overly thick, his eyes a disconcerting yellow. If there ever had been a wolf-man, that would be him. Beside him was a purple-haired girl with golden-brown skin, her hair styled in three rings at the back of her head. Her face was unreadable. The bloke standing on the other side of her had inky black hair and piercing electric-blue eyes.

As I took in "my" people, Priscilla's menacing voice speared the silence. She'd turned her attention back to Saffron.

"I am disappointed in you. I would expect more from any fae regarding the company they keep, even if they are a half-breed Underhill," she purred viciously, lips twisting as she looked us up and down from side-on, arms crossed.

I opened my mouth to argue, but Saffron spoke first.

"Your buttocks and chest are looking abnormally disproportionate, Priscilla. You haven't been magically enhancing yourself again, have you? If being full fae is the be-all and end-all, why are you so desperately trying to look more human? Can't expect much more than hypocrisy from a fae born in a tree-shack, I suppose."

"I was born in the Grand Ash Palace, barrow-dweller!" Priscilla snarled, her beautiful face distorted and grotesque.

"Your arse is eclipsing my view, Priscilla. Move along," I interjected sharply, waving her away from our table with my hand. My own arse had a similar effect, so I fully expected a similar retort. Instead, she slammed her hands on our table, toppling our salt and pepper shakers, and moved menacingly towards me.

My fingers curled into fists. Yes, there were bitchy people at my school, but they were mostly interested in their own lives. They didn't go out of their way to name-call and stir up trouble. They'd just slap you with sly remarks now and again.

My drink started boiling, then everyone pushed back from Priscilla's table as theirs started to boil and spit as well.

Charlie's voice boomed. "That's two days of combat drills now, Priscilla. Keep going with this and so will I, until you can't wait to leave this academy – before you've even taken the trials!" She nodded over to me.

In the narie world, I wouldn't have run from a fight, but Saffron had said the fae learned magic from puberty. Mine had been released for a day or so, and I couldn't control it whatsoever. I nodded back and focused on slowing my breathing. *The fae girl is just a pathetic, petty, vicious cow, getting revenge for what Charlie said.* The inner name-calling was cathartic. The boiling changed to a simmer, then stopped.

Feeling unexpectedly drained, I watched as Priscilla got a handle on her own anger. She glared daggers and arrows at me and Saffron, a promise that this was not finished.

Turning to Saffron, I told her I was going up to our dorm. She said she'd come up with me.

People had come out from the dining hall to find out what the commotion was about. As I stood at the bottom of the stairs leading to the patio doors, a light-haired boy standing next to a ginger-haired one blocked my path. I barely raised my eyes to them and waited for them to move aside.

I felt deflated. Priscilla's words about my alius parents not wanting me stung, as did the whole *you're a killer spy* thing. It was unbearable. I was still trying to fully accept I had magical powers, that I was part alien, and that I couldn't see or even speak to my parents or Vita, let alone the trials tomorrow. There was too much – just too much in my head and in my heart to deal with.

Saffron stepped forward up the stairs; the boys blocking us moved aside. Their eyes, along with everyone else's on the patio, bored into me. I headed to our dorms, body heavy, heart hollow.

CHAPTER TEN

I got ready for bed, the day's events replaying in my mind. My pyjamas fitted perfectly, and I noticed my initials were embroidered on the tag. The brand of toothpaste was my usual, and my brush was anti-frizz. It was a surprisingly good ending to what, overall, had been a hideous day. I hauled up the cabin bed ladder and collapsed on the mattress.

Saffron handed me the two books she promised, and I thanked her, but didn't open them.

"So, everyone thinks I'm a spy?" I said finally.

Saffron rifled through her cupboard and pulled out yet another pair of shoes, exchanging them for her boots. "It's more that they don't know why you weren't registered, and with the recent killings, they're more suspicious than ever. *I* don't think you're a spy. And Priscilla and I have never got on; her attack was aimed more at me, I think."

I told her about what had happened with Charlie earlier today.

"Then she hates both of us," Saffron said, "but there is no love lost."

I nodded. There wasn't any from my end – I wanted to knock Priscilla's perfect teeth out. "If you're half fae, what's your other half?" I asked.

"My father is human. Half-fae are considered lowly, but my court is more powerful than hers, and she resents that."

"Do the other fae give you a hard time?"

"They have, but they don't usually get the opportunity. If you'd met my mother, you'd know why. When fae royals turn sixteen, we are of age, and we must start considering potential consorts. As well as my court being more powerful, my magic is too, so I am seen as a more worthy prize than Priscilla. Since we were young, she has always thought of herself as my better, but she is not – and she certainly hasn't learned to hold her tongue, even when she is facing a mightier foe." Saffron sighed.

"Some people are elitist, bigoted, self-absorbed pricks!" I scoffed.

She laughed. "I couldn't agree more, Lori Fields. I'll get even, you'll see." Her eyes grew so dark they almost appeared black, sending a shiver down my spine. "I'm going back downstairs to, er... socialise. Don't wait up," she added, with a broad, enigmatic smile.

I nodded, wondering whether she was meeting up with one of her potential consorts or enacting Priscilla's downfall. But I had too much reading to do to ask.

The book I opened was named *Alius: The Differences and Similarities Between Our Species*, by Cranberry Willow. It was bound in green velvet cloth and stamped with silver lettering, and best of all, it was short. I loved reading, but with trials starting tomorrow, I needed to learn quickly.

The first chapter was about fae. It answered my earlier question to Saffron of whether all fae could coerce people to their will with a few simple words. It was a form of mind-magic, under influencing magic, and termed 'compulsion'. Of the fae, only noble elder fae had this power. That meant the man named Rhode who'd stopped me in my tracks as I ran from the light-reaper must be one of those. However, elder vampires and chosen vampires were endowed with this magic too. I flipped to the front and back of the book, looking for a glossary, but there was nothing about what 'chosen' meant.

All younger noble fae could use fae influencing magic alone. It was a mixture of influencing and illusion magic used to make their prey find them irresistibly attractive, and far more susceptible to their suggestions. That must be what Zale had used on me. Sure, he'd been beautiful without the magic, but when he'd cast himself in that sea-blue glow, he was almost all I could focus on, despite being desperate to escape. New vampires would develop this magic too.

There was nothing to explain how I could protect myself from compulsion or this influencing magic.

My stomach growled. I was starving now, and reading was keeping my mind off my hunger. Fae had excellent senses, but the vampires' and shifters' senses were superior. Fae had a lifespan of 2000 to 2500 years. I blinked at that – who would want to live that long? Vampires were immortal. I couldn't help but notice a lot of comparisons being made between fae and vampires.

An interesting fact was that fae couldn't lie. They could sense when others were lying, as could vampires and shifters, and they couldn't abide being lied to. My thoughts spun back to my conversation with Saffron and the white Yule thing. She'd *known* I was lying! That cheeky mare – she had mentioned nothing about it. Well, hell's bloody bells, I couldn't even tell a white lie without being discovered! These alius were a tricky lot.

Then I thought about that a bit more. If fae couldn't lie, then Priscilla really believed that I might be a spy. If she didn't, she couldn't have said it. But if I told her the truth, she'd have to believe me, wouldn't she? She could tell if I was lying or not.

Ugh, why should I even feel the need to explain it to her? She'd spoken so loudly... everyone had heard, and if they hadn't, the gossips among the invitees would surely fill them in. There had been many sets of eyes boring into me tonight, and most of them had felt unfriendly.

Saffron had mentioned there'd been many deaths at the trials, and I'd signed a death waiver. I'd fudged over that fact – until now.

Tomorrow, or in the next three to five days, I could be dead. Livia certainly didn't have any love for me. Priscilla would like to tear me to pieces – I'd read that in her searing glare before she had once again been silenced by Charlie. But there would be no Charlie to save the day at the trials.

And now the Eassusians were likely to want to dispose of me. The unregistered spy. Assassin. Priscilla had done her utmost to make sure of that. And the alius could simply wipe my family and friends' memories of me away without a second thought.

Fatigue from the stress of the past two days stole over me. I had escaped death from the light-reaper, only to be thrown into another very real and different possibility of death. Feeling like I hadn't slept properly for ten thousand years, I laid the book down on my chest and rested.

I thought of the Voice. Who *was* the Voice? How did they know I had magic? And why had they released it? If I hadn't heard that voice, I'd have been to a party last night, seen Rob for the first time in years, and hung out with Vita today. I already missed them all.

As I pictured my parents, I could almost hear my dad saying – with bright eyes and a wicked cheeky grin in his sunken, whey-coloured face – "Don't let the buggers get you down, Lori."

That image was replaced by the light-reaper outside my home, followed by the report on the news of the father and son murdered in their mansion. The chancellor had said that the strangler reported on the narie news had been the light-reaper. And the murdered father and son must have been alius, probably Eassusians.

Could the academy really guarantee my magic-less, defenceless parents' safety when even powerful magical alius were murdered by the light-reapers? I doubted it. And could I trust them to help my family financially, as the chancellor had mentioned? Probably not.

I realised I should have asked that burning question. Why let me attend the trials at all? Why not send me directly to the detention facility? Could it be so they, or an invitee, could get rid of the potential assassin during the trials?

I sighed. I'd never fall asleep with all these life-threatening thoughts colliding and tripping over one another. I went through the stages of my meditation app.

It failed miserably.

There was a firm knock at the door. My heart thumped. Who the hell could that be? Saffron wouldn't bother knocking, would she? Had someone come to dispose of me – an Eassusian? I remained silent, quietly shuffling down to the ladder on my bed. But my globe, now flashing orange, flew to the doorknob and flashed green to open it.

"No!" I hissed too late.

I smelled it before I registered what it was. A box of pizza, a can of cola and a stack of paper napkins drifted toward me as the door gently closed. My racing pulse calmed. A note was attached to the box, signed from Saffron.

I imagine you're hungry. Enjoy, friend. See you on the morrow.

My brows shot up at the last sentence. Perhaps she had met a suitable consort after all. Well, good on her. When I opened the box, my stomach rumbled and squealed like it was trying to speak to me. I didn't recognise the type of meat on the pizza; I thought it might be duck, but having never tried duck, there was no way to be sure. It was hot and tasty, and that was all that mattered at this stage of hunger.

I stuffed my face with half the pizza and downed the cola. Thoroughly satiated, I dropped the pizza box on the table beneath my bed.

Everything felt that little bit rosier now. I laid my head back on my pillow and remembered my dad's wise words once more, deciding to focus on the positives.

I'd met Art. Yes, he was a teacher... sort of... and I was sure Charlie had been teasing me when she said he liked me, but a girl could dream. Saffron was my friend; she'd furnished me with relevant reading materials for the trials and remembered that I'd probably be hungry. Charlie was a friend... kind of... I thought. At the very least, she was on my side... I hoped. Talis and Lilliput, of course.

And I had travelled abroad for the first time ever. I could now stick a green pin in my corkboard outside of Britain. *Not everyone gets to stay on a travelling island.*

If I died tomorrow, at least I had achieved that. But I would *not* die tomorrow. I would survive and fight against any of those buggers who tried to bring me down! With teeth, nails, and whatever boiling-drinks magic I could muster.

There. I smiled to myself – that was more like it. I would repeat that mantra until I drifted into...

CHAPTER ELEVEN

When I next opened my eyes, it was morning.

I jerked up, heart racing, disorientated. *Oh my God, I've overslept! Wait – what's that smell of strawberries? Where am I, and why is my face so near the ceiling?*

Memories of the past two days came flooding back with a visceral vengeance. It was the morning of the trials.

My heart dived into the pit of my stomach and wove a tight knot. What time was it? My globe read 6.30 a.m. Saffron was asleep in her cabin bed; she must have slipped in after I'd fallen asleep. Her globe gave off a subtle light, and I whispered for mine to glow too.

It blazed bright white light, like a room prepped for surgery.

"Tone it down!" I whispered loudly, and the globe adjusted to a warm, soft yellow light.

I picked up *Alius: The Differences and Similarities* and crammed. For what? I didn't know, but any information had to be useful in a world I knew nothing of.

I studied the chapter on vampires. They were the only alius species I hadn't yet run across. And as I read, I became increasingly concerned about how powerful they were. Not only did they have the power of compulsion, but I discovered they were faster than any other alius, despite what Charlie had said about their level-pegging. Wolf-shifters were only as fast or faster over shorter distances. Vampires were the strongest, with the sharpest senses. They were undead – having died and been brought back to life with the blood of a vampire. They drank human and alius blood, and the only alius whose blood they didn't drink were shifters. They wore charms that allowed them to walk in the sun, and they had power over mist and air.

It was fun to watch vampires romanticised in movies, but in reality, the prospect of them was terrifying. I flicked through the pages, looking for ways to defend myself against them. Would it be a crucifix, holy water, garlic, stakes, iron nails, ultra-violet bullets, or tearing off their heads and setting fire to their bodies? That was if there was *any* way to kill or harm a vampire. But there was no such information.

I breathed a frustrated sigh and turned to the chapter regarding Eassusians. It wasn't really a chapter, but merely a page. The book was more of a pamphlet or wiki page without the links, wrapped in beautiful bindings.

The Lakoliin are the elementals of Eassus of land, air, fire, and water. They often supplement their powers by using the magical symbols of the Eassusian witches, such as an oval symbol used for an apporting gate, or circles used as a protection barrier.

The light-reaper had called me 'Fire Lakoliin', and I remembered that Art had used an oval symbol on his palm to create that portal. I found nothing on light-reapers, and little on Eassusian witches.

Another section mentioned shimmerers. Shimmerers could shift into anything, including inanimate objects, and they were all blessed with the ability for powerful mind-magic. No explanation on what type of mind-magic it was. I shivered.

At 7 a.m. a harp tune sounded from Saffron's globe. I closed the book and put it to one side.

Saffron didn't so much as yawn when she woke up. She tapped her globe and the harp tune, to my relief, stopped. Then she glanced over at me, as fresh-faced as a daisy.

"Morning, Lori," she said, pulling her covers aside and dropping from her bed to the floor as gracefully as a cat. She glided over to the sink.

"Morning," I replied, peeking over the guard rails of the cabin bed. I decided against jumping down, imagining the resultant twisted ankle and trying to complete the trials with an injury. I climbed down the ladder, opened my wardrobe, and fished out my black combat suit. Saffron had neatly laid hers over the chair at her desk.

I tied my hair back into a high ponytail and started getting changed, feeling a little self-conscious. I didn't know Saffron well – but she was brushing her teeth, oblivious to me, and I was changing with my back to her. Whatever I felt about it, I knew this would be strange for her too. She had a dozen rooms to herself in her palace, and I had only a box room at home.

When I'd pulled on my combat trousers, Saffron made her way back to the bunk and I took my turn at the sink, brushing my teeth and washing my face with freezing cold water to add some colour to my otherwise pasty visage. Then I rolled on my deodorant and put on my black combat top. This was not my usual morning routine; I found it disconcerting, alien even. But then everything that had happened yesterday had been alien, disconcerting and worse. I was entirely unprepared for the trials. What was I doing here?

"How was your socialising last night?" I asked to distract myself. "I didn't hear you come in."

"I came in at one-thirty, after talking to potential allies for the trials. We'll need them to get ahead," Saffron said, purple eyes bright as gems, from where she sat at the dressing table.

My gaze snapped to her in bewilderment. "Allies?"

"Of course. The more allies the better, particularly after Priscilla said that spy nonsense last night."

My adrenaline spiked as I pulled on a boot. Pausing, I turned to her. "Do you think she's turned everyone against me? You said you didn't think I was a spy, but were you just... being kind?" Fae couldn't lie, but what about half-fae?

Saffron scowled at me in the mirror's reflection as she slammed her hairbrush down. Her fiery red hair was twisted to perfection, two wisps falling around a delicate, elfin face.

"I certainly was not just being kind; I am *fae*, Lori Fields!" The way she said it made me think that being fae and being kind ran in opposition to one another. She went on, "I have allied us to a vampire, and I spoke to the Eassusians to gauge their thoughts."

Ice lanced up my spine. Allying with a vampire was the last thing I wanted to do, and after last night and my recent reading, I'd include Eassusians and shimmerers on that list. Then again, being their foe would be far worse. "And what did they say?"

"Undecided, but I think I can work on one or two." She curled her lips up as she picked up some liquid eyeliner and started applying it.

I braced myself for a harrowing day – if I survived at all. "Do you know how I could stop compulsion and influencing magic?"

Saffron picked up a lip brush and a pot of lipstick and blinked at me. "I'm not sure how you would do it, Lori. I use fae magic. It's similar to mage and Eussusian magic, but our approach is often different. It is likely you would develop a shield through your magic, but there are charms and brews that would help resist it."

"Do you think it would be an idea to ask Healer Gale to give me some charms and brews to ward against it?"

"As far as I'm aware, brews or charms concocted at the trials are only permitted if you know how to produce them and use your own ingredients," she explained, with a hard luck expression.

I clenched my fists to stop the adrenaline shakes. Saffron stood up from the dressing table, war paint expertly applied; I looked dull and plain in comparison. But I was in no way an expert at makeup application, and makeup worn during exertion (such as my PE lessons) and the resultant panda eyes was a way worse look for me.

"Ready to get some breakfast?" I asked.

"Absolutely. I could eat a sow and drink a full two udders of cow's milk," she replied, donning her sunglasses.

"I'm peckish too," I agreed, wrinkling my nose. Pigs and cows' udders weren't exactly what I wanted to think of before breakfast.

I grabbed my globe and we made our way to the dining hall, bats swooping around my stomach in anticipation.

The dining hall was buzzing. A small furry creature, like Thistlebloom but with a reddish hue to her fur, stood behind the hot buffet. She was wearing chef whites, a hair net, and a beard net! I couldn't help but think that at four-foot-nothing she must be standing on a box to see above the counter.

I took a croissant, a warm roll, and some scrambled eggs and made myself some English breakfast tea. Saffron picked up two large, boiled eggs labelled 'Duck Eggs', a few spears of asparagus, and an enormous slice of luxurious bread-and-butter pudding. We sat at the round tables nearest the food counter and the French doors out to the combat field.

"Thanks so much for the books you lent me, they really helped."

"Did you get through them?" Saffron asked, cracking the tops of her duck eggs open with a teaspoon.

"Partially, but I couldn't find anything about why you always wear sunglasses." I wanted to ask if half-fae could lie, but if she *could* lie and lied about it, that would leave me none the wiser. If I passed the trials, I'd raid the library to find out.

Saffron hovered a spoonful of egg at her mouth. "Fae are nocturnal, as are vampires. We wear sunglasses to deal with the ravages of sunshine on our eyes until we become accustomed to it. Fae have always been naturally nocturnal. But when vampires change from humans to undead parasites feasting on the living…"

She ate the spoonful as a few sunglasses-clad faces with rounded ears whipped to face our direction. I avoided what I imagined were the glares beneath their shades and turned away.

Saffron carried on, oblivious. "They tend to explode into ash at contact with sunlight, unless wearing a charm. So, they sleep during the day and wake at night, as we do."

I'd thought Saffron more tactful than Charlie; it seemed I was wrong. Clearly the wolf-shifters and fae did not understand tact, yet she was getting a vampire to be an ally? Maybe none of the alius had tact. In fact, it was possible I was the most diplomatic person here. The prospect tickled me.

"Since you're nocturnal, do you and the vampires have your lessons at night?"

"That was the previous arrangement, but if we never see other species because we are asleep and they are awake and vice-versa, how can we become familiar with one another? This academy is very forward-thinking about us integrating. It's diverse, and that's one of the reasons I accepted the invitation for the trials here."

I nodded at her, which spurred her on to a fuller explanation.

"Some academies are entirely segregated, and others are solely for one species, but as we get older, we find alius mix for work, for politics, and events. It's better to nurture the relationships earlier on." She looked up and fixed her gaze on something.

I followed her line of sight; it landed on Zale, the river god. He was standing with Priscilla and her entourage.

"That's what my mother thinks anyway!" Saffron threw down her spoon, bits of orange duck egg yolk splattering on the table. She crossed her arms and growled.

"You're not keen on the whole integration thing?" I asked, shuffling uneasily in my seat.

"No, that's not the problem. It's refreshing to meet new people, of all species." She lifted her purple gaze to mine. "It's vexing to have to do what my mother wants – court who she wants, *marry* who she wants."

Zale sauntered over to us as if on cue.

"Hello, Lori, it's a pleasure to see you again." He smiled widely, dark eyelashes framing light blue eyes. Shimmering blue light enveloped him, accompanied by the smell of the salty ocean. He was achingly beautiful.

He looked away from me to Saffron. Why was he looking at *her*?

"So, you finally came out of your dungeon and joined us up top?" he goaded Saffron with a cheeky smile. I laughed at his wit.

Saffron narrowed suspicious eyes at me. "I certainly wouldn't describe Underhill as a dungeon, and since your watery abode is the reef left of the abyss, I'd hardly call that 'up top', *Zale*."

From my peripherals, I could see her frowning and glancing between us. My tongue would hold no longer. All it wanted to do was spout sweet, meaningful words of love for him.

"Your voice is a melody in my heart," I gushed like a fountain, voice quavering, emotions set to burst if I didn't tell him all I was feeling. "Your eyes a well, as deep as the ocean—"

"Boiled daisies, and a saucer of milk, Zale! Stop using influencing magic on my dorm-mate!" Saffron yelled.

I couldn't seem to look anywhere else but the glorious Zale, although I seriously wanted to scold Saffron for her impertinence. I drank him in. His gleaming wet muscles in the river flashed through my memories, although he looked equally comely with clothes on. His teeth glittered like foam bubbles on a cresting wave, kissed by the sunshine.

Then I caught sight of Charlie behind Zale. She'd appeared from nowhere – she really could hear from miles away.

Zale craned his neck round at her, his mouth in the shape of an O.

"I was simply making her feel comfortable with me. It was entirely harmless," he said as I focused on his sweet lips.

Charlie's eyes flashed a glittering grey, and she bared her teeth. The film of blue-bathed starshine and the sweet smell of the ocean brine vanished. He was as beautiful as ever, but I could look away now. He hadn't denied using influencing magic. *Fae can't lie.*

"Using influencing magic against other students outside of trials and lessons is prohibited," Charlie said, checking her globe. "This is your first... no, second warning, Zale. You will receive corporal punishment on your third, whether during the trials or as a student."

Zale lifted his chin. "I'll be sure there are no further infractions, Prefect Savage." He turned back to me. "I enjoy our exchanges. You're most enticing to behold, Lori Fields," he purred, with no hint of embarrassment, eyes intent on me.

My face heated – not just at the compliment and blatant manipulation, but in realisation. The compliment to me was designed to make Saffron jealous.

There was a hiss from behind him. Priscilla was glaring at me, Saffron, and Charlie. "It's not fair. He uses magic and gets a warning. I say one little thing" – she held up her forefinger in demonstration – "and I get combat drills!"

Other students in the dining hall around us were taking a keen interest in the developments.

"If you don't understand that speciesist speech is wrong, I'm sure there are more combat drills waiting to teach you," Charlie growled through clenched teeth.

Priscilla's eyes sparked as she stalked off to the seating area outside. Doubtless I'd get some abuse later for this. Between Charlie, Saffron, and me, I was the weakest link. I just hoped she waited until after the trials.

Art approached our table and looked around, assessing the situation. The tension in the air palpable. He gestured to the seat next to me.

"May I?" He threw a frosty glare at Zale.

I tried, unsuccessfully, to suppress a bright smile at him.

"In the middle of the action again, Lori?" he breathed in a low voice, eyes alight with amusement.

"Why, what have you heard?" I asked, thinking about Priscilla's accusations last night.

Zale eyed the seat next to Saffron, and said to her, "See you tonight?"

She gave an exaggerated sigh and faced Art, ignoring Zale. He curled his lips up, standing before her and waiting for a reply.

"Good morning, Art. How are you?" Saffron asked, continuing to ignore him.

Zale gave us a nod, and with dignified poise, glided off after Priscilla.

Art watched the exchange with interest. "Very well, Saffron. And how are you both feeling about the trials?"

"You wouldn't have any tips for us, would you?" I asked, feeling my chest tighten.

"Use anything you've learned to your benefit. You overcame a light-reaper – use that experience." There was a hint of admiration in his eyes and tone.

"I'm not sure how I did that," I said as memories of translucent fire snakes choking me flashed through my memories. My hand went to my throat and I closed my eyes, trying to block it out.

Saffron stood up and told me she had to talk to someone and that she'd meet me at the combat field.

Art waited until she left. "Lori, I stopped by to wish you good luck. Try to follow your instincts today. If I hadn't been called away yesterday, I would have offered to help with your elemental magic. So, providing nothing unexpected happens, I can help you tonight if you wish?"

"Yes... I wish, I do wish," I almost shouted. "I think I could use all the help I can get."

He lifted one corner of his mouth in a half-smile and put a warm, broad hand over mine. I felt anticipation and worry coming from him. My pulse raced at his touch. Or was it because the trials started in fifteen minutes?

"I must go. See you out there. Good luck!" He removed his hand and strode toward the French doors.

My stomach roiled, and a sudden wave of nausea and the desperate need to urinate hit me. I rushed off to the facilities.

There were girls in the stalls talking. As I entered the toilets, they hushed up. I washed my face, entered a stall, then heard them leaving, speaking in low murmurs in a language I didn't recognise. Eassusian? Fae? They left, and the toilets were quiet.

When I came out of the stall, one of them was waiting for me.

She had dark purple velvety hair, swept back, and three hoops of plaits sprang from the back of her head like Olympic rings. The shade of her hair matched her eyes: while Saffron's eyes were a light purple, like lilacs, this girls' eyes were the shade of a violet. I recognised her. She'd been amongst the group of Eassusians last night.

"Lori Fields. Part mage, part Eassusian." Her voice echoed in the emptiness of the toilets.

I waited for her to add 'unregistered', but as she refrained, I said as I washed my hands, "And you are?"

"Arameen Miamar. We heard the fae princess talking to you last night."

I sighed inwardly, noticing she didn't have an Eassusian accent and spoke perfect English.

"The way she was screeching it would have been hard to avoid," I replied. She gave a wry smile. "Did Saffron speak to you... about being allies?" I flicked my gaze to her.

"She did. She mentioned a light-reaper attacked you and that, despite knowing nothing of magic, you survived. Both of which we were aware."

She faced me and put a finger marked with circular symbols to her lips, then blew. The faintest twist of colours wrapped around us before clearing.

"I've placed protection barriers around us; you never know who might be listening." She glanced at the main toilet door.

"Do you believe I'm a spy, like Priscilla mentioned?" I asked, folding my arms across my chest.

"We haven't decided. If you are an assassin, then know we'll be ready for you." She looked at me levelly as I tried not to flinch at her frankness. "If not, you should know – the mages hold sway here. As an unregistered Eassusian, it is they you should be worried about... and I'd look out for Priscilla – the screeching fae with the disproportionately large rear," she added, and released a low, rumbling laugh.

I returned a tentative half-grin.

She pointed to a loose hair on my clothes, picked it off my shoulder, but didn't drop it, as I expected. Instead, she twirled it round a finger.

Weird, creepy, and why? I wanted to ask for it back, but I didn't want to get off on the wrong foot. I thought of protesting my innocence regarding being a spy, but if I were in her shoes, I wouldn't trust me either.

"My main advice to you is to trust no one," she said, her eyes large and round.

"I'll keep that in mind."

She dropped my hair, squared up to me, and held her arm outstretched in front of her. I went to shake her hand, but she gave me a wan smile and withdrew from it. I frowned in confusion.

"If you are simply unregistered, in time you'll learn our ways. If you are a spy, it will not end well for you."

She spun on her heel and stalked out the door.

CHAPTER TWELVE

I stared after Arameen, wondering what to make of that encounter. Fortunately for me, since I'd arrived at the academy, I'd been in an almost constant state of fear, so her warning added nothing to my stress levels. *Don't let the buggers get you down.*

I was still alive, so I was winning so far today.

My list of enemies was growing, but now I knew who they were. That was if Arameen Miamar was on the level. I had to watch out for Priscilla, mages, Eassusians... and everyone else! I'd keep an eye on Maester Imod too – I didn't want him anywhere near my memories. If I escaped this place, I would almost certainly face death from light-reapers. Rock, hard place. There were no other options. I had to learn.

I checked the time on my globe: ten minutes to get to the combat field. Exiting the toilets at speed, I collided into the back of someone. A large, broad, solid someone.

"Sorry," I muttered as I back-pedalled a little to walk round him.

The solid mass reached an arm out to block me. He wore a combat uniform and a large rectangular ring on his finger with a crystal in it, like the chancellor. *Mage!*

He turned to face me with a scowl. "Let's have a look at you," he said, in a posh accent.

I stared back at him. He looked around my age; his hair was dark blonde, and he had the good looks of a movie star. He clasped his hands behind his back and rocked back on his feet, bending at the waist to peer into my eyes. His were hazel, framed in thick dark lashes and dark eyebrows. I tilted my head to the side; he looked familiar.

He moved his head from side to side, my eyes following him in some sort of hypnotic, pendulous rhythm. Like he was a snake charmer and I the snake.

"Hmm... eyes easily following me. It seems you do have your sight. In that case, apology not accepted." His too-dark eyebrows lowered further, and his eyes darkened.

I didn't have time for whatever this was. I stepped to the side to walk around him, and he side-stepped to block me.

"The trials are starting soon; I need to get through." I side-stepped the other way. He blocked me again.

"We can keep doing this dance all day long," he sing-songed, still bent down to my level and talking to me as if I was a child.

But I had already done this dance before with the light-reaper. I feinted a side-step and dodged around him.

He caught me by the shoulders, spun me, and pinned me against the wall. My breath flew out of my lungs, and I wheezed, unable to speak. Rage permeated from him and burned into me. He tried to hold my gaze, but I scanned for the best way out. The guy was obviously unhinged.

I took a breath and, being a sturdy sort of girl, threw my weight forward. I rammed him in the ribs with my shoulder and drove him back. He flailed, off-balance, and caught me with an elbow hard across my cheek, snapping my head to the side. The world swayed and shifted, in a burst of stars, but at least I was free now.

It hurt like hell, but I wasn't about to scream and give him the satisfaction of knowing that. I darted off, getting away from him as fast as I could, conscious that he might try to grab me again. What the hell was his problem?

Arameen's assessment of my enemies so far seemed accurate. *Beware the mages* – it had taken all of ten seconds to learn that she was right. Was this what I could expect from this place? Random attacks, hatred, suspicion, and not being able to trust anyone? I thought the elbow crack might have been accidental, but throwing me up against the wall was definitely intentional. At least, he'd learned I wasn't an easy target now. But why should I have to defend myself at all? My parents flickered up in my thoughts. If I was to survive, I needed to stay vigilant and focused.

"What in the Mother was that about?" asked another plummy voice.

I stole a glance over my shoulder. A ginger-haired boy had joined my attacker from the men's toilets. Now I recognised them; they were the boys who'd stared at me from the coach at the barbican gate. The boys who'd blocked my path last night after Priscilla humiliated me.

The first one held his ribs and stared after me, nostrils flaring. "People just blindly ramming into me," he gasped.

His friend raised his brows in surprise. "What?" He pointed in my direction. "That tiny little speck?"

"She's the unregistered."

"Ah, I see. Now, Sebastian... perhaps we should take time for a quick two-minute meditation," he reasoned, grabbing Sebastian by the shoulders, who was still staring after me.

I bit my lip to stop myself laughing as I turned into the dining hall. At least his friend seemed saner and more reasonable than him. I wondered if this was the same Sebastian that Livia had been crying about in the shower room. If he was, it was a shame – they were perfect for each other.

As I run-marched to the combat field, Sebastian and his friend, both long-legged, steamed past me. Sebastian's too-dark brows were stark on his face in the daylight as he glowered my way. His friend swapped the side he was walking on to my near side, blocking me from Sebastian's heated gaze. I kept my eyes beaded on them all the same, ready to defend myself if necessary.

When I neared the combat field, the crowd had thickened around a podium on a raised dais. I spotted Saffron's fiery red hair. My shoulders sagged in relief – a friendly face. She was walking between a toffee-haired, tall guy and a small girl with a mousy brown single plait down her back. A taller girl with black hair tied back into three diamond-shaped buns walked beside her, making up a quartet.

Saffron glanced around, scanning the crowd as if looking for someone. She waved when she caught sight of me. I weaved through the throng of around eighty students as she hung back, waiting for me, then she towed me to the third row from the front of the crowd.

I wanted to tell her about what just happened, but there were too many ears listening... and if Arameen was right, I had to assume I couldn't trust anyone, perhaps not even Saffron. Time would tell.

The chancellor stepped onto the podium, wearing a black trouser suit and a loose white blouse. Professors and older students stood behind her; among them I spotted Charlie and Art, wearing neon yellow jackets.

I heard a tumult of exclamations and expletives behind me, and Sebastian appeared at my right side. My pulse quickened. Was he trying to start something again?! Stepping aside, I accidentally knocked into Saffron, and ended up back to where I'd been standing. His gaze remained fixed ahead, arms folded, not acknowledging me. It was such a change from our last encounter that I gazed sideways at him, perplexed. What was he doing? I looked at all the places he could have been standing where I was not.

What the hell was this, silent intimidation? Indignation and anger sparked in my chest. I inhaled vigorously and shouted, "Are you stalking—?"

Suddenly an arm shot out between us, and a broad shoulder levered Sebastian to the side. It belonged to Sebastian's ginger friend, who squeezed himself – with tremendous pushback from Sebastian – into the very snug space he'd created. "He apologises for his behavi—"

Sebastian cut off his friend. "Not bloody likely." He widened his stance and folded his arms across his chest.

Arrogant git!

Sebastian snapped his gaze to me with a scowl. He must not be right in the head.

His friend rolled his eyes at him and tilted his lips up at the corners. "Archer. Pleased to meet you." He leaned forward and offered a ginger double-eyebrow bounce to Saffron.

I edged to my left to allow him more space. "Lori," I said, grudgingly. To be fair, he had defended me from his friend, and at least if he knew my name, he'd be less likely to refer to me as 'the unregistered'.

The chancellor raised a globe, and all eyes fixed on her at the podium. She projected an enormous scoreboard. The left-hand column of the scoreboard displayed numbers from 1 to 84; the central column held invitees' names in alphabetical order. The points column next to it held scores that all currently read zero.

"I am Chancellor Wutterhorn. Welcome to the Alius Trials. Behind me is the trial scoreboard, clearly divided into three sections. From top to bottom, the upper in gold, middling in silver, and underling in bronze." The sections highlighted and rippled in the respective colours as she spoke.

A highly offended voice sounded from somewhere behind me to the right. "Underling?!"

"We, as alius, all strive to be in the upper section." The upper section rippled in gold once more. "When trials are complete, you will choose the house you wish to belong to. Choose wisely; the house stones will reject you if you are not suitable for that house. If you're rejected, you will be assigned to the house that most closely matches your skills and abilities.

"Those of you who complete the trials and rise to the upper section will each earn fifty points for your house," Chancellor Wutterhorn went on, looking in the direction of Sebastian, the mages and the fae as the golden section gleamed again. "Those of you in the middling section will earn five points," she said, looking at the dwarves and vampires as the middling section shone silver. "And those of you in underling section..." She eyed the Eassusians and shifters. The section did not ripple. "Will each lose fifty points for your houses."

A murmur rose from the invitees.

"Well, that's a new delight we're faced with," Saffron moaned, frowning. Her expression was echoed among the other invitees.

I didn't know much about this world, but Charlie had explained there was a social hierarchy, where shifters and Eassusians were at the bottom. It seemed that despite the alius claiming the academy was progressive and integrated, that hierarchy had filtered into the trials. I hadn't been here long, but not much seemed fair about this world.

"Today we begin the trials with the Revealing!" Chancellor Wutterhorn yelled to cut off the chatter. When it died down, she clasped her hands together and added, "Regina Wyrmglas will now take over."

"This'll be a short reveal for the shifters," someone said in a snide tone in front of me. I frowned at the back of their head in distaste.

A low rumbling throaty growl issued from behind me, accompanied by the scent of smoke and burning, causing the hair on the back of my neck to rise.

"I suppose everyone will see Saffron's wings and finally see her for her true colours." Priscilla's voice came from the front row to my left. There was a derisive titter from her fae friends. I scowled at them all.

Eugenia, Livia, and Karina were standing in front of me to the right. Eugenia's untowelled blonde head turned to look behind her, revealing wide blue eyes and spidery eyelashes.

"Hi, Sebastian," she breathed, sweeping her lashes down.

"Hey," he answered with a smirk, as if this always happened. Karina elbowed Eugenia in the ribs.

"Ow!" Her face scrunched and her jaw dropped in shock. "For the Mother's sake, I was only saying *hi*, Karina."

Livia stared, stony-faced, ahead. I leaned forward, remembering he'd broken up with her and interested, despite myself, to gauge Sebastian's reaction. He stared at the back of her head, and a darkness touched his eyes. Then he lifted his gaze to the dais, looking resolved, pursing his lips.

The stunning Dragon-Shifter Queen of the North, adorned with sparkling gems and golden jewellery, wore a golden sequined evening dress to match. Her blonde hair loose, bouncing curls tumbling down her shoulders and back. She stepped down from the dais and asked her globe to cast a large projection of her. It did so, making her twenty feet tall.

"If all students could take ten steps back, please." Her clear voice boomed across the field.

The front row shuffled back, and the rest of us followed. Regina raised her hand; a warm gold light exuded from it, levitating a large, cloth-covered object at the side of the dais. It settled in front of her as she lowered her hand. She removed the cloth to reveal a table of smoky-white-veined quartz.

"I am Regina Roberta Wyrmglas, Dragon-Shifter Queen of the North. I am your counsellor here at the academy. Any problems you may have, I'm your dragon." She chuckled, flashing her perfect ivory teeth. "To mark the start of your trials, we will first discern your magical abilities and any potential abilities you may gain. Some abilities may evolve past your potential, or adversely, they may not come into being. Most of you are recently emerged or magically unbound; others have an unfair advantage, in that you have trained from an earlier age," she said, giving a pointed look at the fae, including Saffron, and the mages. Her gaze settled on Sebastian. His too-dark eyebrows lowered and creased into yet another scowl.

I will name him Eyebrows, I declared internally.

Regina had delivered a public gibe if I ever heard one. I was delighted she'd had a go at Eyebrows, but I felt for Saffron. She showed no emotional reaction. Poker face slotted into place, but I was sure she felt something about it.

Regina went on with an optimistic smile. "However, invitees at a disadvantage should not be discouraged. Many have risen to the challenge and entered the upper section during the trials despite this." She eyed me brightly before her gaze landed on several other invitees.

My cheeks flared with heat, and a strangled sound escaped from Eyebrows. I allowed myself an ever so slight and humble grin. It grew from ear to ear as I leaned forward to look at him. Archer cleared his throat and puffed out his chest to block any interaction.

Regina pressed her finger to her globe, and it projected a new image: invitees standing in a ring, holding hands, with two at one end placing their hands on the quartz table.

"Please release your globes and arrange yourselves in accordance with this image. Form a ring and join hands with invitees either side of you. The two invitees nearest me," she looked at each in turn, "place your free hand on the crystal table."

CHAPTER THIRTEEN

I pulled Saffron away from Eyebrows and we ended up directly opposite Regina, Saffron holding my left hand in a cool grasp. I felt fear and excitement coming from her. To my right, the overly warm hand of a huge, well-built guy with dark hair and moss-green eyes engulfed mine. Only excitement, streamed into me from him.

Once we'd positioned ourselves in the correct formation, Regina Wyrmglas pressed her palms to the quartz table. Golden light shot out and encased everyone linked to the circle in her golden magic. Our globes ignited gold, rose and floated above our heads, infusing the air with a scent of smoke.

"Memorise all you see; it will help us in the trials," Saffron murmured, leaning down to me. I nodded and observed the many faces forming the circle.

"I will now call the powers," Regina Wyrmglas said in a calm, reverent manner. "Mage magic!"

My globe flashed and made a fizzing sound, emitting a projection of a ring – like the chancellor's crystal sword ring. It faintly glowed white above my head.

I scanned around, finding all the ring-wielders in the sea of faces.

Eyebrows, standing ten people to my right, had a blindingly white ring revolving above his head. It shone the brightest; doubtless that meant he was the strongest mage. A rock formed in the pit of my stomach. Sure, I'd shouldered him in the ribs, but it had only been to escape him after he'd slammed me up against the wall. Why did the strongest mage of the invitees seem to hate me?

Glancing around, I searched for Arameen Miamar. Her eyes met mine. She inclined her head to the side. I mirrored the gesture as if to say; *You were right.*

This ceremony was a public display of our strengths and weaknesses. My ring barely shone; Eyebrows' was so bright it was blinding. He sneered as his eyes settled on mine. I shifted on my feet, uncomfortable. It was like hanging a dunce sign on the village idiot, or branding A on an adulterer. Mine was W for weak.

I memorised the faces of the people who had a ring above their heads: Livia, Karina, Eugenia, Eyebrows, Archer, and so many more. At least half of the invitees were mages. *How can that be?*

Saffron whispered, "The crystal rings of the mages are called mage rings. Yours is dull, so you have either the potential for mage magic, or you presently have a low-power use of it... but you heard what she said. Your mage magic could evolve from the potential."

Or I may never have the ability to use it, I mentally added. The mage rings disappeared.

"Now," Regina said, building the suspense. Her eyes were wide as she beamed at us. She certainly had a flair for the dramatic. "Shifter magic!" Her voice rang out as she pressed her palms to the quartz once more, her sequined dress, cloaked in golden light, making her shine like some sort of star beacon.

The golden globes fizzed once more. Some rings rotating above mages were replaced by an image of an animal; Livia had a ferret, Karina a mouse, another a cat, Archer a turtle. I sucked in a sharp intake of breath. Mages could be shifters too?

The guy holding my hand had a huge white wolf appear above him. He smiled up at it, eyes bathed and eerie in the silvery golden light. My eyebrows shot up past my hairline as I saw that the even larger blonde-haired guy next to him had a massive blue and black speckled dragon rotating above him, with six sharp, curved horns sprouting from its head, as well as fire, earth, and air symbols.

I glanced around. There were four wolves, a fox, a snow leopard, a lion, a tiger and another two dragons rotating above two redheads – a boy and a girl standing together over to my left. My palms were slick. I felt out of my depth, and I hoped the people holding my hands didn't think I was a sweaty mess.

The wolf-shifter beside me smiled, and the phrase '*Oh, what big teeth you have*' sprang to mind. He squeezed my hand, and I felt compassion coming from him, which was oddly comforting, despite what I was looking at. He could probably see or smell my fear. I wondered what colour fear was – probably yellow for coward. I pushed that thought away and returned to memorising powers to faces as the revolving animals vanished.

"Fae magic!" Regina boomed.

Wings, seals, scaled bodies, bows and arrows, tridents, earth, air, or water symbols appeared above the heads of the fae. Zale had a red, orange, and purple-scaled figure, a water sign and a trident rotating above him. Priscilla had delicate, iridescent-green gossamer wings, a bow and arrow, and both earth and air signs. But the person to the left of me drew the fae's attention.

Saffron had a bow and arrow, an earth and air symbol, and an enormous set of black feathery wings above her. She kept her gaze fixed straight ahead. I felt her grip tighten, and her fear rushed into me. I squeezed back in response, and her hand relaxed slightly, her fear receding with reassurance.

I scanned the rest of the fae. They had wings of all different shapes and sizes – some feathered, some gossamer – but only hers were black. Priscilla had mentioned the Revealing would show her true colours. I'd ask Saffron about it later.

"There are loads of healers amongst the fae and dwarves," the wolf boy standing to my right said randomly. Any information was appreciated. He had a square jaw and reminded me of someone.

"Thanks," I replied. It seemed late for an introduction, since we'd skipped pleasantries and moved straight into hand-holding. But what the heck! "I'm Lori. Pleased to meet you."

"Francis. I'm Charlie's brother." He nodded his head in her direction.

I flicked my gaze between them, seeing the resemblance. "I thought you looked familiar," I breathed with a wide grin.

"Well, in a ruggedly handsome, masculine sort of way." He gripped my hand tighter as I sucked down a laugh.

We both returned our attention to the proceedings as the assorted wings, fins, and symbols disappeared.

"Vampire magic!" Regina spewed the words out, pressing her palms on the stone. Her eyes shone an insanely bright gold.

A blood-red colour filled the vampires' globes, and a dark mist rose to obscure them as an air elemental symbol appeared over their heads. I looked around at the vampires and shuddered. There were only seven in all. One had long spikes of toffee-coloured hair. Was that the guy Saffron had been walking beside when I'd first arrived at the combat field?

He dropped his gaze and caught mine. He lifted the corners of his lips and lurched forward, baring his fangs with a hiss. I stepped back, crying out in fear.

Francis gripped my hand tight and growled in return, as did his dragon friend. I felt anger coming from him, mixing with my fright. The other vampires standing on either side of the first guy hissed back at them.

It was nice the shifters had come to my defence, but it made me feel weak. I needed to prepare myself for anything. My fear made me an easy target, and I'd done the same thing with Charlie when she'd partially shifted. Heart hammering, I lunged forward, in a fighting stance, and hissed right back at him. I must have looked demented, but a seed of dignity swelled up and spread through me. I would not keep being intimidated.

He lifted his lip in a sneer, exposing long, sharp fangs. The mist around the globes dissipated.

The vampire swung his eyes to Saffron with the corner of his lip, curling up in an altogether different type of expression, then winked. A smile played around her mouth.

I felt excitement, happiness, and anticipation coming from her. My mouth hung open. What was *that?* Ergh... the answer dawned on me. Was that *lust?* And after he'd been such a d-hole to me!

The word *traitor* popped into my head. I stared between them, watching her bite her lip as he shared a satisfied smile. They were totally checking each other out. I rolled my eyes and stopped myself from releasing her hand and vomiting.

"Is that the vampire ally you were talking about?" I asked Saffron pointedly.

"Yes. He's being playful – it's his way," she said as her eyes swung back to him flirtatiously. She giggled. I wondered what had gone on between them last night and decided she needed to seriously rethink her taste in men. She reminded me of Vita; my best friend was stunning and charming and she had her pick of anyone. She always chose the lady's man, the unobtainable guy, or the bad boy.

Regina's clear voice cut through my thoughts as she cried, "Dwarf magic!"

An earth elemental sign rose above the dwarves, who were standing to my right, next to the vampires. Along with it, a range of weaponry and tools – hammers, swords, axes, and anvils –appeared, and a sign I didn't recognise: a diamond shape with an I in the middle.

The males were smaller than me and they all had thick beards, sideburns, or moustaches. The females were smaller yet; I spied Cassidy from the shower incident. She sensed my gaze and grinned at me. I smiled widely in return.

The largest of the males stood beside her. His beard was long, black, and lustrous, as was his hair. He narrowed his pale green eyes at me from beneath round, gold-rimmed spectacles. The symbols vanished.

"Eassusian magic," Regina Wyrmglas said, in a tone like she was revealing a secret. I smiled despite myself at her playful spirit.

My globe glowed brighter and fizzed. Above my head were four elemental symbols emanating brightly. Fire, air, earth, water. A heated gaze prickled on my face, coming from my right; it was Eyebrows. He jutted his jaw out, and his hazel eyes turned molten and scorched into me. I willed myself to ignore him and surveyed the other Eassusians lined up beside each other, to my left.

Two of them, like me, had four elements. One of them was the purple-haired Arameen Miamar; she glanced at me with a smooth expression and a nod. The other was the black-haired guy with electric-blue eyes next to her.

His expression last night hadn't been friendly, and today it was one of bewilderment. He narrowed his gaze at me, then leaned over to speak to Arameen, keeping his eyes trained on me. Her face remained smooth and unreadable as he spoke.

They were undecided about me, but perhaps that sentiment was shifting. *Do not trust anyone,* Arameen had warned.

The Eassusian wolf-man had earth, air, and an additional symbol of an enormous silver wolf with a spiked mane around its head and folded wings tucked in at its side. The book I'd read last night had omitted maned, winged wolves. If I were to remain in this academy, I'd have to hit the library and find information on each species, the magic of each species, how it worked, how *mine* worked, and how all of it interacted.

The mousy-brown-haired girl with a single plait, standing on the other side of Saffron, must have been a shimmerer. Her elements were fire, air, and water, and she had one other symbol of changing figures – from a hawk, to a whale, to a man – then inanimate objects: a rosebush, a golf ball, a combine harvester.

Whaaa! Transformer reloaded.

It went on changing. She avoided looking around, her eyes cast down, as her light brown skin turned a dark shade of red. My heart stuttered and leapt into a gallop. This girl could turn into *anything*! According to the chancellor, I could never return home; this was now my life. I *had* to survive and pass the trials, or I'd end up in a detention facility in a low-paying job in service to these creatures.

I leaned over to Saffron. "Is that the girl you were trying to recruit as an ally?"

"Yes, her name is Shaidel. She is strong in magic. The girl next to her is Kaylissa, and neither of them seemed against allying with us."

I shifted my glance over to the black-haired girl with the three diamond-shaped buns. She had two elements: fire and air.

The symbols vanished. All species had been called. I tried to release Saffron and Francis's hands, but they both gripped me tighter.

"Wait, there's more," Francis said.

I puffed out my cheeks in irritation. My nose had an itch.

CHAPTER FOURTEEN

"Affinity animals!" Regina cried, with the same zest as when she'd announced mage magic. Globes fizzed, and animals popped up over a multitude of heads. Loads of invitees had affinity animals.

I gaped in awe at the one swirling above my head. It looked like the dragons of the dragon-shifters, but not quite. It was smaller and sleeker, in gold and white, and it had long horns and ears curving back from its head. As I stared up at it, I felt a strong stir in my elements.

There was a collective intake of breath from the Eassusians, and I snapped my gaze over to them. They gaped at me, some in shock, others in horror. Arameen initially gaped with eyes rounded, but she schooled her expression back to unreadable. Her animal was a heavily muscled black-and-white striped cat. It was roaring as it rotated, revealing long, sharp teeth.

When my gaze travelled to the haughty Eassusian standing next to her, his eyes sparked at me in anger. I looked up at his affinity animal, a beautiful, long-tailed blue and silver bird.

Saffron had the same trouble as me. There was a similar intake of breath and chattering amongst the fae when her affinity animals appeared. She had a stag with golden horns and wings, an alicorn, a winged horse, a crow, a cat, an owl, a moth, a vulture, and a bat.

I cast around the fae. A few of them had more animals than Saffron. Priscilla had a whole variety of birds, including crows, hawks, and eagles. Zale appeared to have every creature of the ocean. And another fae with dark-brown hair tied back in a top-knot, had every woodland creature you could think of, aside from the golden-horned stag.

I didn't understand the uproar. I could feel my and Saffron's palm sweat intermingling, and I wondered whose fear I was feeling, mine or hers.

Scanning ahead, I searched for Art on the podium. He was looking at my affinity animal, interest lighting his eyes. His gaze dropped to mine and held it for a moment, the corners of his lips tilting up, then he bent his head over his globe, giving no clues as to what this was about.

Beside me, I watched a wolf rotating above Francis. "Do you have any idea what the big deal is about my affinity animal?"

He shook his head. "I don't know much about Eassusian animals... not yet." His eyes swung over to Saffron.

"The animal that represents Eassus is a legendary creature named the trokket," she said. "It is like an earth-dragon. I'm uncertain what it's supposed to represent other than that, but your affinity animal is one of them."

I blew out the breath I'd been holding. Was that all? But why the response?

"So why are the fae surprised about your affinity animals?"

She spoke hesitantly, as if she didn't want to say the words out loud. "The fae worship the golden-horned hart. It is our most revered creature."

I squeezed her hand, still failing to see the significance, and glanced back to the Eassusians. A boy with nut-brown hair and hypnotic, bright aquamarine eyes smiled at me. I looked away shyly, then back at him. He widened his grin. I smiled stupidly, then reminded myself what I was here to do, and it wasn't playing eye-footsie with the gorgeous Eassusian.

Tearing my gaze away, I mentally noted that the winged wolf-man had a winged wolf and a variety of what seemed to be land animals, but they looked a little different to any animals I'd ever seen. Shaidel had one symbol above her that was changing into different animals over and over. Above Cassidy and the dwarves to my right were a worm, bat, ants, and a swift.

I felt someone's eyes on me. Certain they belonged to Eyebrows and afraid of what I'd see there, filled with trepidation, my eyes slipped up to meet his. As sure as eggs were eggs, they were filled with scorn. Why did I bother? With a frustrated sigh, I raised my gaze to search above his head and found a dragon and winged horse rotating.

Why did the strongest mage my age hate me? And why was my mage magic weak and my Eassusian magic strong? Did that mean I was more alien than Earth-being? Here was my home, yet I didn't belong to it. It left an ache in my chest. My parents loved me. But would they keep on loving me if they knew I wasn't their biological child *and* part alien?

None of it mattered. Either way, it was likely I'd never see or speak to them again. A hollow feeling took hold.

As I emerged from my thoughts, I still felt the weight of Eyebrows' stare. I raised my eyes to his with enough venom in my glower to stop the stalker from looking. An expression of confusion rooted on his face. Was that sadness I detected in his eyes? I tilted my head, wondering what had brought on this change.

There was a flicker, and the intense glare of spewing, rotting, loathing hatred returned. I turned away.

The symbols blinked out.

"This is the final revealing. Mind-magic!"

Like the animal affinities, symbols rose above many heads, though I didn't know what they meant.

Above my head was a disc. A golden orb lay at its centre. Surrounding it were eight other orbs, connected to the central one by a cone shape. It was like eight ice-cream cones with balls of ice cream radiating out from a central circle, or a strange golden flower. I frowned in confusion.

"You have, or are likely to gain, empathic abilities," Saffron whispered.

"Oh, is that what it means? I knew that already."

Saffron drew her head back with an expression of astonishment. I detected panic coming from her. "You can feel my emotions right now?"

"Yes, but I won't share them with anyone, promise," I said.

Her lips pointed ever so slightly up at the corners. She squeezed my hand. I felt relief and happiness coming from her.

I gazed at everyone else's powers. Saffron and all the other fae had three mind-magic symbols above them. I observed Priscilla's.

"The wheel symbol means we have the potential of power over humans' fates. The second represents compulsion and influencing magic, and the third the power of illusion," Saffron explained with a proud gleam in her eyes.

Two of their symbols were faint – the wheel and the power of illusion. It would be something they developed over time. Saffron's influencing magic was bright, the brightest, aside from one fae – the dark-haired one who had had the host of woodland creatures as affinity animals.

The vampires had influencing symbols spinning above their heads, but they were weak too, except for two of them: Saffron's devilish, flirty friend, and the dark-haired girl standing next to him. They had compulsion symbols above their heads. Usually only the elder vampires held that power, I remembered; that must mean the two of them were 'chosen'. I shuddered at the sight of them. I had to find out what that really meant.

Shaidel had two bright symbols above her. One was mind-control; the other, Saffron explained, was mind-walking. Mind-walking allowed her to look through people's memories and see through her mark's eyes. Saffron explained we would learn to guard against all these intrusions.

A dream-walking symbol had appeared above Arameen Miamar, and an emotion-control symbol appeared above the dragon-shifter next to Francis. I knew that emotion control was Regina Wyrmglas's power. Francis explained that dream-walking was like mind-walking, but could only be done while the mark was asleep.

I glanced over to the other side of the circle; Eyebrows had two symbols above his head. His gaze jerked to mine as I observed his symbols.

Francis bowed his head toward mine and pointed his chin in Eyebrows' direction. "Sebastian's symbol is telepathy; his family is famous for mind-magic. Until we learn how to shield against it, he knows what we're all thinking, all the time. The other symbol means he has the potential for mind-walking."

My face flamed as I stared at Sebastian.

"I saw you guys, er... exchanging glances?" Francis added, looking between us, eyebrows arched in question.

Sebastian's glare intensified on my face.

"We were exchanging glances of loathing," I replied, a bit too sharply. I remembered what Charlie had told me. Wolf-shifters could sense physical attraction. Was that what Francis was sensing? Not on my part, surely. *I would never be interested in a guy who hates me.* "He slammed me up against a wall, then elbowed me in the face before we came out here. I just wondered why he hates me so much." I shrugged.

Francis squeezed my hand. A surge of anger lanced from him to me. Sebastian's face drained of colour, but he managed to keep scowling.

I glanced at Art. He was watching the interplay, eyes darting between me, Francis, and Eyebrows. His face was calm and expressionless. He bent his head down to his globe, and I wondered what his powers were.

The symbols disappeared, as did Regina Wyrmglas's golden magic. My head felt light. How long had this gone on for?

The chancellor appeared in a ginormous globe projection, towering over us. "We will now disperse for a twenty-minute break. We will meet back here at eleven a.m. for your next trial."

Our globes flashed green and revealed a countdown for twenty minutes.

CHAPTER FIFTEEN

Everyone dropped their hands. I sighed in relief, thankful I had my numb hands back. The left one was cool from Saffron's hand, the other overly hot from Francis's. Their bodies seemed to run at different temperatures to mine.

"Shall we go to the dining hall?" I asked Saffron as I wiped sweat off on my combat trousers.

"Absolutely. I could eat a flock of wild geese and inhale a barrel of liquorice tea," she replied, setting off at speed.

"Thank you for explaining things to me," I said to Francis, scurrying along to keep up with Saffron. "And keeping hold of my sweaty hand."

Francis walked in a leisurely saunter next to me along with his dragon-shifter friend, who was bigger than my garden shed.

"It was a pleasure. My sister instructed me to help you under pain of death." His eyes widened on the last word.

A giggle bubbled up. "I wouldn't like to say no to your sister, either."

"Well, when we're away from home, she happens to be my alpha, but it's not the only reason. It's better we have non-shifter allies for the trials. The mages make up half the invitees here. Some invitees will fail, but they're usually non-mages. If we work together, we're stronger – there's less chance of failure."

"Like the academy motto, right?"

"Yes, you're right, the motto makes sense."

"Wait a minute. Are you asking if we'll be your allies?" I needed to be direct as possible, because according to the globes we had eighteen minutes and thirty seconds until the next trial.

Francis turned to his friend, and I followed his gaze.

"Hey. I'm Victor Wyrmglas," the dragon-shifter said to me.

"Lori Fields, and this is Saffron Underhill. Are you, uh... related to Queen Regina Wyrmglas?"

He nodded. "I call her Mum in private. And yes, we want to be your allies."

Saffron flicked a sideways glance at me. We silently agreed, and she turned to the shifters. "We are likely to be allied with a vampire and maybe some Eassusians. Is that acceptable to you?"

"The more variety, the better chance of passing," Francis replied.

I grinned. "Great – it's a deal!"

He raised his fist to me, and I bumped it. *Then there were five.*

"Now, let's eat!" Saffron said, like she was on a mission.

"So, Victor," I asked, "what do you call your mum at the academy?"

"You know, when she's not doing titles, she likes to be called Rob."

In the dining hall, a long queue had already formed for the hot food counter. Table service would be slow. I picked up a chicken and pesto wrap and a bottle of water at the cold counter and met with the others at the snack counter, where I opened the wrap and took a bite.

Francis looked around the dining hall furtively and hunched down, looking really suspect. He pitched his voice low. "So, here's the line-up for the trials."

I sucked in a breath and whisper-shouted, "What line-up? Do you know what our trials are?"

"For the sake of the moon, Lori, keep your voice down," he whispered back, and did a shushing motion with his hands. "Shifters, vampires, and even fae can hear you!"

"Sorry, I forgot," I said, taking another bite of my wrap.

Just then the idiot vampire from the Revealing appeared. "We certainly can hear you," he warned, edging his way next to Saffron. As he winked at me, a twinkle in his eyes, he added, "Hello, sweet-cheeks."

"Don't call me sweet-cheeks," I replied with my mouth full, stepping away from him.

He was carrying a lidded paper coffee cup and an apple. Whatever was in the cup smelled metallic, like blood. Suddenly my sandwich tasted like rice-paper. I saw Francis and Victor both eye the cup dubiously.

"But you do... have sweet cheeks," he repeated, as he bit into his apple and leaned back to check out my rear.

Saffron gently smacked him on the arm, and he grinned smugly. My face burned in embarrassment. I'd always had an ample bottom – just ask my mother. It was something I was self-conscious about.

The vampire noticed everyone eyeing his cup and pointed to it. "Vampire – need the blood to survive. I'm Ollie, by the way; Ollie Oddy." He introduced himself with a self-satisfied grin.

"I *like* your cheeks," Victor said in my defence, way too late.

"Can everyone stop talking about my arse?!" My face flared so red that if it had been night, it could have been used as a docking beacon.

"I didn't say a word," Francis said, leaning back as if to check out my rear as well. I backed up towards the table behind me so no one could see anything, and Ollie cackled with mirth.

I tried to get the conversation back on track. "Should I eat this whole sandwich now, or are we going to be doing something physical? I don't wanna yak."

"Have a few bites and leave it. Here are some protein bars. Stuff them in your pocket," Francis instructed, handing me a couple of them – chocolate-covered, yum. "Are the two Eassusians you mentioned joining us?"

Casting around in search of them, my gaze tripped on the first pair of eyes staring back at me. It was Eyebrows, the bloody stalker. I deliberately looked away.

Kaylissa and Shaidel were talking to that stunning aquamarine-eyed Eassusian guy in the far corner of the dining hall. Away from everyone else, including the other Eassusians. There were groups all over the dining hall forming alliances, as we were.

"Doesn't look like it for today, but the offer is there if they want to." Saffron shrugged.

"Will you do us a protection barrier?" Francis asked Victor, who stepped back from us in preparation. I watched, holding my breath.

"*Ee Kor! Ee Arwa! Ee Lev!*" Victor enunciated each phrase.

I stared in open-mouthed awe. Each phrase formed as symbols of red ash fire that shot a foot or so from his mouth and lingered for a moment, then dispersed around us in a fiery swirl and vanished.

"Thanks mate," Francis said.

"No probs mate," Victor answered.

Francis scanned around once more and leaned low into our circle. "Some people may have lip-reading capabilities, so I'm ducking down. Ok... I have the trial events in order, as planned at this moment in time. We'll have a non-combat trial to test fitness, fears, and magic. Then a written test. Next, a magical skills assessment; last, a combat trial that also tests fitness, fears, and magic. Just so you're aware, they may make last-minute changes to avoid cheating. These are the plans for now."

My shoulders slumped in relief at the information.

Ollie whistled and gave a sideways smile. "I didn't take you for a cheater, Franny."

Francis frowned at him, as did I.

"It's Francis, silly, not Franny." Saffron rebuked him with a smile.

"Well, I'm ecstatic I joined this group already." He cozied up to Saffron, and I thought I heard him purr.

"I think we all know why you joined the group," I said, folding my arms and looking between him and Saffron, recalling their sickening flirtation during the Revealing. Saffron stuck her tongue out at me. I flicked them both the Vs. We giggled and Ollie rolled his eyes, looking vaguely peeved.

Our globes vibrated and showed five minutes remaining.

"Time's up. On to the trials," Ollie said, and we trudged back to the combat field.

Chancellor Wutterhorn stood at the dais as we gathered around. "Your powers and potential powers have been revealed. Some invitees, unfortunately, were less powerful than expected. Do remember that the trials separate the grain from the chaff."

She supersized the board behind her; two students had a line through their names. I didn't recognise them, but Sebastian Hale was first on the board. Saffron and I were in the upper section too. They'd positioned me ninth and Saffron fifth. There was an increase in chatter from the invitees at the news.

"I've never heard of students being cut based on the results of the Revealing," Francis said to us all darkly, shaking his head. "Both of them were shifters – a wolf and a fox."

"Did you know them?" I asked.

"I knew the wolf-shifter. His father is an alpha!"

I searched for Francis's name on the scoreboard and found it in the underling section. That made me feel uneasy. But his sister Charlie was a prefect; she was strong and a little scary. That had to count for something, and the trials were far from over.

"Quiet! Settle down!" the chancellor said, as the crowd returned their attention to her. "Your second trial is the Alius Chase. The trial rules are as on the globe projection above me."

I looked up and read:

1. *Winged alius are prohibited from using their wings in flight.*

2. *With the exception of rule one, invitees are encouraged to use their magic.*

3. *Working with or helping fellow students, in any regard, is forbidden.*

My heart plummeted. "We're not allowed allies?" Now I really was in trouble, and I had no idea how to use my magic!

"What is happening this year?" Saffron demanded.

A voice cried behind us, "These new rules aren't fair!"

There were a lot of protests coming from the crowd. I wasn't the only one whining.

The chancellor raised her hand for quiet. "Invitees, release your globes!"

I did so, and everywhere around me crystal orbs glittered rainbows as the sun shone through them above our heads.

"Your globes will guide you through the trial. This is a race. You will be timed, and in order to continue in the trials, you must complete it. If you do not complete the race, you'll be ejected from the trials."

Chancellor Wutterhorn closed her eyes and held her hands up to the heavens, as if in prayer. Her ring crystals glowed white; she opened her eyes and pointed towards the ground behind her. There was a tremor underfoot, and a thirty-foot hedge and a wide arched doorway erupted from the earth, followed by hoots and cheers from the invitees.

"You will be timed from entering the arch. Please queue behind it," the chancellor finished.

We made our way to the hedge arch. I couldn't see anything beyond it; there was a silvery, magical swirl in place of a door. It was broad enough for six people to enter at once. The five of us lined up – me, Saffron, Ollie, Francis, Victor – a few rows from the front.

Sebastian and his friends queued in front of us, Priscilla and her friends in front of them. And somehow Arameen Miamar and friends, including the gorgeous one, were queuing directly behind us. I was the filling in an enemy triple sandwich.

I gulped so loudly I feared all could hear it. Arameen had looked shocked at my animal affinity in the Revealing. Her raven-haired friend had looked bewildered, then pissed-off, and he'd been talking in her ear about me.

I wondered if my powers had swayed her against me... or swayed the Eassusians against me. I'd wanted to ask Art about my affinity animal, but making allies and completing trials had taken priority.

We stepped forward as invitees advanced through the apporting arch.

"You are strong in elements. Remember to use your magic if you need it," Saffron advised.

"I don't know how to use it," I told her, feeling hopeless. "Since the light-reaper attack, the only thing I've been able to do is boil drinks!" I laughed at my own ridiculous statement. I didn't think the next trial would call for that talent – though I was still astounded I had any magic at all. We stepped forward in the queue, my heart palpitating.

"That's a handy ability. I often wish there was a faster way to heat my tepid cup of tea, and now I have you," Saffron reassured me, and I released another nervous laugh, glad of the distraction.

Victor overheard our conversation and stepped to put an arm around my shoulders. I felt positivity and calm being pushed into me, and leaned into him as he relieved my tension.

Eyebrows spun round to face us, brows furrowed, and peered down his nose at me, glancing in disdain between me and Victor. His friends stepped forward, but he remained. He said nothing.

I shifted my gaze between him and where his friends waited, a few paces ahead, at the silvery gate. "Did you want something, or…? What are you…? You're holding up the queue."

He smirked as if he wouldn't fall for that one, then noticed his friends had gone from his side. He flared his nostrils, spun on his heel, and stormed up to Archer and the three other waiting mages to disappear through the silvery swirl. And the dude was a mind-reader?

We were up next. I searched for Art and Charlie on the dais. They waved, and Charlie gave us a thumbs-up. "Go, you lot, you're gonna kill it!" She whooped and waved her fist above her head. I laughed at her enthusiasm.

Our globes went from clear to flashing green and sounded a low tone.

"Thanks Victor," I said, gulping once more.

"That's what allies are for." He gave me a final push of calm and comfort, then released me.

As I stepped through the silvery swirl, goosebumps coated my arms and my face tingled and numbed. I now looked upon a vast expanse of field, not unlike the academy grounds behind us.

When I glanced over my shoulder, the academy and hedge had vanished. Our globes flashed green, starting their timers, and zoomed ahead, revealing our paths.

"Are we still at the academy?" I asked as we chased after them.

"Maybe... They can form whatever magical constructs are needed for the trials," Francis called as he pulled ahead.

Our paths diverged into six different directions, lightly marked out with white magical tracks. My heart sank. There'd be no help or company on this trial; I was alone.

"See ya at the finish line," I said, as cheerfully as I could muster. We exchanged another chorus of good lucks and ran our separate ways.

As I stepped onto my individual path the other invitees vanished, but I spotted someone running ahead of me in the distance. My globe whizzed around my head like an infuriated bee, urging me on.

I ran as fast as I could, but without knowing when it would end or how far I'd be running, it was difficult to know what pace to keep. I didn't want to burn out too quickly, so I pushed myself slightly faster than a jog.

After twenty minutes, as my breathing became strained, a structure finally appeared ahead. It looked like a magical hurdle/obstacle course set between two hedges. The hedges stood about a storey high and a road-width apart, and the hurdles weren't the flimsy things I'd seen on an athletics field. They were heavy, thick, enchanted wooden planks.

The first hurdle levitated slowly up from the ground to over twice my height and slammed back to earth with the force of a guillotine, leaving a deep indentation in the ground. Then it repeated the action. Beyond it was a whole series of varying lethal-looking obstacles.

"These alius are bloody insane," I said aloud to my globe.

The rule against the winged alius flying made sense now. They could easily just flap their way over... if only.

My globe zoomed through the obstacles to the other side and bobbed up and down through the gaps of the animated hurdles, flashing green as if to say, *Get going*.

I took a deep breath, waited for the first hurdle to fall, and stepped over it... kind of. It rose faster than I expected and caught my trailing foot. I nose-dived into a sprawl on the grass.

As the plank hurtled down toward my head, I tucked from a wide sprawl into a ball and squeezed my eyes shut. A rush of air whooshed past as it belted the earth. I opened one eye, then the other, then rolled to my feet to examine the obstacle behind me.

"Did that rise faster than it did before, just when I stepped over it?" I said to my globe. It whizzed down next to me and facelessly inspected the plank. It swivelled to 'look' at me, then to face the next obstacle.

"Alright! Give me a second!" I glared at it and rubbed my grass-covered palms on my combats. With my heart in my mouth and all colour drained from my face, I observed the next obstacle.

This hurdle shot up from the ground like a dart, hung in the air, then slammed back down. I let it go twice to get the timings. As it hung in the air, I held my breath and nipped under it. What could be simpler? Easy!

The next obstacle involved two planks edged on either side with four-inch serrated, curved, saw-like teeth. Each plank began in an upright position beside a hedge, then fell toward the centre. After a second, they returned to an upright position, then back, like the windshield wipers on a car. This wasn't so easy.

I watched them for timings, half expecting a spray of water to squirt out, positioning myself to the right side. Once the hurdle hurtled down, this area would give me the most time to jump through. But I'd have to allow for the added length of the serrations on both sides, giving me less time and little margin for error.

Here it goes!

The hurdles fell. I leapt through, but one blade on its journey back up shaved the skin off my lagging elbow, causing me to spring away from the obstacle with a gasp.

Spikes the size of kitchen knives shot through the earth where I'd just been standing. I ignored the sting of exposed flesh and dry-gulped, heart thundering, pulse racing so hard I could hear blood rushing in my ears.

The spikes sank back down, leaving no indication they'd ever been there. Panting, I stared at the ground hard, searching for signs of another set of spikes. I had to be more careful. I hadn't seen them before I jumped.

I faced the next obstacle, wanting to get out of this death trap as fast as possible, checking high and low for any other surprises. The academy certainly seemed intent on maiming its prospective students, if not killing us.

My globe floated beyond the next obstacle and flashed green at me, but I had to give myself a talking to first. *I am Alius, strong in all four elements, with empathic abilities and the potential for mage magic. I can do this.*

I wondered how Saffron and the others were doing. They'd probably finished already.

This penultimate obstacle had two planks lowering and rising, one after another, at different speeds. There was a two-second gap when I could jump through them both. On the other side another set of spikes, longer this time, appeared two seconds after that. I breathed deeply to settle my nerves. The two-second gap was coming.

I jumped and caught my foot once more on the last plank. Falling into a sprawl, I pushed off the ground like an arched bridge. The spikes thrust at my mid-section and lightly jabbed the skin on my stomach. I sucked in my stomach as far as it would go, holding my breath, remaining motionless, bottom up, hands and tips of my toes on the ground, arms shaking until they subsided again.

How was this a race? It was one near-death experience after another.

I thought of the light-reaper and all alius. It was vital I learned how to defend both myself and my loved ones from them. I only wished the academy had taught us magic *before* they tried to eliminate us. This was all I could do for now.

I steeled myself. Complete this trial or die trying.

The final challenge comprised three obstacles in quick succession, with varying levels of lethalness. Falling to my knees, I checked for spikes coming out the ground. There were two rows at the very end.

There was no way to jump straight through all three obstacles, and there was minimal space between each one. I'd have to step through each one with perfect timing without mistakenly overstepping into the next one. *I have faith in myself! I can do this!* My globe buzzed in loops on the opposite end, waiting for me.

The first hurdle shot so fast from left to right that it stole my breath. I stepped through as it slowly made its way back. There was a foot of space both in front and behind me. Taking deep breaths, I tried to slow my racing heart as I observed the second obstacle.

Two verticals snapped together in the centre, while another two horizontal hurdles drifted slowly together to the centre. There had to be a space I could step through quickly, without hurling myself into the last set of hurdles.

And there it was! I moved to the left hedge, turning ninety degrees as the horizontal plank rose to just below knee height and the verticals snapped together. I bent over from the waist, side-stepping over it with an exhalation.

Last one. Two vertical and two horizontal planks moved in a dance of circular movements against each other. I found the pattern to the movement and watched the double row of spikes come up on the other side.

The gap I found was high and brief. I shuffled to the side, waiting for the right moment, then dived through the gap head-first into a double tumble and sprang back up to my feet. The spikes came up behind me.

That was something I hadn't done since gymnastics lessons when I was ten years old. *Still got it – never lost it!* I searched ahead for the next obstacle and saw nothing. Was it over?

The globe winked green at me and zigzagged in the air as if in a celebration dance, then zoomed forward, showing I should chase. I ran after it, relieved to be alive and intact.

CHAPTER SIXTEEN

Conscious of how long I'd taken to complete the hurdles, I ran as fast as I could in search of the finish line or the next obstacle. It felt like it took an hour, but according to my globe it was only fifteen minutes before I reached an arched door that stood unsupported in the middle of the path on the field. My globe zipped up to it.

I pushed the door open, entering a deciduous forest, and followed the path to the sound of running water and another invitee ahead. My globe met with his and bobbed a hello.

As I neared, I took in the wide, fast-flowing river running across our path. I nodded at the dark-haired invitee with teak-coloured skin, casting my mind back to the Revealing. He was a shifter – a snow-leopard-shifter, to be exact.

"Hi. Been here long?" I asked.

"Longer than I wanted. Seb Hale overtook me and crossed in less than five seconds," he said, shaking his head. "I'm not keen on water." He eyed it, lips tight, forehead furrowed.

My globe zoomed across the river, waiting for me. The width of the river was about the length of a tennis court. There was no visible bridge, steppingstones, or fallen log to cross it.

What the globe did hover next to was a rope, suspended from high on the trunk of one leafy tree on my side of the river to high up on another tree across the river. The rope dipped low, hanging into the water in the centre.

But the rope was too high and too far from the water's edge for me to reach, and the tree was bereft of lower branches. Maybe I could take a run at the rope as it descended into the river and try to catch it? But if I missed, I might land on the rocky outcrops below. I needed to check the depth of the water. If it was shallow, I could seriously injure myself.

I cast around for a long stick in the woods, returned when I found a likely candidate, and stabbed down into the water to determine the depth. The water flow was too strong and tried to suck the stick downriver.

An alternative method would be a magical one. One of my elements should get me across – not that I knew how to use them. I felt like a fool, attempting it in front of the snow-leopard-shifter. He watched me with one brow arched, folding his arms.

I smiled nervously. "Gonna try the magic for this one."

He nodded and returned his attention to the water with a scowl.

Closing my eyes, I felt for the air buoyant in my chest, the fiery flames below it, and slow-moving icy water beneath. Earth I couldn't feel one bit.

How had I accessed them before? I'd been angry when I boiled the drinks. That was a no-no. I would likely end up with a river of boiled fish – though that would make a decent meal. Yum, salmon... I smiled to myself.

Cracking an eye open, I observed the snow leopard staring mournfully at the water. That meant he wasn't focusing on me and thinking I was a total freak. I closed my eyes again in concentration.

The light-reaper had delivered me to his feet in a gale of wind. But how? Could I expand my air out? I raised my hand in front of me like he had. Had he said anything? The chancellor and Regina Wyrmglas had said nothing for *their* magic. But in folklore, movies, and books, people spoke magical words or rhyming spells. *Yes, I'll try that.* I formulated my magical rhyming words.

"I raise a mighty zephyr to blow me across the river," I muttered. It sort of rhymed.

I felt a slight stirring of breeze in my hair and opened my eyes.

Maybe louder? I lifted my hand higher and raised my voice. "I raise a mighty zephyr to blow me across the river!"

Nothing had changed. No wind except for the slight breeze.

My globe zoomed over to me and hovered in front of my face. I sighed and waved it away. I had to get on with the trial. It might take me all day trying to use my magic, and this was supposed to be a race. I'd do it the narie way. I moved beneath the rope that trailed across the river.

"Magic is a no-go," I said to the shifter, feeling I had to explain my failure.

The corner of his lips pulled downward, and he nodded. "Are you gonna try the rope?" he asked, his dark eyes sparkling.

"Can't see another way."

I took a few steps back. I'd learned from my athletic classes at school that I had very little flight in my leaps. If I missed, I risked hitting the boulders below – *So I just won't miss*. I blew my cheeks out.

One. Two. Three.

I sped to the bank's edge and leapt, arms spreadeagle, groping for the rope. I caught hold of it. Its roughness bit into my hands and I stifled a cry.

Yes, did it! But I was just hanging there suspended, feet dangling down. What to do?

I lifted my legs to hook onto the rope and missed, but I had a pendulous movement going now. I swung back, lifted my knees forward, and wrapped my legs around the descending rope.

Unfortunately, my hands slipped, plunging my head and arms into the river, narrowly missing the jagged rocks.

My senses screamed at me. The river was icy cold. My head was deep frozen in a second, and there was the minor problem of drowning.

Squeezing my stomach muscles, I pulled my head out of the water, spitting water out and blinking. Upside down, I looked at the shifter on the bank's edge and realised that my shirt had fallen to just above my chin, exposing my sports bra. He'd covered his mouth with his hand, but not enough to hide a smirk and a barely repressed chortle.

"Are you ok?" I heard amusement in his voice.

"Will be in a sec." The blood rushed to my head, and I felt veins standing out on my neck as I attempted to tuck my shirt into my combat trousers. It fell back to my chin. I frowned. *Who really cares? Girls walk around with barely any clothing during the summer.* Focusing on the task, I rocked my body backward to slide further down the descending rope. It worked. It wasn't the most dignified crossing, but needs must. One more should do it.

Now immersed in the icy water, my skin stung. The rope was within easy reach of my hands, but I needed to work on sit-ups and upper body strength. I mentally added them to my list of my many physical deficiencies as my teeth chattered.

The water was flowing fast around me, trying to pull me down the river. I pushed my legs down to find the riverbed, but the flowing water just pushed them sideways. Instead, I pulled myself across, hand over hand, for thirty feet.

When the rope ascended, I crossed my legs at the ankles and pulled my way up with my hands and legs, hanging from the rope like a monkey, but far less nimble. I was cold and sodden, adrenaline rushing through me.

The ascent steepened; I slid back toward the middle, shredding my raw palms further. I needed a plan. I'd climb further up, and before I slipped back down, I'd fling myself backwards toward the bank's edge. I dragged myself up the rope.

Now! I swung back and curled myself, guarding my head with my arms, hoping I'd swung to the left side enough to avoid that slippery-looking boulder.

I hit the water, and the river slammed me into the boulder head-first.

Spots danced across my vision; the water temperature numbed any pain. I'd check for wounds when I'd reached the bank. I braced myself against the boulder. Once steady, I pushed with my legs, driving myself to the river's edge, and pulled myself onto the slippery, muddy bank.

My globe zoomed from side to side and spun in place. I took that as a *Huzzah!*

"Thanks," I said aloud as I knelt down to wash my hands, trying not to think about how that could have gone so much worse.

"What!?" shouted the shifter over the rush of the water.

"I was talking to my globe!" I swiped my hand across my forehead, checking for blood. I found some on my fingers and washed the wound with the water, then pressed the bottom of my shirt to it to staunch the flow.

"You're bleeding?" he called, sniffing at the air with a look of concern. "That was one hell of a crossing!" he added, bubbling with laughter.

"Thanks. Yeah, I cut my head on the boulder." It would be a while before I saw the funny side of it, though.

Another invitee appeared from the woods beside the shifter. It was that gorgeous Eassusian. My breath caught in my throat.

He waved at me and smiled. "Good day to you both. You took a dip in the river, I see. How was it?" His voice was deep, rich, and carried easily over the rushing water.

"Surprisingly refreshing," I replied in an equally bright and cheery tone. Thankfully, the cut on my head had stopped bleeding. Head wounds could be a real pain to staunch.

"Good one, girlie! My turn now," the snow leopard said.

I was happy he'd found the courage to cross and hoping he wouldn't drown. "Good luck. Maybe I'll see you ahead!"

Perhaps I should wait for him, but I couldn't help him; I'd fail the trials if I did. Surely the professors had eyes on us and would rescue him if it came down to it? But hadn't they said people had died in these trials? I turned back to watch his progress.

"You get on, girlie, I'll catch you up!" He waved me onward.

Reluctantly turning away, I moved on. He sounded confident. My globe flashed green, urging me on, and when I still didn't move, it zoomed ahead and zoomed back. That meant I wasn't going quick enough for his liking. It was definitely a *he*.

"I will name you Maximus," I told the globe. He stared blankly at me and spun sideways as if cocking his head.

I started jogging, wondering if I was becoming like that guy in the film whose plane had crashed on an island and he developed a close relationship with his basketball.

The shifter's voice pierced my thoughts. "Piece of piss, mate."

Was he talking to the Eassusian? Or did he talk to his globe too? I glanced over my shoulder as he came into view, relieved he was in one piece.

"Hey, girlie – your crossing was the most entertaining I've ever seen. I'm Jay, by the way." He held out his hand, and I took it in a firm handshake. My dad had always told me to make sure my handshake was firm and dry. Nothing on me was dry right now, so I was happy with the former.

I felt elation and happiness coming from Jay, no feelings of apprehension or suspicion. The guy was alright.

"Lori. How many crossings have you seen?"

"A few." He smirked.

I fell into a jog, and he jogged alongside me.

"Thanks," he said.

"For what?"

"Making me laugh after I was faced with my worst nightmare."

"Yep, that was fun… and you're welcome. So happy I could be here to amuse you."

"I'm not the only one." He snorted, shaking his head, beginning to pull ahead of me.

"What does that mean? Who else was I amusing?"

"The globes are filming us right now. So pretty much everyone in the academy can view this." His grin broadened as my head whipped back, and my mouth and eyes flung open wide. His expression sobered. "But thanks again… really. See you around, girlie."

He sped off, kicking up dirt in his wake.

Speechless for a few seconds, I eventually found my voice. "Not if I see you first!" I shouted after him, cheeks flaming. *Everyone* had seen the upside-down-head-in-the-water incident with boob flash? I felt like crawling into a cave and dying there.

I shook my head to dislodge that thought. *Focus, dammit. It's the trials!*

My clothes were drenched, but it was a fine, sunny day, and they must have had some sort of spell on them because they were drying out exceptionally fast. After ten minutes of pelting it and trying to catch up with the shifter, who was out of sight in no time, I was totally dry, and I'd arrived at another door.

As I stepped through, my surroundings changed again. A few hundred metres in front of me was a wall so wide, that there was no visible end in either direction. As I approached cautiously, it looked to be around a hundred and fifty feet high, or roughly fifteen floors up.

If water wasn't the snow leopard's thing, then heights weren't mine. I'd once gone with Vita and her mum to Wainwright Castle, excited to climb the tower and see the view, all the while fantasising that I was a princess enjoying the sight of my kingdom.

That didn't happen. I'd climbed the first cramped, claustrophobic spiral stone staircase and found I had to cross a walkway to the lofty tower with no railing to one side, a thirty-foot drop to the ground, and an overzealous wind blowing. I'd pressed my back up against the wall and slid across, closing my eyes and praying no one would notice the scared-to-death freak. I made it three sideway steps before a hefty gust of wind blew. I'd shuffled back along to the cramped staircase and descended, then found a bench to sit on for thirty minutes and tried to wrestle my hyperventilation under control.

Now I had to climb *this* beast.

My mouth had gone dry. There were handholds on the wall, and a few rope-ladders to the summit, but forget about a safety net. I willed myself to grow a climbing backbone.

I'd completed the first two obstacles and come out with a few scrapes, but one wrong footing here and I'd go splat. I wondered if I could tell the globe to get me out of here, like in Celebrity Jungle. I pondered all the pros and cons of leaving at this stage. It didn't seem like any other alius had tried to kill me yet – aside from possibly the academy itself during the hurdle trial. So that was a pro. Wind speed was minimal – also a pro.

I opted for the ladder and started my climb. My hands were raw from rope burns, but I made my way steadily up, ignoring the pain in my palms and the drop below. My heart was hammering so fast I thought I'd faint, throw up, or both, but it couldn't keep up that speed forever. After about ten minutes it settled down to a manageable rate.

At halfway up, a crow flew down from nowhere and used my head as a landing perch. Birds were almost as bad as heights. I clung to the rope ladder and shook my head to dislodge it, hoping it wouldn't scratch me or take a dump on my head. Luckily, it flew away.

Unluckily, it came back with some friends.

My heart was beating like the flapping of their terrible wings. Birds and all their ceaseless fluttering! Three more crows swooped from the sky and descended on me, one landing on my head. Two settled on the rungs above me, and one tried to land on my arm.

"You have got to be kidding!" I exclaimed, trembling. The bird on my head pulled at my hair with its beak, its claws digging painfully into my scalp. If I waved my arms, I could lose my footing, and I didn't want a sudden movement to make it try to peck out my eyes.

Between the birds and this nauseating height, I wanted to tear myself out of my skin, it was crawling so badly. My globe bobbed a few feet away, surveying all that was going on. Frozen, I clung to the ladder like a gibbon to its mother.

After a few stationary, terror-filled minutes, the gorgeous Eassusian appeared at the bottom of the wall below me.

Just start moving, I convinced myself, *and they'll flap away*. I looked above me to grope for the next rung. The prehistoric, beady eyes of the crows glared at me in a death warning. Heeding that, I settled back to clinging to the ladder.

Giggling sounded from above. Reluctant to face the birds, I kept my head down. My face burned with heat. Was someone watching me? An indignant fit of rage consumed me. "Bugger off!" I yelled.

The beasts all spread their wings and took to the skies.

Relief washed over me. I waited to see if they'd swarm back at me, but they didn't. Pulling myself up the next rung, I recalled that Priscilla had been two rows in front of me in the queue at the hedge gate. And in the Revealing ceremony, she'd had an affinity with birds. What birds had they been? I felt my anger flaring and took deep, long breaths, so I could concentrate on not plummeting to my death. I climbed another forty feet. Only about thirty-five more to the top.

A bird called. I looked up to find more diving toward me.

The gorgeous Eassusian pulled up level to me on a rope ladder to my right.

"What the—?" He frowned up at the birds and climbed double speed up his ladder.

A hawk glided down and slashed my arm. I hit out at it and missed, my foot sliding off the rung. Prickles of heat replaced icy dread as I held to the ladder like my life depended on it. Because it did!

I hunched my head and shoulders as more crows landed on the rungs above me. Blood was dripping from the gouged flesh. The hawk dive-bombed for another attack.

"*Stop!*" I shouted desperately at it.

To my astonishment, it glided past me and flapped off. Wait. Were the birds listening to my instructions? My pulse raced in hope and excitement. "Fly away, birds, and don't come back!"

The crows, like a plague in reverse, all took to the air and disappeared. I searched the skies and blew a wobbly breath out.

I climbed shakily up and made it the last few feet, pulling myself over and dropping to hug the solid, paved area at the summit. Adrenaline trembles consumed me as I lay.

I looked up and noticed a highly polished set of boots in front of me. The gorgeous Eassusian was gazing down at me. I kept my eye on him; the Eassusians weren't to be trusted.

"Someone sent the birds after you," he said, frowning, in his odd Eassusian accent.

"I think I know who." I slitted my eyes, envisioning sweet revenge.

He raised his brows in question. "Then I suggest you give them a thorough thrashing when you next see them." He smiled warmly.

Laughing, I noticed his lips were full and sumptuous, like a treasure amongst his stubble, then shook my head. My palms were raw. The hawk gouge was stinging, as were the scrapes on my elbow and my head, and lactic acid was cramping my muscles. So why the hell was I thinking about this gorgeous man's lips and wondering what it'd be like to kiss them?

Maximus zipped around my head and drew my attention to another unsupported arched door. Getting to my feet, I walked over to it and responded before I stepped through the door.

"I intend to."

I omitted the fact that I had no idea how to achieve that.

CHAPTER SEVENTEEN

THE DOOR OPENED TO a pine forest with a fresh scent and verdant vibrancy I had never seen before. I didn't wait for the Eassusian – in fact, keeping away from him was my new goal. Eassusians weren't to be trusted! And the man was like Zale when he used his influencing magic on me. I thought back to the Revealing. I didn't remember the Eassusian having that type of magic, but there had been a lot of invitees and multiple abilities; it was difficult to keep track. Perhaps it had slipped my attention.

I tore a strip from the hem of my top and wrapped it around the hawk gouge on my arm as a makeshift bandage, then chased after my globe with all the speed I could muster.

He brought me to a beautiful expanse of meadow. To my left was a large herd of winged horses. I'd seen the teacup versions and they were super cute, but these were spine-tinglingly out of this world. They, too, came in all the colours of the rainbow.

I crept cautiously to them when I remembered that this was a trial. Was I expected to ride them?

As if he'd heard my question, Maximus zoomed over and above the winged horses and back to me, then projected an image of a genderless person mounting one.

I had only been riding once with Vita. I'd gone with her to her riding school, and we'd gone on a horse trail outside the school. We should have been trotting, but the pony I rode kept going into a canter and then a gallop. I wasn't sure if it was my beginner riding skills – or that underlying the feeling of freedom in cantering and galloping, there had been distinct fear. I'd felt like I had no control and could be thrown and trampled at any minute.

Feeling out of control at a height was not something I was looking forward to.

"Have you ever ridden one of these magnificent creatures?" the gorgeous Eassusian said at my elbow.

I jumped at his voice and shook my head. How could I get away from him? "No, I've never seen a full-sized one before. They're stunning."

He looked at me sidelong.

"They are indeed," he said, keeping his eyes on me.

I took a half step away; he was infecting me with his masculine hotness. I shook my head. No Eassusians, no hotness!

A girly giggle rippled out from somewhere close to the treeline ahead. I saw a tall figure with broad shoulders mount a winged horse in one easy motion. I made a beeline for them: first to get away from the Eassusian, and secondly to watch how they mounted them. It wasn't like the winged horses were wearing saddles, stirrups, or reins. I was sure that narie combat academies would have had some regard for safety. I knew a riding hat might not be very effective from five hundred feet up, but it wouldn't do any harm, either.

As I neared the treeline, I regretted my decision. It was the murderous Priscilla, her blonde friend whose name I didn't know, Archer, and my other nemesis – *Eyebrows*. He alone had mounted his winged horse, while the others stood beside theirs.

I about-turned to escape and the gorgeous Eassusian barrelled into me, but he caught me and prevented me from falling. I felt a rush of excitement and deep satisfaction coming from him and mixing with my own. His aquamarine eyes lit up, and his pupils dilated as he held me close.

A winged horse stomped the ground behind me. I tipped back my head at the noise.

"You're not supposed to help anyone in these trials, Eassusian. You should have let her fall," Eyebrows said coolly from atop his gleaming white winged horse.

"It was I who knocked into her. I simply caught her; it was my mistake." He pulled me up from the old-movie lover's embrace.

I straightened my clothes awkwardly, then suddenly remembered Eyebrows could read my thoughts and promptly tried to erase all thoughts I had knocking around my head. The Eassusian's lips, for example.

As that seemed impossible, I decided to watch him set off in flight. I didn't know where we were supposed to be going. Maybe the globe would show me the route when I climbed aboard. I studied his winged horse; it had an intelligent, knowing glint in its dark brown eyes.

"Pegasus," Eyebrows said to me.

The Eassusian and I exchanged furrowed glances.

"They're not called winged horses, they're called pegasuses," he added, in explanation.

"Did you just read my thoughts? Because that's a huge invasion of privacy, and frankly it should be illegal," I snapped, though I didn't know if he could stop reading thoughts any more than I could stop people's emotions flooding into me.

"What they should make illegal is unregistered alius being invited to the trials." He sneered as he stared down his nose at me, eyes trailing over me from head to toes and back up. His brows bunched as he looked just above my head, probably at the nest of fly-away hair that undoubtedly had sprung up after the watery challenge.

"You'd have to take that up with the chancellor. I'm certain ramming someone up against a wall and elbowing them in the face is against the rules," I argued, mocking his overly posh accent. "Besides, it's not my fault the chancellor invited me. I would have happily stayed at home, given a choice." I ran my hand over my hair in an attempt to smooth it.

"A likely story – and elbowing your face was accidental after you rammed me like a rabid harpy." He turned his attention to his pegasus. "Shall we fly, Megalos?" He spoke in a calm, soothing voice.

I wanted to protest about the name-calling, but instead backed away and quickly pulled out my hairband, brushed fingers through my hair, then tied it back up again. If I was being recorded, I didn't want to be a larger target for derision than I already was.

Megalos spread out his wings high and gracefully swept them down in an arc. A rush of wind blew outward and around me in all directions. They were long, powerful wingbeats, that increased in a graceful, majestic way, rather than the fluttering of small birds. I shivered at the memory on the wall and stopped myself from glaring at Priscilla. Her comeuppance would have to wait – probably a few years until I learned how to use my magic.

Eyebrows and his pegasus were high in the sky now, soaring over the meadow. My skin prickled and the hair on my arms stood erect.

"We haven't officially been introduced. I'm Vil, Vil Vinn," the Eassusian said to me.

"Lori Fields... pleased to officially meet you. Have you ever ridden one of these before?" I gestured to the pegasuses.

"Unfortunately not, as it would certainly aid us in these trials."

"Then, I think it best we watch people who've done it before," I said, inclining my head to Priscilla and friends, now resigned to his company. It wasn't likely I could stop him following me; it was a field, after all.

We crept nearer to them, using various pegasuses to shield our advance whilst crouching in the long meadow grass. Unfortunately, it seemed stealth was something else I had to work on, as the pollen caused me to sneeze. The quiet murmurs between Priscilla, her friend, and Archer ceased.

"Oh crap!" I whispered loudly, slowly backing away.

Priscilla moved like a serpent through the tall grass to catch us in the spying act.

"The unregistered assassin. Your hair looks akin to a frenzied cat attack on an unsuspecting ball of cotton, but less appealing. And I have news for you," she said, eyes narrowing, as my hand went to my head. "Eavesdropping on us is cheating, unregistered. You must work out how to mount the pegasus *alone*." Her voice dripped with honey but stung like hornets.

"I would say sending birds to attack me is cheating, Priscilla, and perhaps even attempted murder," I shot back, straightening from my crouched position and squaring my shoulders at her. She really got my goat.

She tittered, glancing at her friend, who joined in. "As I recall, there were no rules against attacking others – only against helping others. Besides, many alius have affinity animals."

I knew she couldn't lie, so she was neither admitting nor denying it. "*Did* you use your affinity animals to attack me? A simple yes or no would suffice."

"Your accusation is naïve and shows you know nothing of the alius. Now run along, we have a trial to finish. I'm astonished you've progressed this far."

"I'll leave when I'm good and ready. You don't own this space, so off you trot on your pegasus if it's so easy."

"I think it would be useful to give you the lie of the land. Fae are far superior to Eassusians—"

"When she says Eassusians, we're talking about Lori, not you, Vil," Priscilla's friend cut in, batting her eyes at Vil.

"Quite. Of course, we're not referring to you, Vil," Priscilla said tightly, then she flicked her shining black locks over her shoulders and flashed him a coquettish smile. The strange display confirmed to me that Vil had influencing magic.

Her gaze swooped back to mine.

"As I was saying before Gwen interrupted me..." She glanced at her friend with a glare so sharp, it could crack a diamond into dust. "You'll soon learn your place in this world, half-breed, and to hold your tongue when your betters are speaking, or it will never end well for you." A saccharine smile crept across her lips, her hard jade eyes sending a chill up my spine as a green glow emanated from her back.

"Learning your place, Priscilla, one might say, is a lesson *you* have trouble learning," Saffron snarled, from behind me.

I turned to her with a relieved smile.

"Well, it won't be a half-breed who teaches me. And you'd have to catch me first," Priscilla snarled. She gracefully sprang up and mounted the dappled forest-green pegasus she'd been standing next to.

I wanted to smack her in her smug face.

"Very well," Saffron said. "Challenge accepted." Her pale purple eyes turned to slits.

Priscilla whispered something to her mount. I wasn't sure what it was, but her pegasus's eyes rounded, its nostrils flaring as it reared. Priscilla's expression changed from leering to terrified as she held on for dear life.

What did she say? My jaw hung open in surprise, and Saffron and I exchanged a hearty laugh at Priscilla's expense. It seemed pegasuses weren't her thing, or at least she wasn't theirs. Her mount grounded its forelegs, and we backed away as it arched its wings and beat down as Sebastian's pegasus had, flattening the grass and flowers surrounding it.

Saffron eyed me briefly, then smoothed my hair, whispering something. I felt amusement mixed with anger coming from her. Black magic emanated from her back and made her whole eyes, even the whites, shine black. Woah! I felt a warmth on my head; she was drying and hopefully straightening my hair. *My very own demon fae*, I thought to myself.

I heard screams from above as Priscilla's pegasus dived back toward the earth, her screeching all the while. Gwen and Archer then both mounted their pegasuses.

Vil turned to me. "I think we simply choose one and see if it allows us to ride?"

I thought an introduction was in order, though time was ticking away, and I'd wasted loads of it already. "Saffron, this is Vil – Vil, Saffron."

Saffron dropped her hand from my head.

Vil spoke first. "Pleased to meet you, Saffron. Have you ridden any of these fine creatures before?"

She smiled at him and answered in a breathy voice. "Pleasure's mine, and yes, I have," she said, giggling. "Unfortunately, I have to fly, but I'll be seeing *you* later." She put her hand on his bicep and squeezed. The blatant seduction made me squirm, but he seemed entirely nonplussed.

Saffron moved to stand directly in front of a lilac pegasus and looked into its eyes, then held her palm out. The pegasus eyed her and walked off, its wing feathers bristling.

She went onto the next with the same result, then the next. Finally, a jet-black pegasus stared back at her, walked toward her, nuzzled her hand aside, then snorted in her face.

"Thank you, my friend. I am Saffron. Will you carry me to our destination?"

The pegasus blinked at her and spoke. "I will indeed, fair Saffron. I am Dimitra; you are welcome to mount."

I gaped. "Bloody Nora! Pegasuses can talk?"

"We certainly can, young mistress," Dimitra replied, giving me a gummy grin.

Saffron nodded at me and gracefully pulled herself up on Dimitra's back.

After I'd picked my jaw up off the floor, all I could think to say was, "Well, have a safe flight."

I heard chatter from behind me as more invitees entered the meadow. Quite a lot more.

Spurred on, I approached pegasuses as Saffron had, and Vil did the same. The first moved away; the second looked irritated and stamped. The third was golden with white stripes. She nuzzled my hand aside and snorted in my face. I'd been repeating Saffron's words in my head, so I would make the request in the right word order.

"I am—" I stopped, faltering, and started again. "Thank you, my friend. I am Lori, will you carry me to our destination?"

The pegasus's eyes widened. "You don't have to recite word for word what your friend said, flower. Once I snort in your face, it means I think you're alright. Now, hop on. I'm Katerina, but I go by Kat."

"Well, thanks so much for accepting me," I said, trying to find a dignified way to mount without stirrups or saddle, or even a nearby box to stand on. It wasn't like I could ask Vil for a hand up.

She noticed my difficulty and lowered herself to the ground.

"Are you sure you can get back up?" I assessed her legs for strength. I was heavier than I looked.

"Don't you worry about that. We'll be fine."

I straddled her back, tensed in worry, imagining her trembling under my weight and asking me to hop back off. Then none of the pegasuses would let me ride them.

"Are you ready, flower? Get your hands twisted in my mane and let's be off."

I did as she asked. She stood back up, as if I weighed nothing, raised her beautiful velvety, gold-feathered wings to the sky and *whoosh*, down they went in an arc. We lifted, and she quickened her wingbeats, rising higher and higher. To my amazement, I felt safe on her back, as if I knew she'd never let me fall.

We flew up and over the meadow in the same direction Eyebrows and Saffron had gone, sweeping across pine-covered mountains. Craggy tors stretched up from the verdant blanket, and lakes shimmered, kissed by the sun's rays. The air seemed warmer higher up, or did she have some sort of magical power that kept us warm?

"Have you ever been on one of us before?" Kat asked, her voice loud and clear as if we were in some sort of sound bubble.

"This is my first time, and I wish I could stay up here forever," I said, feeling... free. The air element within me was filling me up to bursting, the sensation made my eyes line with tears. My worries and stresses of the last two days seemed to fall away and remain on earth. Up here, it was just me, the pegasus, and Maximus, keeping pace in front of us the whole time. The warm wind was delicious. I sniffed.

"Are you crying, petal? I won't let you fall."

"I know that, Kat. I feel—" I paused, thinking I'd sound stupid.

"Free? If you were gonna say free, do you fancy going faster?"

"I'd love to," I said, a stupid grin plastered across my face.

I didn't regret that answer one bit. She raced through the air and tore through the wispy clouds, soaring and diving. My stomach somersaulted, flipped and dropped. I'd always loved a rollercoaster ride, the weightlessness as I dropped, but you never got a view like this.

"Hold on tight, love, we'll be landing in a jiffy." She descended fast, and we touched down lightly in a forest clearing below.

"That was the most amazing ride I've ever had. Ever. I can't thank you enough, Kat." I leaned forward to lift my leg over and dismount.

"You haven't finished your trial yet," she informed me. I belatedly realised that Art was standing off to the side. He held a long, pointed stick.

"Hi, Kat." He walked up to us and stroked her neck.

"Hi, Art, how have you been keeping?" she said, nuzzling his neck and snorting.

"Keeping well. Was Lori a good passenger?"

"The best. She's a natural, this one. She's one to watch out for."

He turned to me, all business. "Well done, Lori, for getting this far. Kat will be with you for the next part of the trial. Follow your globe, and you'll come upon hoops suspended in the air. You must use this lance to spear the hoops and get as many as you can. If you miss any, you are not to turn around to try again; one attempt and move on. If you fall off Kat, just get back on and continue."

He lifted it up to me. I grabbed it and held it level; it was lighter than I'd expected. I didn't know how long I could hold it for, especially with my palms raw. I heaved it up to a vertical position, trying to balance on Kat's back.

"I've given you a shorter one than usual to match your height. Just do your best," Art said, looking into my eyes. I gazed at him and drank him in – his ocean-blue eyes, flecked with gold, his long dark lashes, and the day-old stubble that gave him a more rugged look.

He cleared his throat, looking away. I snapped out of it, remembering we were being filmed and he was a teacher... kind of.

"Thanks. I'll do my best. See ya." I fired out my words to escape the awkwardness. Maximus floated to attention, spun, and whizzed ahead. Kat trotted after him.

I will not fall for the unattainable teacher-slash-student, I thought to myself. But what if he was like Zale and Vil? Was he casting some sort of attraction spell on me, like they were? I didn't feel like he had, but that didn't mean it wasn't the case.

Kat shifted from a trot to a canter, following Maximus as we cut through the forest, her wings tucked close to her body. "That Art – he's so bloody lovely, isn't he, and he's great with us pegasuses. My Megalos adores him, and he's very picky with passengers, you know. Same as me."

"Well, I'm honoured to be your passenger."

"Likewise, flower, likewise."

"And Megalos... does that mean he really liked Sebastian Hale?"

"He's a special boy, as is Art – powerful ones. Like you."

I wanted to ask what she meant, but the hoops came into view as we entered a wide clearing. There were seven lined up, several meters apart.

"We'll take it slow, so you can practice."

This pegasus was the sweetest thing. I lowered my lance to horizontal. Kat lined us up with the first levitating ring and walked to it. I tried to spear it, but almost fell off Kat instead.

I composed myself, held the lance vertical in my right hand, then lowered it again to horizontal. Kat walked to the next hoop. *Almost got it.* I scraped the outer area of the ring. I thought I had it now – balancing with the weight of the lance, staying on Kat. She lined up again, and I got the next ring. They were more spread out now; Kat picked up speed. We got all the rest. Five rings in total.

"You're one to watch, young Lori. Few who've never had a go before get five rings. I'll be seeing you again – maybe at Zeus Ring practice?"

The lance disappeared from my hand. I blinked, then dismounted.

"Thanks again, Kat. I don't really know what Zeus Ring is, but it seems... popular," I said, remembering how Charlie's hotspot in the academy had been the Zeus Ring Stadium. "If I never get to fly on you again, I will remember this day forever."

"Anytime, flower. Good luck in your trials." She beat her wings. I watched for a minute, waving as she rose and flew back to where we'd come from.

Another door appeared in front of us. Maximus – no, Max was less of a mouthful – zoomed to it, and I stepped through. The scenery changed: we were back on the combat field.

Max buzzed, and took me over the two posts marking the finish line. *4 hrs 03 mins 56 secs* flashed on his face.

CHAPTER EIGHTEEN

It looked as if most invitees had already finished and they gathered by the dais, where the professors stood, chatting to them as they waited. Chancellor Wutterhorn gave me a tight smile as I passed her.

Saffron glided up to me. "I knew you could do it," she said, flipping my ponytail with a flash of teeth.

"Well done, Fields!" Charlie called to me.

"Thanks, Charlie. Has Francis finished?"

She cupped her hands around her mouth and shouted, "Yeah! He's in the healer's tent." She pointed to a large white tent on my right.

I gave her a thumbs up.

Regina Wyrmglas floated to my side. "Excellent performance for someone who knows little of our world. Wouldn't you agree, Chancellor?"

"Yes, I wouldn't have extended an invitation if I didn't think her capable," the chancellor said from a few feet behind me, training her eye on me. "I'm looking forward to seeing how you fare in the rest of the trials, Lori. You made effective use of your animal affinity today."

As she turned away, I frowned. "I thought my affinity is to a trok – what's-it-called... dragon trokket?"

"Trokkets are a legendary animal of your world," Regina answered. "They are the masters of all the beasts, birds, and animals. It is curious that their magic holds sway on Earth, and your affinity to that animal seems to give you affinity to all animals."

As she finished, my emotions shifted – from confusion and overwhelm to ease and clarity of mind. I guessed Regina was tinkering with my feelings again. "Like the shimmerers?" I asked.

"In part. Shimmerers shift into anything they wish, and they have affinities to all living things. Whereas your affinity creature rules over them, and they must obey your commands."

"How about if another invitee sent their affinity animals after me? Why would they listen to me over them?"

"If you are speaking of Priscilla, I suspect that your command to the crows and hawk was more powerful than her request to them," she said, spreading her lips into an infectious grin. She shoved positivity and calm into me. She went on, "You will undoubtedly do very well here, but I know it's caused significant upheaval to your life. Knock on my door any time. I am perfectly qualified to help you as counsellor, even though I'm Regina Wyrmglas, Dragon-Shifter Queen of the North."

"Thank you, and if I pass the trials, I'll come to you for help if I need it." I meant it sincerely.

"If you pass!" She tittered. "Of course, you'll pass. Honestly, Laurel-Leah Fields, you're so amusing." She waltzed off to speak to another invitee who had just crossed the finish line. I laughed at her unreserved cheerfulness, feeling lighter than a minute ago.

"What's happening now then?" I asked Saffron.

"We're waiting for the rest of the invitees to finish." Her brows furrowed as she looked at my forehead and the bandage covering my arm. "You're injured?"

"You didn't see them on the pegasus meadow? Just a few scratches and bumps."

"I was busy facing off with our friend Priscilla and sorting out the bird's nest on top of your head. Come on, we'd better get you healed and whole," she said, pulling me towards the healer tent.

The tent was partitioned into sections. We sat on the chairs at the entrance marked 'Waiting Area'. Moans and cries of pain issued from several directions. I jumped up, changing my mind – I only had a few scratches – just as Healer Gale emerged from one section and waved me over.

As I entered, I found Cassidy, the dwarf from the shower incident, standing near the bed.

"Oh, sorry!" I said as I backed away, thinking I'd gone into the wrong section.

"Lori, hello! Please don't go – I finished the trial over an hour ago and since I want to be a healer, I asked Healer Gale if I could assist today. Do you mind if I watch and help?" Cassidy gestured to the bed.

"Not at all. Heal away."

Healer Gale drew the curtains and marched up to me. "Let's have a look at you. I've just fixed you up and here you are in front of me again!" she chided me. "Up you get on the bed."

I slid up on the bed in a seated position. "Nothing terrible – I hit my head on a rock. There's a bird scratch on my arm, lost some skin off my elbow, rope burn on my hands."

"Hmm, bruising on your cheek as well. Not to worry, we'll patch you right up," Healer Gale said, with a kind yet evaluating look in her eye. She turned and nearly walked into the diminutive Cassidy. "Come along, Cassidy, we'll mix some suitable salves. Be right back, girls."

They left the cubicle. I flopped down on the bed, exhausted, and Saffron sat on the chair next to me. My stomach growled. I searched in my pocket for a protein bar, but the river water had penetrated the wrapper, creating a packet of brown, chocolatey slop. Revolting! Saffron plucked it from my hands and disposed of it with disgust in the bin.

"Do you think we'll have another trial today?" I asked.

"I hope not. We're not machines, after all, and I could eat a herd of wild horses."

"Ew!" I said. "Do fae eat horse?"

"It's an expression, Lori, and only as a starter." She shrugged her shoulders dismissively.

"I've never met fae before I came here, but in the narie fairy tales, the fairies are usually one with nature. How does Lilliput feel about you chomping on his kind?"

"We can't all be the same, Lori. Variety makes our worlds interesting and tasty."

"Like vampire tasty?" I asked pointedly.

"He's so dreamy, exciting, and different, isn't he?" she said, with starshine in her eyes.

"I suppose he's got to be someone's cup of tea. What do you think about Vil?"

"Well, there's something about him, too. I saw you making doe eyes at him." She waved a suggestive brow at me.

"Was I? But you were too, and you weren't too subtle about it!" I giggled; she joined me. "Wasn't it strange – it's like he cast a spell on us, like Zale did to me. I don't understand it."

Saffron crinkled her brow. "You're right, but I didn't know Eassusians had that power."

"Me neither, but I know nothing about this world."

"Well, no argument from me on that account."

"Rude!" I said, laughing.

"You call it rudeness; fae call it truth." She flashed a devilish grin on that angelic face.

We sniggered.

After they'd slathered on salves and poured blue healing energy into me, I asked Healer Gale if I could have one of her rejuvenation brews. She explained they were forbidden during the trials, raising my suspicion that they had some dodgy illegal stimulants in them. It really gave you an almighty buzz.

Cassidy escorted us out of the tent. "Will you sit with me in the dining hall for our next meal? I suspect our next big trial will allow allies." She gave me an exaggerated wink, her eyes glittering like sapphires with anticipation.

"Of course – great," I said as I caught her meaning. "Who have you got in your crew? So far, we're allied with a dragon-shifter, a wolf-shifter, a vampire, and possibly two Eassusians, but they haven't confirmed yet."

"My mate Owain and I have only talked with dwarves so far," she told me. "It's not dwarvish nature to mix with other species or even other dwarf tribes, unless by kin or marriage. But we decided we should broaden our horizons, and I mentioned to Owain about meeting with you. After all, one reason we accepted the invitations to these trials was to break free of our mould and mingle with other species." Her voice became progressively softer as we reached the exit and ended in a whisper as she eyed a group of dwarves approaching.

"Okay – see you at dinner then. Thanks for the healing and everything," I said, raising my arm to show my now-smooth skin, no longer marked by the hawk attack.

"You're perfectly welcome," she replied, heading back into the tent.

I turned to Saffron. "She's worried about dwarves overhearing our conversation about being allies, but she wants to sit with us in the dining hall in front of all the dwarves. I don't get it – what's the difference?"

"I'm uncertain, but I know they distrust all non-dwarves and stick to their own, as most alius do, and that they're as bad as the mages for not wanting to mix species or bloodlines," Saffron explained in a hushed tone as we walked away.

"Bloodlines? So... mages don't get with other species? Cos if that's true, how do I exist?"

Saffron looked darkly at me. "They tend not to mix. It happens, but it's frowned upon."

"And how about the Eassusians? How do they view it?" I asked, suddenly thinking of Art. I scanned around for him. Instead of finding him, my eyes landed on the last person I wanted to see: my personal stalker.

Eyebrows.

Sighing, I gestured to Saffron to move away from him. It didn't matter how far away we stood from Eyebrows; he knew all our thoughts, regardless. But not seeing his stupid face everywhere I went gave me peace of mind.

I was leading the way around the tent when we heard a bloodcurdling screech, followed by a serious amount of blubbing. The ruckus appeared to come from a dark-haired fae professor, who'd flooded his back and hands with green magic. He was standing in front of a yellow rose bush. His green magic attempted to envelop the bush, but it was fighting back with black, magical barbs.

"Get me out of here! I've been trapped in here for millennia!" a muffled voice belonging to Priscilla screeched from amid the trembling roses.

The bush rustled and shrank a little, then grew to twice its original size, resulting in another shriek. Saffron bit back a laugh. Chancellor Wutterhorn looked very put out as she marched up to the professor, nearly elbowing him aside.

"Never fear, Bill, I'll deal with this," she said, raising her mage ring. Her lips moved silently as the white crystals glowed and seemed to unpick the black barbs. With a blinding glow from the crystals, she shrivelled the plant to compost.

Priscilla appeared in its place, crouched and covered in it. The rose thorns had scratched and bloodied her hands and face. She looked up and around, and stopped when she settled on Saffron.

"It was her!" she squealed, pointing at Saffron. She got to her feet shakily, giving my dorm-mate a glare of pure hatred, which was slightly ruined by the way soil kept falling out of her hair at every movement.

Saffron's black magic was already seeping from her back and running down to her hands, but Regina Wyrmglas cut across Priscilla's path.

"Do pipe down, Priscilla. There are no rules against attacking other invitees during trials. By rights, your professor should not have revealed or aided you. You and Saffron have both been trained to a high standard in your magic. She defeated you in a challenge fair and square," she told her, not unkindly.

Priscilla's friends gathered around her, looking unconcerned or outright bored; Zale was inspecting his manicured nails.

"But we'd completed the trial, so she was attacking me *outside* the trial. She deserves punishment!"

"You invited her to the challenge. We all saw it on our globes, Priscilla. Now, I suggest you get your scratches seen to in the healer's tent," Regina Wyrmglas said, lowering her voice. "She's already defeated you once today, and if you invite further challenges, I will ensure no one intervenes." She flicked her gaze over to Saffron, whose black magic shrouded her in shadows, and abruptly stalked away.

Saffron seemed entirely unfazed, but something wedged in my throat. Priscilla was right. There were no rules against attacking another invitee.

"So, Priscilla was within her rights to send affinity birds to knock me off the wall?" I asked quietly. I'd wanted to ask Regina Wyrmglas before, but she'd been pushing all that feel-good calm into me. Perhaps she'd been trying to distract me.

"Not exactly. If she wanted to attack you, she would have to do it in a non-lethal way. Err... do you have a fear of birds?" Saffron asked delicately, clearly trying not to sound too judgemental about anyone having such a pathetic fear. "It's just that you... looked like you did."

"Yes," I admitted, hunching slightly in shame. "So, she wasn't trying to kill me?"

"I think sending birds to someone climbing a wall who is both afraid of heights *and* birds can be lethal. Like if you'd pushed Jay into the water that he fears – that could have been lethal."

"Did you watch that on your globe? Jay mentioned it was all recorded." I was hoping it wasn't true.

She nodded. "When I arrived at the pegasus meadow, I heard you talking about the affinity bird attack, but I wanted to see what happened for myself. So, I reviewed the footage. Incidentally, your fall from the rope at the river was classic. It will be on the top ten highlights for the trials, I'm certain!" she exclaimed eagerly, radiating enthusiasm.

My face heated. To change the subject to something far less humiliating, I asked a question I found increasingly perplexing. "And since I saw you in the pegasus meadow, you've managed to view that and trap Priscilla? I didn't think you were that far ahead of me!"

"Yes. The trials are held in a magical construct, so timings may not run as you'd usually expect. What was your time for the trial?"

"Over four hours," I admitted.

"Mine was one hour and thirty minutes," she said humbly. My jaw dropped. "So, although we met in the meadow, you couldn't measure if you were ahead or behind in the trial – the academy likes to keep you on your toes."

I blinked at that, trying to compute it. Since I couldn't make sense of it, I would add it to my list of things to read about. "And after you viewed the footage, you challenged Priscilla to a duel?"

Saffron's expression changed from kind to vengeful.

"Priscilla issued the challenge on the meadow. I merely accepted. I waited for her to finish, and as soon as she crossed the line, I trapped her in the rosebush and encased it with an anti-reversal charm, interwoven with a timed invisibility and sound-barrier enchantment, so no one could hear her cries," she said triumphantly.

A giggle bubbled out of me. "Check you out! Maybe you and the vampire make sense after all."

"This I know. It is you who needs to grasp an understanding of the alius. Which reminds me, you asked me a question before Priscilla interrupted," she said, as if she'd had nothing to do with the interruption.

She cast her gaze around, then a black swirl of magic inked its way from her back and shot down to her hands. She raised a hand above her head and traced a circle.

"I've cast a silence barrier so no one can hear us." She glanced over her shoulder at Eyebrows, who was still hovering nearby.

"You know he can read our thoughts, though, right?"

She nodded. Her black magic appeared again, and she put her hand on my shoulder, whispering something in a language I didn't recognise.

"Now we can talk in private. I've made a barrier to deflect his magic, but I can't hold it for long. I wanted to explain to you about relations between species. Alius do, occasionally, have inter-species relations. But they tend to stick to their own to ensure survival of their species. Fae have very few or occasionally no children in their immortal lives, so we mix with other species, usually humans, to ensure our survival. Other mixed alius are rare."

"So, my existence is not acceptable as part-mage, part-Eassusian. Is that what you're saying?"

"Look, you're perfectly acceptable to me – and you're making allies, so who is to say you're not acceptable?"

"Well, there's the whole people-think-I'm-a-killer-sent-by-Emperor-Valeconiss, unregistered thing."

Saffron waved that away. "Same answer. You're making allies and forging friendships," she said, gesturing to herself. "And Lilliput likes you, and so did Thistlebloom."

I gave her a long look.

"You can stare all you want, but it is near impossible to get approval from my lady's maid. I barely have it, and I've known her since birth. And how was your pegasus during the trials? Did she rear like Priscilla's did?"

"No, she was lovely. Kat is the best."

"Alius are comprised of all sorts. Cassidy wants to ally with you, as did Francis and Victor. Just think – in only two days and without control of your magic, you have accomplished this."

"I have to admit, you've made some excellent points there." I replied, tension drifted out my shoulders. "Thanks, Saffron."

"Of course, many alius find me to be excellent, and that's what friends are for."

I snapped my attention to her. Friends… she was my friend. And I was hers. I smiled. Then my thoughts returned to the trials. "I know it only took you an hour and thirty minutes, but how did *you* find the trials?"

"It was easy," she admitted with a shrug.

"How did you cross the river?"

"I suggested the boulders on the riverbed should rise in a straight line across. They granted my request, and I stepped on them over the river. Fae are, as you said, one with nature. We ask nature for help and nature does as we ask. Eassusians, as I understand it, use will, but I know little of that."

"I tried to use my magic, but I didn't know how to access it. I don't know what I'm doing."

"The way you access and manipulate magic is different to mine. We're going to have to find an Eassusian to help you."

"Art offered."

"Oh... lucky you," she said with a smirk.

Chancellor Wutterhorn cleared her throat from the dais. I spun to see a supersized image of her projected in the air. Saffron dispersed her magical barriers.

"The Alius Chase is complete. We have counted your scores, and they are available to view in your globes. For those of you who have recently completed the trial, I suggest you rejuvenate yourself at the healers. Everyone else should get something to eat in the dining hall. Trials are complete for today. It's a seven a.m. start tomorrow morning. Your globes will sound an alarm and give you the destination an hour before the trial begins. Dismissed."

I called Max; he flew over and projected the scoreboard. Three further names were crossed off the list, plus the two from the Revealing. Perhaps they hadn't completed the trials... I didn't want to think of any other reason. Seventy-nine invitees remained.

Sebastian Hale's name was at the top of the upper section. Typical. And I was now thirty-eighth.

"They've demoted me to the middle of the middling section, but I'm just glad I crossed the finish line at all. But *you're* still in the upper section!" I showed Saffron the projection. She scowled at the scoreboard. "You're not happy with that?"

She clicked her tongue. "I've dropped five places. And why do mages always come first?" She slitted her eyes at Eyebrows. "You're new to the alius world. Did they take that into consideration when scoring you? Why have they ranked you so much lower?"

"I don't know. How do they even calculate it?"

Eyebrows interrupted our conversation, stepping far too close to me. I took a step back.

"They consider how you've used your magic and faced your fears, your times, and if you've stuck to the rules," he said. "Did you indirectly help anyone, Saffron?"

He glanced between us, and his eyes settled on me. Saffron tsked at him.

"How did you make use of your magic, Lori?" He bent down, talking to me as if I was a child, like he had this morning – tempting me to take a swipe at his perfectly chiselled chin. "I'm yet to see the footage, but I heard it was highly entertaining." He glanced at Jay, who was talking to a mixed group of alius near the dais and returned his gaze to mine. His eyes were a dark storm, so deep you could lose yourself in them. Just before I did, he straightened and walked away.

I narrowed my gaze at him, feeling bad for Saffron. She hadn't directly helped us, but she *had* allowed me and Vil to watch her find a suitable pegasus.

"Sorry," I said to her.

"If they scored me lower for letting people watch me mount a pegasus, so be it. And don't be sorry. You've had magic for two days; most alius were unbound or emerged weeks ago," she said. "They've had more time to get used to their powers. I would have thought they'd take that into account." Her eyes changed colour in a flash, from light purple to what now looked like hot coals. "Let's get some food!" she added in a hangry tone.

CHAPTER NINETEEN

We found Francis and Victor already eating in the dining hall. Dozens of platters of buffet-style food covered the tables. As we weaved through the tables to join them, Art approached me.

"Well done, Lori, you made it through the first two trials," he said, with a half-smile.

"They've downgraded me to the middling section, but I completed the trial and I'm still here." I shrugged and offered my own half-smile.

"Why didn't you use your magic?"

"When I tried to summon the winds, it didn't work."

"You have four elements. There were several ways you could use your magic in every phase of that trial. So, when you want to summon your magic, what are you doing?"

My stomach growled. "Art, I need to eat first."

"Me too," he said, patting his belly.

We took a seat at the nearest vacant table, one of the round ones near the food service counter. I waved at Saffron and pointed to where I was sitting. She nodded and settled down with the shifter boys, Ollie joining their table too.

Biting into a chicken wrap, I felt my tension draining away. I was hungrier than I'd thought. Art piled up his own plate full of sandwiches, a pasty, sausage rolls, and two giant scotch eggs. We ate silently for a minute or two.

"I've been called away again this evening," he told me. "I leave in ten minutes, but if I get back before ten tonight, shall I knock for you and do a brief training session? As you mentioned before, you could use all the help you can get." His tone was serious.

"Sounds like you agree with that, and yes please." I gave a nervous laugh. *What flew up his nose?* "Where do you go when you're called away? Are you going out to fight light-reapers?"

"It's not something I can discuss," he said shortly.

"Ok," I said, raising my brows. He was either in a bad mood or he was annoyed at me, but I needed training from someone, and he was it.

He wiped his mouth as he finished chewing. "So, tell me what you're doing to summon your magic, because not using magic is why you scored so low."

I found myself narrowing my eyes at him, accompanied by a sinking feeling. "When I fought the light-reaper, I don't recall how I accessed my magic. In TV shows and books, they use a spell to do magic, so... I tried doing that. No one's taught me how to do it, so I don't know how to access it." I took another bite of my wrap.

He pursed his lips and scraped a hand through rich, dark hair, ocean-blue eyes fixed on me. "Your elemental symbols were bright in the Revealing. This shows you have a high-level power in all four elements. You can access it by using your will. Visualise what you want to do as you will it to happen."

His eyes darkened as he ploughed on, voice rising.

"You have earth element. In the first obstacle, simply willing the hurdles to stop moving through intent, using visualisation, would have gotten you through that quickly." He was talking rapid-fire and doing a chopping motion with his hand to punctuate each point he made. "During the river obstacle, you could have used any element. Your power level will allow it, you need to—"

I cut him off. "Wait a minute, Art. Are you angry with me?"

"Why would I be angry with you?"

"Because you're practically frothing at the mouth."

He leaned forward in his chair and back again. "I'm not angry, and there's no frothiness in sight. I'm trying to help you get through the trials, so let me help you. With your water magic alone, you could have visualised the water freezing to ice so you could walk over it. You could have heated the water so you didn't feel so cold."

I flung my arms in the air. He wasn't the only one getting angry and frustrated. "But the water was fast-flowing. As soon as I'd heated it, it would have run away downriver."

"You're thinking like a narie, Lori!" He thumped his fist on the table.

Several of the invitees' heads popped up like meerkats, listening out for the next drama. He barely seemed to notice. What was happening? Aside from Saffron, he was the one I trusted the most, yet he was coming at me like this.

"This is enniar, Lori – it's magic, no? You could have visualised stones rising from the river, or even a fully formed bridge to cross it. You could have used your air magic to levitate to the top of the wall. Or earth magic to grow a tree from beneath you to get up that wall."

"You *are* angry with me... with how I did the trials."

"I'm not angry, Lori," he said in a lighter tone, looking around as if finally realising his outburst had attracted an audience.

I was indignant. "You realise that until two days ago, I *was* a magic-less narie? So yes, I think like a narie, and no, I didn't know and still don't fully know what's possible in magic. And I think you and the academy are wrong in expecting me to know how to do it!"

He folded his arms, squinted, and shook his head. "But Lori, to pass the trials you must *try to* use your magic. You've used it before, and you must admit that you could have tried harder to experiment," he said, folding his arms across his chest like the know-it-all he was turning out to be.

Why did he even care? My shoulders sagged. I felt a brush against my elbow, and anger along with the contact.

It was Saffron, glaring at Art. "She's right. Trials are supposed to be scored on potential, but we're being scored based on having prior knowledge of magic. Most of us have lived with it our entire lives. I've studied magic all my life in readiness for when it emerged. She is brand new to it and has not had the benefit of studying, watching her parents, or talking about magic. She is at a marked disadvantage!"

"It doesn't change the fact that Lori needs to pass the trials and must work within the current scoring system. I want her to pass the trials, and I'm trying to help her with that. If I'm coming over a little overzealous, that's why." He turned to me. "I'm really not angry with you, I'm just frustrated. I want you to pass."

Saffron folded her arms and gazed evenly down her nose at Art. I blinked. It seemed he was much more of a turd than I'd initially thought... but at least he was trying to help me.

His globe played a tune I wasn't familiar with. He tapped it, and the tune halted. "I must go. Maybe I'll see you before ten tonight. If not, we plan to train tomorrow after dinner." He picked up a pasty and strode out the dining hall.

"He has repressed rage issues, but he's exceedingly... well-proportioned," Saffron admitted as we watched him leave.

I stared after him, feeling more than a little crushed. I consciously straightened my spine against it.

"Come sit with us." Saffron gestured to her long table further down the hall. Cassidy had joined them with the male dwarf she'd been standing next to during the Revealing. He was the tallest of the male dwarves, with pale green eyes and a black, lustrous beard. Vampire Ollie was sitting next to Cassidy with the two shifters opposite.

I picked up my plate and drink. As we approached, Francis gave me a wave; he was talking to Cassidy.

"Take a pew, little Lori," he said, gesturing to the space next to Victor. Saffron and I sat down.

"Hi, Lori. I want to introduce you—" Cassidy started.

"Free space right here next to me," Ollie said to Saffron, cutting Cassidy off while patting the space beside him. I watched Saffron for her reaction. The vampire was needy. I hadn't seen that one coming.

"Maybe after dinner. I need to speak with Lori. Can you pass my drink over?" Saffron asked.

Ollie tongued the inside of his cheek. Francis reached over and handed Saffron what looked like a cup of water with a dandelion floating in it. Bleh!

"Lover's tiff?" Ollie asked, his eyes glinting at me.

I stared at him blankly and looked behind me in case he was addressing someone else.

"Vampire hearing," he said, pulling an ear. "Tiff with your lover-boy teacher's assistant? I heard every word."

"I think most people overheard that conversation. He wasn't exactly whispering, and where did you get 'lover boy' from? All he did was have a go at me."

Francis coughed, looking somewhere over and around me. I sighed; shifters could see my aura. What did he see there? Red for embarrassment and frustration? What colours had he see above Art's head? *And how did they get 'lovers' from that exchange?*

"Now, now, boys," Cassidy said, flicking back her wheat-coloured hair. She leaned over Saffron and peered at me, her indigo eyes sharp in her round, sweet face. "Lori, I want to introduce you to my boyfriend, Owain Ore," she said, squeezing his arm.

Owain slid his stern, bespectacled eyes from Ollie to Francis to me. "Pleased to meet you, Lori. Cassidy has said *good things*."

His voice was far deeper than I expected, and he spoke in a way that implied he would wait to see the *good things* for himself. He offered me a hand larger than my own, although he was an inch or two shorter. I gave it a shake and felt distrust and suspicion coming from him.

"It's very good to meet you, too." I gave him a wide, bright grin. "How are you finding the trials?"

"Simple at the moment, but it will get more difficult as we go along, I assure you."

I tried not to gulp. Maybe that was what Art was concerned about. "So, do you want to train to be a healer like Cassidy or are you interested in something else?" I asked.

"Well," he said, pushing back his glasses. "I'm more interested in making things and weapon design."

I couldn't contain my surprise at that. "That's different. What sort of weapons?"

"It's not that different. We are at a combat academy, after all."

Cassidy looked at him adoringly.

Saffron whispered, "Prickly bugger, isn't he?"

I covered my mouth to hold back a chuckle.

He carried on talking, oblivious to the exchange. "As to the kind of weapons, I have a few ideas. I'm interested in improving designs for all alius weaponry, and I'd especially like a stab at improving mage rings and energy weapons," he said, eyes brightening.

"What are energy weapons? Are we talking a hammer wielding lightning bolts, Thor-style?" I asked.

He gave me an appraising look. "Yes... that's an idea. I'd like to work with lightning, and additionally develop weapons for Eassusian elementals, for example. When most alius, aside from mages, produce their magic, they burn out after a while. So why not design a weapon that acts more like a mage ring and stores your powers to release them whenever you want?"

"I don't know about Eassusians burning out or any of that yet, but anything we could use to fight light-reapers would be useful," I said, lamely.

"Uh-hm," he grunted, folding his arms across his chest, lips pursed. If it was a test, I thought I might have failed.

Ollie chimed in. "Interesting. Do you think you could design weapons for vampires?"

Owain cleared his throat and frowned over his glasses at him, eyeing the paper cup of blood.

"Ollie, I would be interested in your reasoning for some of your actions during the pegasus trial. I'll play it on my globe and ask the questions as I find them." Owain flung his globe into the air. "Globe, play number three of '*Ten Ways How NOT To Fly Your Pegasus*' on AliusTube."

His globe flung up a projection.

The video began with Ollie nearing the pegasuses in the meadow. Like gazelles sensing a lion, all of them scattered away as he neared. Ollie's globe zoomed in on his face, getting increasingly irate at each attempt.

"Globe, pause the recording. Turn up the volume by three points, then replay. Thank you." Owain's eyes, shining with amusement, slid to observe Ollie. Ollie growled.

The globe projection rolled to the next scene. Ollie looked set to explode with rage by the seventh attempt. "You bastard pegasus cowards, one of you get over here now or I'll rip your throats out!"

he hissed, pointing at all of them with a mad gleam in his eye. The pegasuses continued to scatter and avoid him.

Ollie had his elbows on the table and was hiding his expression behind his hands. I bit back a laugh. Instead of getting redder, he looked even paler than usual.

I returned my attention to the recording, where Ollie had lost all patience and made his move. He leapt thirty feet, his goal seemingly to land on a bay-coloured stallion. I gasped at the power of his leap. The pegasus snorted, manoeuvred itself square to him, and backed up a few paces. Its wings shot out at its sides. Just before Ollie landed, the pegasus charged toward him and turned, sweeping a wing across Ollie's path, belting him through the air toward the treeline.

Ollie's globe kept pace with his flight as numerous tree branches slapped him in the face, before he eventually slammed with a bone-crunching crack into a giant tree trunk and ricocheted off. He dropped like an anchor, forty feet down. When he stood up, his arm hung at a weird angle from his body, and his head had a twig imbedded in it. He removed it and sped back to the meadow, all while his skin knitted back together and his arm unbroke itself.

I shuddered. The Revealing and the books Saffron had lent me clearly had not highlighted all the powers each alius species had.

"Globe off!" Ollie commanded. Owain raised his hand, and his globe paused play but continued projecting.

"It'll only listen to me, as you well know," Owain lectured Ollie in a patronising tone. "We haven't reached the part I wanted to ask you about yet."

"Why don't we have a look at Lori's fine use of magic, epic brain-freeze, and peep-show incident at the river obstacle?" Ollie urged, raising his eyebrows hopefully.

"I'd prefer to keep watching this. We haven't yet reached my favourite part," Victor chimed in, to my relief.

"You are all utter bastards, every single one of you!" Ollie snapped.

A giggle rose in me that couldn't be suppressed.

"I don't know what *you're* laughing at. We'll be viewing yours next," Ollie warned, folding his arms with a smirk. I stopped laughing.

Owain asked his globe to resume the recording. Ollie didn't stop when he sped back to the meadow; he raced on so quickly that his globe could barely detect his movements. A pink mare with purple spots snorted and started in the opposite direction, but Ollie toppled her easily, placing his disproportionately small mouth and fangs against her thick, muscular throat.

I couldn't help giggling at the ridiculous size difference, but cut off as the mare's eyes rolled wildly. Her legs kicked as he pinned her to the ground. Surrounding pegasuses stomped and prepared to attack.

I looked hard at Ollie. He gave me a fanged grin.

The pegasus spoke in a panicked voice. "I submit – I submit... I allow you to ride me, young demon spawn." She turned to snort in his face. Ollie smiled a triumphant smile, hopped on her back, and off they went, as she stormed into the sky.

Then she started spinning.

Ollie had no saddle or anything to hold on to. On every rotation, he crawled like a spider around her. When she was belly-up, he crawled onto her belly; when she was belly-down, he looped round her wings and crawled on her back. She spun for the entire journey. The globe played in slow motion at every spin with epic timing, zooming in on the terror on his face and the mare's expression of elation at every one of his screams. The globe then sped up the recording, giving the impression that he was the rings orbiting Saturn.

Everyone erupted in laughter.

"Globe off," Owain said impatiently and swivelled to turn to Ollie. "Ollie, I'm not willing to ally myself with individuals of sub-par intelligence, so, tell me... after attacking numerous pegasuses and threatening their lives, were you under the impression it would be a comfortable ride? What were you thinking, exactly?"

I sucked my lips between my teeth to wrestle down another bout of giggles. Saffron didn't even try to hide hers.

Ollie trained an accusing pair of eyes upon her. When she didn't take the hint, he inspected his nails for a moment, pursing his lips. "I'm a predator. The pegasuses, although vicious, *dangerous* animals, behave as prey do." He stared Owain in the eye. "My aim was to finish the trial, and I did it in one piece."

"Barely... and the indignity of it all!" Owain bristled at Ollie, pushing his spectacles back up his nose.

Ollie rolled his eyes and bowed his head with a sigh, pushing a thumb over each of his eyebrows as if relieving internal pressure.

Francis interjected. "I'm a predator. All three of us are predators – you, me, and Victor," he said, jerking a thumb at all of them. "But we didn't have to put our fangs into one of them to persuade them to let us ride them."

"There's one subtle difference," Ollie said, shaking his blood cup at them. "Undead. Demon spawn, in fact, is what that cheeky bloody mare called me." He exhaled deeply.

Saffron piped up, seemingly oblivious to the tension. "It was tremendously done, Ollie – bravo. I haven't laughed so hard in ages. Thank you." She squeezed his arm, eyes shining with tears. "Top three on AliusTube! Outstanding!" She clapped enthusiastically.

"Saffron... why?" Ollie asked with a pained expression.

She frowned. "What? I was congratulating you... what?" She turned to everyone around the table in question.

The rest of us exchanged glances, then flicked our gazes between them. Francis was looking above and around them, probably observing their auras. He sucked in air through his teeth and blew a low whistle, pulling a large hand through his dark hair.

"What?" Saffron whispered to me.

"Tell you later," I said, and changed the subject to spare her any further indignity. "So, how did everyone else do in the trials? And can anyone tell me what the other trials might be like? Feel free to share with all."

Victor answered, to my surprise. I had the impression he wasn't always the most talkative person. He was a kindred spirit to me in that way. I wasn't always this talkative; I was only compelled to become a keen conversationalist because I was new to this world and knew literally nothing.

"I'll give you a run-down of my Alius Chase. I have earth magic, so I halted movement of the hurdle obstacles and walked through. At the river, I used the ropes and leapt across." He glanced sideways at me with a hint of amusement twinkling in his eye. He'd probably seen my crossing. I looked away from him, a prickle of heat sweeping up my neck. "You're probably already aware shifters can partially shift, so our nails can grow and harden. I used my claws to scale the wall. My main problem was the pegasuses. I'm a predator, like we just said, but the pegasuses are warriors and don't scare easily. One of them was kind enough to allow me on his back. The hoops I caught."

"What, all of them?" Owain asked.

Victor and Francis both nodded as if it was nothing. Owain returned a nod of approval, quirking his lips up at the corners.

A knot of tension released from my shoulders. All of this was valuable information; even watching Ollie in action gave great insight into what a vampire could do. "Thanks, Victor, I can't tell you how much that helps."

"It's a pleasure to help. Anything for my allies."

"And their sweet cheeks," Ollie needled me.

Victor was kind, but I felt he wasn't attracted to me in the slightest. I rolled my eyes at Ollie and shook my head at Victor, signalling that I knew he wasn't helping because he like my cheeks.

Owain glared at Ollie, then cleared his throat and stroked his beard while staring hard into space. I downed my drink and ate another half-sandwich, wondering if male dwarves came out of the womb with a beard.

"Trials have been running for centuries; they have set previous ones on an archipelago," he said, addressing me. "A desert, a catacomb, a network of caverns, a gladiator arena, even a house or a city or combination of them – it can be any setting. They usually allow us to work in groups, but that changed today. You will fight or try to overcome other alius or any predatory creature, including creatures one would expect to be inanimate. There's usually a winnowing portion of the trial. It is dangerous, and it is typically when invitees are ejected or die, but then again, an invitee was ejected this time based on the strength of the powers at the Revealing. The rules change, so it can really be anything." Owain shrugged. "Anyone else know anything that I don't?"

"Plenty, I should imagine," Ollie drawled.

Owain jabbed an unexpectedly long finger at him. "That's enough out of you."

"Yes, Professor. Now you've told me off, I'll be certain to behave myself," Ollie laughed, and shook his head derisively.

"Give it a rest, Ollie." I sighed. Owain had just embarrassed him, but Ollie was generally unpleasant, anyway.

"We can't all be bland and scared to death of using magic, birds, heights, and a bit of fang like you are," he sneered at me, peeling one side of his lips back.

Saffron leaned forward, eyes glittering, irritated at his gibes for once. "Stop it, Ollie. We're trying to attract allies, not drive them away."

I attempted to respond with diplomacy, or my version of it. "Anyone else have something useful or informative to say instead of derogatory and demeaning?"

Francis chimed in. "As it's a combat academy, their goal is to immerse us in danger, then analyse how we deal with fear, danger, overcoming situations, fighting. How we interact with each other, how we use our magic, the choices we make – it will be like what we've just done, but where we must defend ourselves."

"So, if they record the trials, can we watch past trials tonight?" I asked.

"No. Only people who have passed the trials into the academy can watch them, or like today, we've completed a few, so we can all watch those now," Francis explained, picking up a chicken leg.

Now I was confused. "Jay told me he's watched past trials."

Cassidy raised a brow and rested her chin on her tiny fist. "His parents may have let him watch them, but they shouldn't have. Or he may have hacked the globe network. I know his parents hack security systems for a living, so it would make sense he'd know how to do it too." She tucked her chin in and eyed him with disapproval.

My shoulders sagged in disappointment. "How about the magical assessment? Any tips for that?"

"I'm afraid not, Lori. You'd have to speak to an Eassusian and a mage for that," Saffron said.

I glanced around, wondering who I could find to help me. If Art didn't return in time, I was screwed. I thought about the dreamy Eassusian, Vil, but I was one hundred percent certain he was putting some type of enchantment on me. I scanned for Shaidel and Kaylissa. They'd been in the dining hall earlier, but I couldn't see them now.

"Did you talk to any mages about being allies?" I asked Saffron.

"It would be a futile use of my time. Mages stick to their own. You won't find one willing to join us."

My heart plummeted. Victor placed a hand on mine and pumped happy vibes into me. I squeezed his hand back in gratitude.

A thought occurred to me. Arameen had told me the mages had it in for me. What if the chancellor had offered me a chance at trials to give the appearance of fairness, but would somehow ensure that I failed? If mages didn't like their own mixing with other species, despite the motto of the academy – *together we are stronger*... I was not only a mixed mage, but unregistered. It would make sense they would want me to fail so they could tuck me away somewhere I wouldn't be a danger.

"Was everyone assigned rooms with other alius, or with their own species?"

"I room with a vampire," Ollie supplied. "Why do you ask?"

I was surprised he'd bothered to respond. "Just testing a theory. Anyone else?" My gaze fixed on Victor. "Who have they roomed you with for the trials? Is it a dragon-shifter?"

"Alexandru Solomonari, dragon-shifter," Victor confirmed. My pulse quickened.

"How about you, Cassidy, have you been roomed with a dwarf or other alius?"

She nodded and pointed to a female dwarf with dark hair sitting on the opposite side of the dining hall. "Dwarf. Beatrix Whitegold."

I swivelled my head toward Francis. "Were you roomed with a wolf-shifter?"

He nodded, his eyes sparking. "You're wondering if they roomed you with a different species because it would impose a barrier to learning. Your dorm-mate can't teach you magic," he said, shifting his gaze between me and Saffron.

Saffron frowned and folded her arms. "They may have thought we'd get on, because we're both mixed species?"

I hadn't considered that. "Maybe." We did have that in common, and she had helped me far more than any other. "Are there any other mixed fae invitees?"

"No," she said.

I'd keep that theory under my hat, but it might be nothing either way. I looked at Saffron, but she avoided my gaze. "You're the best dorm-mate ever, just so you know, Saffron."

"I'm your only dorm-mate ever, so neh." She stuck her tongue out at me and giggled. I joined her, and Ollie scrunched up his face in protest.

As everyone talked amongst themselves, I considered candidates I could ask for help. Arameen had said she was monitoring me, so she and her crew were a no.

Karina the mage? She wasn't too bad, a peacekeeper among her friends, but she was loyal to Livia. And Livia didn't like me, but... it couldn't hurt to ask. I glanced around and spotted them sitting together. I sighed, resigned to the fact that it was unlikely Karina would ever be on her own.

But as if by providence, as soon as my eyes settled on her, she stood up, as if she was leaving the dining hall alone.

"I'll be back – just going to the loo," I said to Saffron, and took off after her.

Karina turned left upon leaving the dining hall, glancing around as she went. By the time I got to the door, she'd disappeared somewhere down the left passageway. Had she moved dorms? They'd been using the shower rooms in my wing of the mansion. Why was she walking down in that direction?

As quietly as possible, I rushed down the hall after her, then halted when I heard footsteps from ahead. I'd never been to this area of the building and wasn't sure if I was allowed to be there. In a panic, I hid behind a half-naked male statue, holding my breath.

I realised too late that the statue's crotch was level with my face. I pulled back with a jerk just as one of the mage invitees breezed past. His eyes snapped to me, and he frowned in confusion and distaste before speaking to someone behind me.

"Alright, mate?"

"Good, Blake, I'll see you in a bit." It was Eyebrows.

"Bollocks," I muttered under my breath as I straightened and turned around.

"A fitting choice of words," he said, lips drawing up at the corners. His hazel eyes fixed on me, filled with unspoken accusations. "It appears you were attempting to have relations with the skimpily clad Apollo. You'd have better luck with the marble busts outside the chancellor's office."

"Sounds like you speak from experience, Sebastian," I shot back, getting ready to sidestep him.

"What are you doing down here?" he asked, glancing ahead and returning his gaze to mine.

"You can read my mind. Why don't you tell me?" I challenged, crossing my arms.

He inhaled deeply, as if I was trying his patience. "Not one mage will help you with your mage magic. Of that, I'm certain. The Revealing showed your mage magic would be a trickle. And I doubt it'd be worth any mage's time to train you," he said, stepping so close I had to tilt my head back.

I will not be intimidated. I stood my ground and didn't flinch.

"We'll be finding out for sure if that's true over the coming days. Will it upset you ever so if you're forced to have mage magic lessons with me?" I asked softly in a semi-mocking tone, dropping my arms to my side.

His lips twisted, and he released a barking laugh. "You're about as low on the hierarchy of mage magic as anyone could go. I'm as high as anyone could go. And I promise you…" he breathed, almost tenderly, as he inched his face down to mine. His eyes were soft for once.

His gaze brushed at my lips. My breath hitched. My pulse raced.

I looked down at my feet to hide my eyes, in case my sudden want for him betrayed me. My cheeks heated. Who was I kidding? He could read my mind either way.

"If you end up joining me in class, it will be *you* who is sorry you have mage magic, not me." He spoke softly near my ear as if telling me sweet nothings instead of threats.

I bent my ear to my shoulder and shifted my weight away from him, infuriated that a thrill coursed through my body at his proximity. Was I really *attracted* to him? Even now, I prevented myself from closing the gap between our bodies.

Instead, I stood my ground and waited for him to pull away first. He hovered there, unmoving. What was this change of tack? Why didn't he just shove me against the wall like he did before?

Something shifted in my mind at that memory. I lifted my face. His lips were an inch away. His breath was warm against my mouth, and he smelled of spicy citrus and vanilla custard.

"Why are you hovering?" I asked steadily as I met his gaze. His eyes held a considering glint in them.

"Why aren't you moving away or shoving me back? I attacked you earlier today, and you shouldered me in the ribs. Now I've just threatened you, and you're just standing there and taking it." He searched my face.

I pulled back a little. "Why are you talking threats, but looking at me like you want to kiss me!?" I hissed, angry now. My voice shaking with adrenaline.

He straightened up and leaned back, laughing. "Oh, Lori, don't you know I can read your mind? Ever since you first saw me on the coach, I've known you wanted a bit of this." He gestured to himself, up and down. Arrogant bastard! He bent his head toward me once more. And lowered his voice in a caress. "Are you some sort of masochist? Have you no pride?"

He straightened, turned on his heel, and sauntered away.

I trembled a little after he left. He'd read my mind, and somewhere in my subconscious, he'd found out that I liked him. But I *didn't* like him – I couldn't stand him. Sure, when I'd first seen him on the coach and when I'd run into him, I'd thought he was hot, but I wasn't out of my mind. *It's a physical attraction. It'll be gone in a few days, or weeks, then I'll get over it. I'll just ignore him, and he'll fade away from my thoughts.*

The main problem was his stalking tendencies! And why was he stalking me anyway? Why did he hate me? Simply because I was unregistered? If not, what was it all about? A lot of the alius were wary of me, but no one else followed me around. *And what's going on with the flirting? Does he want me to fall for him, so he can whisper sweet words of loathing in my ear whenever he likes?* I shivered. Why did I always attract the weirdos?!

CHAPTER TWENTY

I AMBLED BACK INTO the dining hall, aware that in my periphery, Eyebrows was talking to Archer at a round table in front of the food counter.

When I was making my way to the long table in the middle, Arameen intercepted me. "Laurel-Leah Fields, can we have a moment to speak to you privately?"

"Umm, what about?" I said, searching around the hall for the rest of her friends.

"It won't take much of your time. We've booked a conference room for a meeting in private, for all Eassusians and part-Eassusians." She inclined her head to the side.

"Can I bring someone?" I asked, looking over at Saffron. She looked up and caught my eye, frowning.

"Unfortunately, it's just for Eassusians, and it concerns us alone."

"Okay. Let me just talk to my friend for a minute," I answered, and sped over to Saffron.

"What's happening?" she asked, looking beyond me at Arameen.

"Arameen has invited me to a meeting for Eassusians in a conference room. I'm just letting you know where I am in case they do something, ok?" I gabbled.

As I walked back to where Arameen was waiting, I could feel Eyebrows' eyes following me.

Saffron glided up behind me with Ollie in tow. He pinned me with a withering gaze. "So happy to spend my free time being your unpaid muscle," he muttered.

Saffron straightened as she spoke to Arameen. "Ollie and I are tagging along to see where the meeting is taking place."

"Very well," Arameen said, with the same tilt of the head.

She led us into North Hall, and we turned right, up the sweeping staircase, only to realise that Eyebrows and Archer were hot on our heels. They shot up the stairs past us and blocked our way as we ascended.

"What's happening here? Where are you taking her?" Eyebrows questioned Arameen, folding his arms and entirely ignoring me.

"Are the comings and goings of Eassusians, vampire, and fae your business?"

He pointed his chin in my direction. "She's part mage, so it is my business."

"And do you track all the mages in this way, or just the half-Eassusian?" Arameen enquired, folding her own arms. "You're neither professor, maester, mentor, prefect, nor lover to Lori. Or do I have my information wrong?" she added with a wry quirk of her lips.

I mirrored her expression, interested in what his answer might be.

His eyes narrowed at her in a poisonous glare. "I'm concerned for her welfare. She is unregistered and unknown. You may perceive her as a threat, due to all the light-reaper attacks."

"And since you consider Lori a mage, will you be extending her an invitation to any mage meetings you hold? I know you had one last night, as did the fae, though I'm certain Lori was not invited. Is that correct, Lori?"

"I wasn't aware of any meeting," I confirmed to Arameen. Having met a few mages, I was pretty sure I wouldn't have gone even if I had been invited. "Wasn't told about a fae meeting either." I eyed Saffron.

She clicked her tongue at me. "I told you I was going downstairs to socialise. Must I describe word for word all that I am doing?"

"Alright, I was teasing – get a grip."

Saffron beaded her eyes on me. I returned her gaze evenly.

"Let's just bloody get on with it!" she said, squaring up to Eyebrows. "Sebastian Hale, you've been at it all day, and it's time you stopped stalking my friend's body and mind. *Eassusian* meetings are not *your* concern, just as *mage* meetings are not *my* concern."

Eyebrows jerked his chin away. "I don't stalk her body and mind!"

Saffron replied with a scary, forced laugh. "Ha, ha, ha! Everywhere she turns, there you are, skulking, blocking her path. This very moment is a good example of it. So, move aside and control your impulses, if that is at all possible!" Her eyes were two burning bright coals. She shook her head and inhaled deeply, turning to Archer. "Archer, you seem the level-headed type to keep him in check. Now move aside before I remove you myself!" She drew her chin in and narrowed her stare in warning.

Archer shrugged, lifted his orange brows, and dragged Eyebrows to the side.

"This academy is worse than the fae courts, and that is really saying something. Let us go forth!" Saffron demanded, spinning round and pulling me up the stairs by my sleeve.

As we reached the top, we turned right down a corridor, then right again. The meeting room was on the left, and benches and chairs lined the corridor.

"The meeting room is here. You're welcome to wait on the chairs outside," Arameen said to Saffron, who nodded. She and Ollie snuggled into a love seat together. Yuck.

The meeting room door had a symbol of a trokket inset on a round plaque. I stepped through to find the room circular, as was the table at its centre. Arameen's friend with electric-blue eyes sat on a throne-like chair opposite the door.

He stood when he caught sight of us. He was of medium height and build, his hair black, his skin tanned, and he wore a long, blue collarless overcoat with blue and silver birds embroidered on it – his affinity bird. There were eight Eassusians present, including Shaidel, Kaylissa, Vil, and the wolf-man. I inclined my head to all of them, and they echoed the gesture.

Arameen ushered me in. Her friend came forward to meet me at the door.

"I'm Loro Arnevcoad. Thank you for coming. We need to speak privately," he said, scanning the room. Like Arameen, he had an English accent. "Follow me."

His expression was tight and no friendlier than it had been at the Revealing. He strode to the wall to the right of his throne chair. Arameen and a blonde guy who was broad in the shoulders followed us.

Loro pressed his hand against the wall. A symbol appeared and a section of the wall swung out. We walked through into a small, dome-shaped chamber. My heart was racing, leg muscles twitching to make a run for it, but the cloak-and-dagger affair intrigued me, and the interior of the room was charming. It had a warm golden glow to it.

I took a seat at a small circular table. Loro sat opposite me, Arameen to my right. The blonde-haired guy stood over me.

"I'm Lasrenn Leissith. Welcome to the den. Would you like a drink?" he asked, moving to pick up a decanter filled with green liquid set on a silver side-table to my left. "Rosemarian mint do for you?"

"Yes please," I said, recalling that it was Art's favourite drink from home.

Lasrenn poured four glasses and placed them in front of us before he took the last chair.

Loro leaned forward and spoke. "I asked Arameen to collect you under the guise of an Eassusian meeting so we could speak privately, as what I'm going to ask you is... sensitive. I understand the mages searched your mind and found your memories altered and that your parentage is unknown. Is that correct?"

"Yes."

The three of them exchanged glances. Loro continued, "As I mentioned, what we will discuss is sensitive. I respectfully request that you make an oath to promise you will not speak of the details of this meeting and allow us to place an enniar oathmark on your skin."

My jaw dropped open. I couldn't respond for a moment or two, so he rushed on.

"I'll explain how it works. The oath binds you from discussing what we speak of outside of the four people in this room. Lasrenn will apply the oathmark, using a paste made in an oath mortar. We will all receive the mark; I will speak the oath, and we all agree to it."

"Does it hurt?"

"No, it's painless."

"What happens if one of us breaks the oath?"

"The mark will burn with the face of the person who broke their oath."

That didn't sound too bad. "Ok," I replied.

I wasn't sure about any of this, but Lasrenn would mark all of us; Arameen seemed to be truthful about what she'd said this morning, and Saffron and Ollie were just outside. Despite that, apprehension had my heart fluttering.

Lasrenn pushed up from his chair and transferred a stone mortar from the silver table to us. Loro pulled up his sleeve and placed an arm prone on the table. Lasrenn scooped up red paste on his finger and drew a mark of four interlocking circles on his forearm. He gestured for me to put my arm out, and he did the same to me. The paste was cold. Lasrenn drew the marks on Arameen, and when he'd drawn the last circle on his own arm, Loro spoke.

"We make the oath that all marked are beholden to it until released. None here shall discuss sensitive matters other than with those who are marked. The matters regarded as sensitive will be outlined and are to follow. Those who make the oath, say aye."

"Aye." All three spoke in unison and turned to me, waiting for a response.

My hands prickled with sweat. Was I doing the right thing? "Aye," I murmured, hesitantly.

The circles shone silver, warmed, and sank into our skin.

"With that being done, I will make my request," Loro said, gazing at me. "I was hoping you would submit to a mind-search by an Eassusian mind-walker so we can uncover your parentage. I understand that a mage did the initial search, but at the Revealing, I noted your enniar, your magic, seems to be stronger with Eassus than Earth. Perhaps one of our mind-walkers would fare better?"

My heart rate spiked as soon as he mentioned mind-searching. "I'd prefer that my mind wasn't searched at all. I'm not a lab-rat, and as a narie-raised person, I felt a mind-search without my permission totally violated my rights," I said, standing up.

"So hasty, Lori. Perhaps you have something to hide, as the fae princess suggested?" Loro said, softly laughing.

I glared at him.

He remained unflinching under my gaze and looked away in thought. "It would be to your benefit to know your parentage.

Knowing your true identity and even possibly restoring your memories would help you know yourself and your capabilities."

"Why can't you just ask me the questions, and I'll answer them if I can, or want to?"

He sighed and stood up, gripping the back of his chair. "Someone altered your memories; you don't know the answers to our questions. If someone had corrupted my memories, I would be curious to know what they'd hidden from me and why. Are you not curious in the least?"

"It's all new to me, and at this moment, I wouldn't care if I never found out," I said, folding my arms. I really wanted to leave, but the door had resealed itself, and I didn't know if I could open it. Loro followed my gaze to the invisible doorway.

"I'll share some information with you that will pique your interest," he said, facing me.

"Go on," I said, deciding to hear him out. I was more likely to get out of the room if I at least listened to them. They'd gone to all this trouble getting me alone.

"Usually, the gods only bless *noble* Eassusians with all four elements. And no one has had a trokket as their bellidora for over a millennium."

My face drained of all blood. Noble? The gods? Bellidora?

"That's why you were all staring at me during the Revealing?"

He nodded.

"And what is a bellidora?"

"It is your affinity animal. The light-reaper you faced, did his magic take the shape of an animal?"

"A snake."

"Most light-reaper bellidoras are snakes. We can create many animal shapes in our magic, but it feels natural and more potent to use our bellidora. So, now you understand why we're interested to learn of your background. We would not complete the mind-walk ourselves. It is my mother – Estrellis Chathun Arnevcoad, the usurped true Empress of Eassus – who will arrange it. We are asking on her behalf."

"Why are you asking? Why doesn't your mother ask me?"

"Since the increase in light-reaper attacks, she must remain protected. Our whole family is a primary target." He spoke gravely, running a hand through jet-black hair.

"It seems strange to me. If it's that important, why doesn't the academy arrange an Eassusian mind-walker to do it?"

"I'm certain they will, but whether they share the information amongst all alius is another matter."

"And what if, when they do it, I share the information with you... if I feel I want to?" I said, immediately regretting the offer. "At least if someone's going to be poking around in my memories, then it only has to happen once."

Loro flicked his gaze between Arameen and Lasrenn, and they both nodded.

"Very well," Loro said.

I eyed the doorway again. I'd had enough of them for the day, but I had a question of my own.

"In return, when I ask for help with my elements, will one of you help me? I know both you and Arameen have four elements."

"Arameen and I will be more than happy to help, providing you share the information," Loro said, narrowing his intense gaze at me.

I needed to learn how to access my elements for the trials, and if the academy wanted to search my mind once more, the chancellor hadn't mentioned it... though Maester Imod had. I didn't know which was worse, having the mages or the Eassusians do it. Who knew what they would find there? It frightened me, so I pushed it out of my mind.

His bargain seemed fruitless, but I wanted out the room. I had lots to do.

"That seems fair," I lied. "Can I mention to other people about being a noble and the bellidora?"

Loro pursed his lips and rubbed the stubble on his chin. "Yes, but you absolutely cannot mention that we asked if we could use our own mind-walker to search your mind. The mages like to hold all the cards, and they wouldn't be happy if they found out."

"Thank you. If you'll excuse me, I must be going now. My friends are waiting for me outside."

I said my goodbyes, and Loro opened the door to release me from the hidden chamber. A hush fell as I entered the meeting room. I inclined my head to Vil, Kaylissa, and Shaidel and left the room, feeling unwanted there.

Closing the door, I found Saffron and Ollie sucking face in a more-than-compromising position on the love seat. Hands resurfaced from under clothes at the sound of the door.

"Get a room, you two!" I bellowed.

"Jealous?" Ollie needled. His face, usually a whiter shade of pale, was all flushed. *Ergh!*

"In your dreams, demon-breath! Now I've got to find a fae elder to scour that from my memories." I turned to walk on, flustered and somewhat disgusted. Then I remembered they'd come to defend me and were acting as bodyguards, so I turned back. "By the way... thanks for coming and waiting for me."

"We haven't got there yet, but we've got all night," Ollie drawled.

Saffron gently nudged him and gave him a coquettish glance.

"Too much information, Oddie!" I snapped. I marched back down the corridor. It had been a long day. I needed time to think, and I didn't want that image lingering any longer than it needed to.

"Lori... Lori," Saffron called, and I heard her running to catch up. "How did it really go?"

"It was fine," I reassured her. Her eyes darkened, and she folded her arms. "Honestly! I don't want to interrupt your... er... session. I'm going back to the dorm; I'll talk to you later."

She nodded reluctantly, and I left.

Eyebrows and Archer were hanging around in North Hall as I descended the sweeping staircase. They were busy chatting up a couple of mage girls, their backs turned to me. I put my head down, hoping Eyebrows would be too busy reading his conquest's mind to notice me. It worked, so I scarpered to Dome Hall to get back to my room.

I needed a warm shower and to study the books Saffron lent me. Art would come or he wouldn't. My plans for getting help elsewhere had failed, but at least I'd made it through the first two trials.

CHAPTER TWENTY-ONE

The showers were empty, so I took my time and let the warmth of the water soak into my muscles. As I didn't know if I'd be reading the rest of the night or doing training with Art, I had no idea whether to dress for sleeping or combat training. In the end, I put on pyjamas. I could always change if Art knocked for a training session.

After settling down to read on my cabin bed, I finished the exceedingly short book on alius, reading about mage rings. They acted like a battery and stored the mage's magic, as Owain had mentioned. Each ring contained something useful with it that would enlarge, or become of use with a word. I thought of the chancellor's mage ring: the intricate two bands holding an oval between them and a sword at its centre. Eyebrows' ring had two crossed swords at its centre.

Then I started on *Beasts of the Alius World*. There was no information about trokkets inside. I checked the time. It was 9.50 p.m. It was unlikely Art would come now. I closed my eyes.

I was likely a noble, but it was uncertain. Trokket bellidoras only occurred once every millennium. What did that mean? My thoughts drifted to the identity of my biological parents. Were they alive and simply didn't want me, or were they dead? They'd chosen a good family for me, so they must have cared a little. Was it betraying my mum and dad to want to know who my biological parents were? Not that I'd see my adoptive parents again anyway – not if things didn't change. Did I truly want to know about my biological parents? The answer was... no.

A high-pitched ringing began in my ear, like at Murray's greasy spoon. My heart pounded. *Not again!*

The Voice that had started all of this off by unbinding my magic and landing me in this heap of crap, spoke in my mind. "You are in danger. Meet me at the amphitheatre at half past ten."

"Hello! Can you hear me? Hello!" I shouted in response, wondering if I could get some dialogue from this guy.

Nothing.

I climbed down the cabin bed ladder and pulled on a black pair of jeans, a top, and trainers. I needed to do some sneaking to get out of the building. Maybe the Voice could give me some answers, because I had more than enough questions.

Flinging Max into the air, I asked him for the map of the academy. The amphitheatre was beyond the Eassusian and fae quadrants, overlooking the ocean. I opened the door and surveyed up and down the corridor. No sign of Art or anyone. I checked my globe. It was 9.55 p.m. All clear.

I rushed down to Dome Hall, then on to the dining hall, where a few people were still milling about. The dining hall door was still open, but the French door leading to the patio was closed. But was it locked?

Priscilla was at the back of the dining hall, chatting with her friends. I didn't have time for any of her shenanigans, so I checked Max for alternative routes and turned right from North Hall, passing the Apollo statue, shuddering at the memory with Eyebrows. He'd been so intimate, yet so hateful.

Pushing him out of my thoughts, I followed the passage, taking a slight right, then an immediate left turn. To my right, doors led to what I assumed were mage dorms, and windows overlooking the grounds lined the wall to my left. I tried opening some of them, but they were locked. As I peered through them, I saw a door back the other way. Maybe that was unlocked?

I approached it, ever hopeful. *Please be open.*

Someone had left it off the latch. I opened it a fraction and listened for a moment, but I heard no movement. Sliding through, I stopped at an alarming thought. If the person who'd left it off the latch returned and closed it, how would I get back in? I stood contemplating that, then heard voices approaching.

I dived behind the hedge beneath the windows, then peeked around it. It was Archer and Eyebrows.

Of course, it would have to be them.

On their arms were the two girls I'd seen them talking to in North Hall. Eyebrows had his arm draped around the blonde one's shoulders. It hadn't taken him long to move on from Livia. I heard kissing sounds and peeked further round. Archer had his tongue down the black-haired girl's throat.

I rolled my eyes. Everyone and their dog were getting action tonight, and I was running out in the dark, evading enemies.

"It's getting cold out. Do you want to bunk with me for the night, Seb?" the blonde-haired girl offered.

"Oh, Zurie... I'd love to, but we've got a lot on tomorrow." He interlaced his fingers with hers. I was sure he glanced my way, so I ducked down, feeling a stab of jealousy and silently cursing my traitorous body for it.

"Well, maybe some other time then," she said. I peered up to see her lacing her arms around his neck. He pulled her tight against him and gave her a long, deep kiss. I wished they'd just bugger off inside.

Archer finally came up for air. "Let's go inside, mate, I've got to get some sleep," he said, holding the black-haired girl's hand and thumping Eyebrows on the arm.

I picked up a twig. If I could wedge it against the latch, perhaps I could stop it closing properly. Credit cards were good for that – I'd learned that the hard way after locking myself out the house one time. But my credit cards were at home, and I realised I was entirely unprepared for this jaunt outside.

The quartet filed through the door. Sebastian took the latch off and let the door self-close. I raced to ram the twig in before it shut, not knowing if the door would open when I returned, but it was too late. I'd have to take my chances.

I sped across the main building, trying to keep to the shadows. Eyebrows kissing that girl popped up in my thoughts, and I chastised myself for even thinking about it. The guy was a total prick, who hated and resented me, and it was highly probable he was the person I was in danger from. *I'll find out soon enough.*

Passing the patio fountain, I tore across the green, with only the glow of the moon to light the way. I should have worn darker footwear; my trainers were white and glowed luminescent in the dark. I threw Max into the air. It was 10.10 p.m. It would take me another fifteen minutes to get there.

I hit the tree line. The wind was picking up and swaying the branches, causing the moonlight that filtered through the canopy to dance in ever-moving spots. I slowed to a walk. It was creepy in the woods at night. I hadn't completed the academy tour with Charlie, so all of this was unfamiliar. I stumbled over an exposed tree root and ended up sprawled on the cold earth. Picking myself up, I cursed under my breath.

"Max, glow," I whispered.

Hopefully now I was under the cover of trees, the light wouldn't be seen by patrolling professors. But the further I ventured into the creepy wood, the more my fear swelled. I began to second-guess my decision to meet the Voice, wondering who he was and why he'd unbound me. How had he even known my magic was bound? How did he know I was in danger?

The glow from Max cast shadows everywhere. The leaves rustled in the wind. At every sound, my heart leapt into a gallop. Finally, I stumbled on to a paved path.

"Max, academy map," I whispered. He projected it. "What is my location?"

I was on the border of the Eassusian and fae quadrants, passing the fae lake to my left and the Eassusian earth section to my right. I should be there in ten minutes. I picked up my pace. This path was paved, and the walking was easier for a while. It ended and led onto a trail. There were no trees now, and the wind buffeted me harshly. There was a dark outline of a structure ahead. Looking up at Max, I realised that nightwalking had slowed my pace and I was already a minute late.

As I approached the dark mass of the amphitheatre, I heard the roar of the ocean. The wind whipped at my hair and moaned in my ears, and a tang of salt touched my lips. The entrance wasn't where I thought it would be. I stalked along the amphitheatre's length to the left side, finding no opening. I headed towards the right-hand side. Just as I thought it might have a hidden door, a burst of light flashed through the wall in front of me, then disappeared.

I raced to where I'd seen it and located the entrance. A stone arch led to stone steps, trailing down to a floor where a stone dais rose up. I cast around, seeing very little in the surrounding darkness. I stepped cautiously over the threshold and stood at the top of the stairs.

A speck of light made its way toward me. A firefly? It moved like an insect. It hovered in front of my face, formless. I backed away.

"What the—"

The speck rushed into my open mouth as I spoke. I coughed as it hit the back of my throat and swallowed. I waited for something, anything – a feeling, like sickness or magic taking root – but there was no reaction. Maybe it had been an actual firefly.

"Hello?" I rasped into the darkness.

The wind howled across the amphitheatre. I glanced at Max; it was 10.42 p.m. Had I missed my meeting?

"Hello!"

A male voice sounded from behind me. "Hello."

I jumped and staggered back; my foot slipped on the stone stairs. I started falling. A large, icy hand caught mine. I felt suspicion, anger, and fear coming from him. He pulled me up and held me close to steady me, the scent of spicy citrus flooding my nostrils. My eyes flung wide open.

"What are you doing out here?" Eyebrows demanded, still holding me.

Holy crap-balls!

He spun me away from the stairs and held me at a distance by my shoulders, as if I was a wayward child.

"Globe, light this place up," he said.

I winced as the light dazzled me, using my hand to shade my eyes. "Thanks for blinding me, and what the hell are you doing here?! I can't go anywhere without you following me. It's creepy as hell!" I yelled, backing away, hoping to bamboozle him by going on the attack.

He clenched his fists, magic ring crystal glowing bright. His eyes were a storm. How was I going to get out of this?

Making a split-second decision, I shot out of the amphitheatre and back out to the field. For once, he wasn't blocking my path. I'd always been fast for a narie. Charlie said Eassusians were faster than mages, so I liked my chances.

A blaze of white light came from behind me, and I was hauled ten feet off the ground by a magical lasso, my legs cycling in mid-air. Eyebrows came into view from below, lit up by his globe.

"I'll ask again. What are you doing out here tonight?"

"Put me down. You're not supposed to attack other invitees outside the trials," I spat.

"Well, maybe we should find Chancellor Wutterhorn and ask her what *she* thinks?"

A shot of fear burned through me as he carried on walking toward the mansion, pulling me alongside him as if on a tether ten feet off the ground.

"I went out for a walk. What's it to you?" I struggled and kicked out, to no avail.

"Who were you saying hello to?"

"No one. I just wanted to see if it echoed. It's an amphitheatre. Now let me down!"

"Not until you tell me the truth."

"I *am* telling the truth!" I bellowed, incensed that I was once again held against my will. I emptied my mind of all my thoughts and secrets. No way was I going to tell him why I was out here.

He swore and lowered me, released me from the lasso, and closed the distance between us. As my feet touched solid ground, he grabbed my shoulders and stared hard into my face. Distrust, rage, and confusion shot from him and into me.

"You're blocking me. You're blocking your thoughts from me – how are you doing that?" he hissed, wildly searching my face.

"I don't even know how to block my thoughts. And you shouldn't be reading them, anyway."

"Look, you can tell *me* the truth, or you can tell the *chancellor* the truth. It's your choice," he said calmly, eyes molten.

The wind was tearing through the open space. I was trembling with cold, my face and hands freezing, and I was sick of this.

"Have it your way. Tell the chancellor." I twisted out of his grasp and headed toward the tree line, heart galloping and sweat coating my hands, despite the cold. I glanced over my shoulder, waiting for the next attack.

He marched up to me from behind and spat in my ear. "You're a lying, half-breed, mongrel spy."

I spun and slapped him hard across the face. His head whipped to the side. He backed away from me, rosy handprint on an otherwise pale face. I waited for retaliation, but he avoided my gaze and stormed off toward the tree line.

Standing still for a moment, I watched him disappear into the eerie woods, surprised I'd hit him, especially with a girly slap. My palm stung.

There was no sign of him as I entered the woods. It was better that way. I felt gutted, empty. Not only at his words; I'd come to get some answers, and I was none the wiser. I knew Eyebrows hated me now more than ever. And he was certain to tell the chancellor. I'd be in the detention facility by morning, or worse. Art hadn't shown up tonight – although he was turning out to be a bit of a toss-pot too. Would I even get to see him, or any of them, before they took me away?

I pushed those thoughts aside. Disaster could be averted. No one had told anyone anything yet. It was his word against mine. I made up all the excuses I could think of for taking a night stroll as I sped back. My fingers were so cold they burned.

As the mansion came into view, I tried to work out how to get back into the building. Eyebrows had probably followed me out through that door and locked it when he arrived back. The chances he'd left it open were minimal, but I had to try it.

To my relief, the door was propped on the latch. My pulse stuttered as I pushed it open, half-expecting Eyebrows and Archer or the chancellor waiting for me as I opened it, but the corridor was empty. Eyebrows was nowhere to be seen. I closed the door behind me and made my way up to my room through silent halls.

I stopped to go into the shower room; if Saffron was asleep, I didn't want to wake her. I tidied my windswept hair and washed my hands, dirtied from my fall, then made my way back to the room.

Art was waiting for me, sitting on a chair outside my door. His face was smooth, his eyes the colour of twilight, dark, with a glint of light in them. My blood ran cold. Maybe Eyebrows had told Art. He looked at his globe. Was he the one taking me to the detention facility? My warden? I opened my mouth to make my excuses.

"I've been waiting for you for over an hour. Did you forget?" he asked, standing up, dragging his ocean-blue gaze over me. "Have you been crying?"

My heart leapt. He didn't know... not yet. "I'm sorry, Art. It got to nine fifty-five with only five minutes to go. I was pretty sure you wouldn't be back. So, I went out for a walk... It helps me think. It's cold outside – the wind picked up and stung my eyes as I made my way back."

"How did you get out? The doors are locked during trials by quarter to ten," he said, furrowing his brow.

"The one I walked out of wasn't, and it wasn't locked when I got back. Look, I'm sorry I wasn't here. I was sure you wouldn't come. It was late to train, and I like to walk when I need to think. Please, Art, I could really use your help – I'm so sorry I wasn't here." I really felt like crying now.

His eyes held my gaze with a hint of disappointment, and he folded his arms across his broad chest. He looked more gorgeous than ever. "I find it hard to believe you were out there on your own at night. Were you with someone?" he asked, eyes fixed on me.

I failed to see the relevance of that.

"Erm... no. Well, I was for a while, but I wasn't with anyone I wanted to be with," I said truthfully.

He sighed, and the tension released from his shoulders.

"If I have time tomorrow, I'll help you. I'll let you know when, but if you're one minute late, I'm leaving." He stalked away.

Relief washed through me. I was safe for now. But the chancellor could still come tonight...

When I entered my room, it was empty. Saffron was out. She must have stayed with Ollie for the night. *Ew!* I kicked off my trainers, but stayed in my clothes. If I was going to be dragged away during the witching hour, I'd do it fully dressed.

I lay down on my bunk, thoughts whirling back and forth. Eyebrows had said I was blocking his thoughts, but how had I done it?

The speck of light that rushed into my mouth – had that blocked my thoughts from him? *Maybe it was magic and not a firefly after all.*

What had happened to the Voice? Who was I in danger from? Would Eyebrows tell the chancellor? I closed my eyes and searched for sleep, but thoughts kept pouring in.

Two trials completed and passed. Tomorrow, I faced two paths. First: remain in the academy and continue the trials. If I failed the trials, the chancellor would send me to the detention facility. I would start at the bottom and never have the opportunity to aspire, to rise. It was working in that greasy café back in the Heights for the rest of my life. No comforts of family. It was knowing, without a doubt, that there was no more to life than this, forever.

The other path was more frightening. If Eyebrows told the chancellor I'd met with someone during the night, it would raise the same suspicions he had. That I was a spy, and worse – an unregistered half-breed spy.

They would make it their mission to search my memories. They'd find out I was unbound, rather than an emergent; that the Voice had unbound me, and it was him I'd been going to meet. They'd know I was hiding things from them, and this would cement their suspicions that I was a spy assassin. And since my mind had been altered, for all I knew, they were right!

I knew I was in danger. Not because the Voice had told me; I felt it hanging over me, like a sword on a thread.

I knew the academy shouldn't know about the Voice – that no one should know about it. I didn't know why; it was an instinct.

But since they had already searched my mind, I wondered how they'd missed him speaking to me in my mind and unbinding my magic. Perhaps their mind-magic search had skipped over it, or they couldn't detect it? Or maybe he had magically protected the memory. I didn't know. All I knew was that the alius specified a clear delineation between an emergent – newly magical – and magic being unbound.

The Voice had told me mine had been unbound, but from what the chancellor had said to me at our first meeting, she and all the others considered me emergent. Unlike Eassusians, who emerged at seven, mages often didn't emerge until they were eighteen. I was part mage, after all, so it wasn't that unusual.

If they found out, what would they do? It would be worse than the detention facility. I was sure of it.

I could try to escape from this travelling island and lead a magicless, colourless life. But where could I go where no alius or light-reaper could find me? I was sure that even if I never used magic again, they had ways to track me down.

Amongst my racing thoughts, my dad's face flickered in my mind. *Don't let the buggers get you down.* I remembered what my mum had said after that kid down the road threw a brick at me and I was scared to go out alone in case he did it again or worse.

One day after school, she'd picked me up in her gym clothes and driven me to a martial arts club nearby. She turned to me and said, "There's no sense in worrying what might happen. You can't control what that boy will do, but only what *you* do. So I thought we could learn how to defend ourselves together. What do you think about a self-defence class with your mum?"

I smiled at the memory and felt a growing warmth spread through my chest. I couldn't control what Eyebrows was going to do or say, nor the chancellor, if he told her. I couldn't even meet the Voice in the academy without being followed, never mind escape this place. What I *could* control was how I dealt with it and learned from things.

The slap to Eyebrows' face had either strengthened his resolve to tell the chancellor or made him realise he was being an utter tool. I wouldn't let the bugger get me down and lose sleep over it.

I nestled my head into my pillow and drifted into sleep.

I hope you enjoyed reading Alius Academy: Elemental Mage Series Book 1!

Want to see a **Map of the Academy**? Find it on my website: **www.larawray.com**

If you'd like to read the **companion novella** to Alius Academy, named **Seeker Mage** for **FREE**, then you can sign up to my Readers' Group Newsletter at **www.larawray.com**

Also By

Join my Readers' Group Newsletter

In signing up to my Readers' Group Newsletter, you'll receive a **FREE companion novella** to Alius Academy, about Lori's friend Vita, and Rhode, named **Seeker Mage: Elemental Mage Series**. You'll also get writing updates, special offers, giveaways and **another series related bonus**. You can sign up at: **www.larawray.com**

Want to see a map of the Academy? Go to my website
www.larawray.com

For more information, head to Lara's website:
www.larawray.com

Connect with Lara on:
Facebook Author Page: Lara Wray
Instagram: @larawrayauthor
Goodreads: @larawrayauthor
Website: www.larawray.com
Email Address: contact@larawray.com

Printed in Great Britain
by Amazon